"Ghosts, murder, speaking to the dead . . . Oh, and a hint of romance. I was glad I had a few days off so I could sit and read this book!"
    -Krista Wallace, author of the *Gatekeeper* series

"Sandra Wickham has filled a world—one much like ours—with well-drawn, vivid, and relatable characters. *Death Coach* grabs the reader from the first chapter and ratchets the tension tighter to a fantastic finale. Full of interesting magic, spooky ghosts and a unique take on the afterlife, Death Coach is slick, fun, and has a heart of gold. Full of fright, family, and phantoms, it's a perfect read for lovers of paranormal mystery and contemporary fantasy. I hope there's many more books in this series!"
    -Chadwick Ginther, Author of the *Thunder Road Trilogy* and *Graveyard Mind*

"This book kept me reading and hoping Amy would banish the dangerous spirits, and reconnect with the beloved ones."
    -Melanie Dixon, author of *The Aquaria Chronicles*

"Reaching into the world of the mystical supernatural yet grounded in the natural lives of modern day society's diversity and bias, *Death Coach* lets us safely grow and appreciate that everyone has a story to tell. It helps us to further our understanding of and apprecriation for different ways to view life and be  successful."
    -Mary Brunk, Contrary Creations

"Sandra Wickham takes you on a captivating, page turning, supernatural adventure. If you pick up this book, be warned, you can't put it down."
    - Judy Dufort, author of *The Sarken Legacy*

# DEATH
# COACH

SANDRA WICKHAM

This book is dedicated to everyone who has ever read my writing and given me feedback, support or encouragement.

It is a much longer list than I can fit here.

Thank you for making me feel like I could be a real writer.

# Chapter 1

The dead hadn't talked to me for twenty years because I refused to let them, but the incessant buzzing in my ears meant they wanted to. They weren't welcome here, never again.

Old fears threatened to overtake me, so I focused through the opening of our antique dressing screens at my cousin Carme. The dividers served to provide a reception area separate from my office and gave it a bohemian feel, lightening up the drab grey carpet and brick walls.

I forced myself to breathe. "You want to be the coach?" I asked my cousin. "We could switch seats."

"Naw. You're awesome at it," Carme replied. Having Down syndrome gave her words a thicker accent, which she worked on by speaking slowly and clearly. "I'm just here to look good." She flipped back her loosely curled hair. "You'll do great." She gave me an even bigger smile.

Today, Carme wore a long black skirt with an orange top, her light brown hair held back with a black-and-orange clip. It was a stealth Halloween outfit; she kept it subtle for my sake. Tomorrow, I would spend Halloween hiding with my cats in my warded apartment.

"Thanks." My ears rang so badly, I winced and had to sit down.

Carme stood. "Are you okay?"

I nodded. "Fine. Really."

"Do you want me to call Mom?"

"No." I slowly stood again. "Maybe. No. I'm fine." I didn't want to pull Aunt Jodene from her shop at the busiest time of year for some ear-ringing.

Carme gave me a bit of side-eye but relented. "Your new client will be here soon."

"Potential client," I pointed out.

"Think positive," she shot back.

For the first time in a long time, I had nerves about a meeting. This person could make a difference in steering my business toward a higher-paying clientèle.

My blouse and slacks were designer and combined well with my favourite black boots, perfect for a rainy October day in Vancouver. I hadn't dyed my hair in a while and felt suddenly self-conscious about the brown roots glaring out from the blond. There wasn't much I could do about it at the moment.

A woman walked through our door. Research told me this was my appointment, Heidi. About my age, early thirties, tall, she emitted a confident presence. She walked toward Carme, who had come out from behind her desk.

Heidi's change in posture suggested she didn't know how to react to Carme. "I'm looking for Amy Cameron?" Her tone hinted she wasn't sure Carme would understand her.

*Important client*, I reminded myself. Plus, Carme could take care of herself. She was a competent seventeen-year-old who had dealt with people's reactions to her all her life. She didn't like when I jumped to her defence.

I walked out between the screens and my cousin pointed at me. "That's Amy. May I take your coat?" Carme asked, with what I knew to be her most formal tone, then added an extra-polite smile. She hadn't missed Heidi's reaction to her.

"No, thank you," Heidi replied, studying Carme closely.

I stuck my hand out. "Hello, Heidi. I'm Amy."

Heidi took my hand in her gloved one. "Nice to meet you."

I opened an arm toward the gap in the screen. "Won't you come in?"

Our office wasn't fancy, and though I had the money to move somewhere else, I felt at home here for many reasons. Sometimes in moments like this, however, I wished it was nicer.

"Yes, thank you." Her brown high-heel boots *thunk*ed on the carpet. She didn't remove her long, stylish coat as she sat down. We probably could've turned the heat up a little; I hadn't thought of it. The office was a bit drafty. I'd been meaning to talk to Charles about getting better windows installed, but we were all busy.

A strong lavender smell wafted around me. I hoped it was her perfume and not a predecessor to the dead visiting. I worked my way around my desk and sat down.

"It smells fabulous in here." Heidi tucked her expensive handbag beside her. For a moment, I thought she meant the lavender, but I could tell by her expression that wasn't it. Only one glorious smell made people's faces radiate bliss like that.

"Yes," I replied. "One of the advantages of being above a coffee shop. The Artful Cup; have you been in?"

She shook her head. The Drive might have been below her usual standards. "You should," I continued. "Charles has the best coffee on the Drive. Possibly in all of Vancouver, maybe even all of the province."

Not only did I believe it, I would always promote him. I owed him big. When I started out, I met clients in his cafe until he'd offered me this space to rent.

"Are those paintings from the cafe?" She pointed at the art behind me.

"Yes, his wife did those." His wife, whom I had coached and who had then left him.

I took a settling breath. "You're interested in working with me while you start a second business?"

"Yes. I've been following your blog since you exposed that event where you got scammed out of your money. I was impressed how you handled it. I've liked what you had to say on a lot of topics. I think you could help me."

"Great," I replied. Those were dark times for me, losing a large chunk of money and fighting to expose those involved, but after many years, I made it out. I never wanted people to go through being scammed like I had and never wanted anyone to ever fear it with me. I decided I would be as transparent as possible in my career as a business and life coach. They would get the true me at all times. Turns out people liked it and it made me successful, which included only working with people I could truly help. "We can discuss what you're looking for from me and see if we would fit as coach and client."

"I appreciate how you openly say you don't have your act completely together. It's real. Not like the others." She leaned forward, conspiratorially. "But tell me. The feud with that meditation teacher, Nik, was that real? Or some sort of publicity stunt?"

Two roads lay ahead of me. The first would take me down a path of defending myself, berating him and reliving the whole experience. The second had far less potholes and potential accidents. "Sadly, it was real," I replied.

The office cell rang and Carme answered it. The smell of lavender overwhelmed me, churning my stomach.

"Why don't you tell me about the second business you'd like to—" I stumbled over my words, distracted by Carme's wide eyes. Her attempts at speaking kept being cut off. Heidi couldn't see Carme without turning fully around.

"Sorry," I said to Heidi. "What areas do you think—" I paused again as Carme grabbed her crystal necklace pendant with her whole fist, a habit when she was upset.

Heidi twisted around to watch Carme. "Is she okay?" she asked.

"Fine." I said. "What would you most like help with in your new business venture?"

Carme took the phone away from her ear and came toward us with an apologetic but desperate expression. Her free hand grasped her necklace hard as she stood next to me.

"Amy, sorry," Carme said, "but you have to talk to them."

"Would you excuse me for a moment?" Heidi gave me a supportive yet curious nod.

I took the phone from Carme, who quickly walked back to her desk. The ringing in my ears increased. I pushed the phone forcefully against my ear.

"Hello, this is Amy Cameron. How may I help you?"

"Help is the last thing I want from you." The voice belonged to an angry, gruff, older male.

"I beg your pardon?" I tried to remain cool and collected.

"Our daughter would be alive if it weren't for you," he shouted.

"I'm sorry sir, I don't know what you're talking about."

"You wouldn't, would you? You fake, self-serving piece of crap. You killed our daughter, Mary."

I'd been about to end the call, until he mentioned her name. "Mary? What do you mean? What's happened?"

Heidi grabbed her purse and pointed over her shoulder to the door. "I'm just going to go," she whispered.

I started to tell her to stay, but she was already headed for the door. Carme did a quick wave good-bye as she left.

The man, Mary's father, kept yelling insults while the ringing in my ears turned up, like an old refrigerator working overtime.

"Please, tell me what happened." I tried to ignore my damn ears to focus on the extremely upset man on the other end of the line.

"She's gone," he said.

"Mary is dead?"

"She is," came his answer, full of hot anger and grief so intense I found it hard to breathe. "My beautiful daughter is gone and it's all your fault."

My fault? What could he possibly be talking about? "Was she in an accident?"

Choked sobs cut off his next words, so I waited, anxiously. Mary had been a client until about a month ago, a young, intelligent and warm woman. She had big dreams to start her own business, all while finding her way after several failed relationships. She'd been grateful for my help and was well on her way to great things. The thought of her no longer existing hurt my entire being. Her hat. She'd left her hat and I'd put it away somewhere to get it to her. Now I would never do that. It felt impossible.

"It wasn't an accident." His words came out tight and forced. "She killed herself."

My chest tightened and I sucked in a sharp breath. That couldn't be right. Unfortunately, his anger and grief forced me to believe it to be true.

"I'm so sorry for your loss," I said, aware it wasn't adequate.

"You should be," he snarled back. "She left us a note. Told us everything. How you made her confused. Unhappy. She blamed you."

His words circled in my head for several breaths before coming to an uneasy rest. "I don't understand." My eyes burned hot with tears. I couldn't fathom why she would blame me.

"You as good as killed her," he said. "I hope you burn in hell."

He hung up.

I lowered the phone and stared at it in disbelief. It had to be some kind of mistake. A prank. It didn't make any sense. Mary had killed herself because of me? She'd been so happy the last several times we'd met, focused on a new career with a fresh outlook on relationships. Had her excitement been fake? A show? Had I missed it somehow?

Carme came to sit where Heidi had been. I told her everything from the side of the conversation she hadn't heard. The ringing in my ears flared, like I was sitting inside an airplane engine. The lavender smell sharpened, assaulting my nose and my stomach.

Carme played with her necklace pendant. "Should I cancel your clients for this afternoon?"

"No," I said too quickly, and she raised her eyebrows at

me. "No," I repeated slower. "I'm okay. Really. I'm fine." Did I believe it? Was I fine?

Carme studied me like she didn't believe me either. "What about Heidi?"

I let out a long exhale. "I'll call her. Do damage control. See if she'll come in again."

How much had Heidi overheard? The accusation I'd killed Mary? Was I to blame for her death? Maybe Carme was right and I should cancel my clients for the afternoon. Maybe forever. A client I had coached for a better life had ended it. I needed space to think, needed to breathe. I also needed coffee and not just for the caffeine. It helped make the ringing in my ears go away.

"Okay, cancel those appointments," I told Carme, admitting to her and myself I needed time off.

Hands shaky, I sent Liam a text to see if he was around. He lived and worked not far, and, as my best friend, was always good about meeting me when I needed it. I could use some of his positive vibes right now.

Carme finished her calls. "All set," she said. "I rescheduled them."

"Thank you." My phone buzzed. Liam would meet us downstairs for his morning break.

A weighty smell of lavender surrounded me. The memory of a different smell, the one that preceded my stepfather's terrifying visits, made me grip the arms of my chair.

My heart thumped, my breathing shallowed and my body became paralyzed. This was not the same, I told myself. It couldn't be.

But it could be. Someone blamed me for their death; what better reason to come after me?

My ears rang so badly, my whole head hurt. The scent of lavender clouded me, so thick I could almost taste it. I got to my feet. "Carme, we have to leave. Right now."

There was no denying it. There was a ghost in the office and I was pretty sure it wasn't happy.

# Chapter 2

The smell didn't follow us and I began to breathe a bit easier.

Carme let out a sad sigh as we descended the stairs. "At least your other clients won't know."

I hadn't even thought of that. Not exactly the best advertisement for life coaching when your clients kill themselves.

"Why won't they know?" I asked.

"The police won't tell anyone but family," Carme said. "I saw it on a cop show."

"Thanks, Carme."

She beamed. "You're welcome."

We went outside to the street through the nondescript glass door and turned left to the entrance to the cafe. Carme held the door open for me.

There was nothing as fabulous as walking into Charles' Artful Cup cafe. It didn't just smell like fresh-brewed coffee ready to wrap you in a comforting, loving embrace. It also held hints of baked goods, pencils, chalk and paper. It made all worries disappear. Usually.

Charles gave us a quick wave from behind the cash register. His son, Darren, also waved then went back to making coffees. In keeping with the season, they'd draped webs on the ceiling, complete with giant, fuzzy spiders. There were jack-o'-lanterns lined on top of the food display case. Some of the paintings on the wall even had a bit of web draped over their corners.

Midmorning, it wasn't too busy, which was nice for my brain space right now. An older woman, around Charles' age, sat at one of the tables with art paper on a spool. For as long as I could remember, I'd seen her in the cafe every morning, drawing. She had a pencil from the mug packed with art supplies and was focused on whatever it was she drew.

Four people sat at the high table in front of the chalk wall at the far end of the cafe, the most popular spot in the place. The chalk artwork had been redone recently, I didn't know by who, but it was magnificent. A beautiful bouquet of flowers, no two quite the same, boasted bright yellows, dark blues, pink and lavender. I thought of the lavender smell from the office and shuddered.

Our turn came at the register. The creases on Charles' face deepened from forehead to chin as he gave us a big smile. "How are you ladies today?"

"We're great," I lied, not wanting him to worry. "We'll take the usual and a latte macchiato for Liam."

Charles rang us up then flicked a hand at us. "Go. Sit. I'll bring it over."

Darren came over from his station and waved. He had new round wire glasses and a fresh haircut.

"Your hair looks great," I told him. His natural blond colour was even nicer than what I had to pay for. He gave me a big smile.

"Hey, Carme," he said, his words thicker than hers.

"Hey, Darren." Carme smiled, but not her usual, genuine one.

Darren shuffled his feet, then gave another, smaller wave. "See ya." He went back down the counter.

Carme and I sat in a booth along the front windows. "What's up with you? I think Darren likes you."

"Yeah," she replied quietly. "I know. But I don't like him. Not like that."

"Why not? You've always gotten along."

She held up her hand. "Let me stop you there," she said with so much attitude, I knew I was in for it. "You think because we both have Down syndrome, we should be a couple?" She didn't give me a chance to answer. "He's addicted to his phone, is obsessed with watching sports and doesn't even play them." Carme herself was a Special Olympics medalist in swimming.

Liam slid in beside Carme. She didn't have to move over. He was taller than us but also thinner. "Hola, how are my favourite amigas doing?" Carme grinned at him.

The ringing in my ears flared so badly, I couldn't hear Carme anymore. I saw her lips moving, but everything became a melded racket of entangled noise. The smell of lavender cloaked me.

"Are you okay?" Carme's voice reached me as the ringing eased off. After a couple deep breaths, I nodded.

Liam studied me. We met four years earlier when a few hundred of us showed up for a prepaid business weekend of seminars which never happened. During the battle to find the people who had ripped us off, we'd become friends. It was one of the best things to come out of the awful experience.

That and my renewed determination to become a coach and help people.

He brushed his hand along the top of his cropped hair. He went to the barber more often than I went to the salon, keeping his dark hair shaved at the sides and only an inch or so at the top. "So, what's up?"

Carme and I exchanged a glance while I tried to work up the words.

Liam leaned in. "What the hell is going on?"

Everyone in the cafe was minding their own business, but I leaned in as well, speaking as low as I could. "One of my clients killed herself."

Liam sat straight up and swore loudly in Spanish. Most of the cafe now watched us. He gave them an apologetic wave, and heads turned back to their own tables.

He leaned back in. "What are you talking about?" he whispered.

It took me a moment to answer because my ears flared up again. I told him about the phone call and Mary. He stared at me for a few seconds, then reached across to touch both my forearms. He'd never met Mary, but you wouldn't have known it from the sadness on his face.

"I'm really sorry to hear that. You know this is not your fault, no matter what, right? Are you okay?"

Carme leaned in to join us. "She's so not okay. But she will be."

They smiled at each other and then me. Great people around me made me a better person. Somehow, I'd been incredibly lucky in my family and friends.

"Thanks, both of you," I said. "Should I send flowers to the family? Or no?"

Liam squeezed my arms again and sat back, using his

eyes to let me know someone was coming from behind me. A heartbeat later, Charles' oldest son, Ethan, tall, dark blond and far too cute for his own good, appeared at our table.

"Greetings," he said with a nod to our table. He had an extra big smile for my cousin. "Carme, what a great outfit. Business Halloween; I like it."

Carme instantly blushed, stared down at the table and muttered a thank-you.

"Hi, Ethan," I said, to give her time to start breathing again. "Visiting from Calgary?"

He shook his head. "Moved back, actually. I've been visiting my mother in the interior for a bit." He held out a hand toward me. "Of course, you know all about that."

A pleasant smile returned to his face, but it was a shot at me and it landed. His mother, Charles' wife, had been one of my first clients, and I'd helped her pursue her dreams. I didn't realize her dream was to pack up her things, leave her husband and move four hours away to the interior. Yes, I felt guilty, but also proud of her at the same time. It was nothing compared to the guilt of having a client kill themselves.

Charles saved me as he came to deliver our delicious-smelling coffees. "Now, Ethan, don't give her a hard time. Your mother is extremely happy. She comes back to visit Darren every week, and he loves going up there to stay with her. You'd know these things if you weren't always moving away." He placed a small plate of scrumptious looking lemon squares on our table. "On the house. Ethan made them. They're quite good." He patted his son on the shoulder and gave us all a crinkled smile.

Ethan gave me a shrug. "I guess I should listen to him. Plus, we need your business."

I twisted to see Charles making his way back around the

counter. "Is the cafe in trouble?"

"Let's just say you might need to look for another office," Ethan said.

When I'd been looking at spaces downtown I couldn't afford, Charles had offered me the upstairs. He gave me a great deal, suggesting it would be great to get Carme more work experience outside of her mom's shop. Now I could afford a place downtown, but I'd been taking my time because I liked it here. Maybe it was time. If I wanted to attract higher-paying clients, I should have a more upscale office space.

Ethan rubbed his hands together and put on a fresh smile. "But that's why I'm here. We're going to turn things around." He smiled at Carme, who blushed wildly again. He gave a small exit wave and headed to the back room.

Liam, who'd kept a friendly smile plastered on his face the entire time, let out an audible breath. "Was it just me or was that a little awkward?"

Carme took a square. "I think he's nice."

"Can't blame him." I also grabbed a square. "It's because of me his mom left his dad. Charles does seem a lot better now, though, right?"

"Charles is a rock," Liam said. "I agree with Carme. Ethan is extremely nice."

I pointed a sugary finger at him. "You just like Ethan because he got Charles to make the bathrooms gender neutral."

Liam reached for the last square. "It's not just for me, you know." He waved his hand to encompass the cafe and Commercial Drive outside. "Lots of people around here. But I think I may have to work on setting you and Ethan up. He's so your type." He waggled his eyebrows at me.

Liam missed the pained look on Carme's face. She waved at him to move out of her way. "I'm going to go."

"Carme, you don't have to," I began.

"No, it's okay," she said as Liam got up to let her out. "I should go help Mom for a bit." Aunt Jodene's shop was up the Drive a few blocks. "I'll see you after to help you."

She wasn't scheduled to work this afternoon. "You don't have to do that," I told her.

"I know," she answered, a smile back on her face. "But you need me. Bye, Liam." She gave a big wave to Charles behind the counter as she left.

I rolled my eyes at Liam as he slid back in.

"What?" he asked.

"For someone who's usually extremely intuitive, you've missed this one? Carme's clearly got a crush on Ethan and you're talking about setting me up with him."

Carme had been in love with Ethan since she was old enough to know what it meant. She and Darren had grown up together, going to the same Down syndrome groups and events.

"Oh." He shoved the square into his mouth. "Sorry." Tufts of white icing sugar flew out and I shook my head at him.

I leaned in again. "Also, Charles told me a few months ago Ethan lost his girlfriend in a car accident. Maybe part of why he's here." We all had our stories.

Liam was right. Ethan was nice to look at, ambitious, smart and usually friendly. Carme's enduring feelings for him made it too complex an avenue to ever pursue, which was probably a good thing.

Someone came into the cafe dressed as a zombie and I must've reacted, because Liam shook his head. "You're the only person I know who doesn't like Halloween."

"I have my reasons." I'd never told Liam about being able to communicate with the dead, afraid I would lose him as a friend.

"Right. Here we go again. Maybe you'll tell me someday." He took a long drink of his latte, watching me the entire time. "Meantime, you're doing a lot of good for a lot of people. Don't let this stop you."

For the first time since the news of Mary, I allowed tears to flow down my cheeks. "I don't understand." I dug for a tissue in my coat pocket but came up empty. "She was happy. She was excited about life."

He set his mug down. "Do you want me to call in sick for the rest of the day, stay with you?"

Wiping the tears with a crumpled napkin, I shook my head. "No, you go. Your office can't survive without you."

He chuckled. "So right. Okay, I will check on you later." He patted the top of my head and waved good-bye to Charles.

Left alone, I took another deep breath. My phone came to life, notifications pinging on everything.

*What?* I tapped into my email.

My stomach clenched at the subject lines from people I knew and didn't know. They were all about Mary's suicide. How was that possible?

I went to my blog. My latest post had been flooded with comments, but not about the post. They were about Mary's suicide. Some offered condolences to Mary's family. Many called me a fake, a fraud, cheat, a scam artist or worse.

All over my social media, people called me a murderer; others told me to go kill myself to make it even.

My heart pounded. This wasn't the onset of an anxiety attack. I knew the difference. Anxiety attacks hit me when the dead knocked on my door. These were real, living people. Them, I could handle.

I called Carme.

"Hey, what's up?" she asked. Her mom chatted with customers in the background.

"Someone leaked the news of Mary's suicide. I've traced a couple of links back to Nik Marson's blog. Someone posted it there in his comments. I think it was him."

"What? Why would he do that?"

"To get traffic to his blog? He gets to slam me again?"

"What are you going to do?" she asked.

"Damage control," I answered.

"I'll be there as soon as I can."

"Thanks." We ended the call and I got to work.

I deleted all the comments on my blog and turned off future commenting on everything. Next, I went through all of my social media, deleting what I could, ignoring what I couldn't.

I thought about emailing Nik. Should I call him out? I didn't have proof it was him. What would I tell a client in this situation? I was in no condition for an emotionally intelligent conversation with him. No, I would focus on what I could do, what I had control over, now. Perhaps after, I could ask him to take the comment down. Would he do it?

I began to work on a statement to post, but the words wouldn't come. Maybe being on my laptop instead of my phone would help. Plus, I could check out the office before Carme arrived, to see if I smelled any ghosts. If I did, we could move back to using the cafe as my office. That wasn't what I wanted. It would be a step backward, not forward.

I sent Carme a text asking her to bring some of her mom's stuff to update the office wards and meet me there.

*Got you covered,* Carme sent back.

Carme had never been able to communicate with the dead, but she had an amazing talent for wards.

After a thorough smell check for ghosts in the office, I opened my file on Mary. She'd had a rough history with men who abused her, but she had come to realize it wasn't her fault. It wasn't a pattern she wanted to repeat. We'd worked on her feelings of self-worth, focused on being kind to herself, loving herself, so she could blossom in her career. She had been doing so well.

A note jumped out at me. One of her favourite self-care things to do was a bath with lavender oils. It was possible the lavender smell was her spirit's scent and she had been haunting me. My heart clenched. My breathing became shallower.

As soon as Carme arrived, she got to work on the wards. The smoke and burning herbs covered the usual smells from the coffee shop below. She moved in a mesmerizing way and I found myself more at ease, despite the horrible day.

When she was done, I went to her desk. "Will you help me write something for my website? A statement, something to counter all the negativity, if we can manage it."

"Sure." She opened her laptop and I stood by her as we talked through it. The office cell rang, and I could tell from Carme's responses it was a client cancelling.

"Your two o'clock tomorrow," she said with an apologetic shrug.

"Thanks." Back at my own desk, I checked for any new activity online. I could deal with the business side of this. It wouldn't ruin my career. I'd post a statement online and write a letter to the family. I would work on a new vlog series, run some social-media ads and hit the pavement with free consultation brochures. It would be fine.

The smell of lavender hit me so strong, I thought I would lose the coffee and lemon square from my stomach.

Our printer whirred into action on the shelf behind me. "Are you printing something?" I asked Carme. She paused her typing and shook her head.

A familiar tightening choked my heart. Slowly, I moved to the printer. The page coming out had one word repeated over and over.

*LIES.*

# Chapter 3

The printer continued its frantic pace.

*LIES. LIES. LIES.*

Carme grabbed her phone. "I'll call Mom."

Aware of my spiraling anxiety, I turned off the printer. It didn't stop. After a quick glance at Carme, I pulled out the power cord. The printer continued to zing along.

I grabbed my coat off our rack, and there was a knock at the door.

"Ghost?" Carme whispered, the same hint of excitement her mother got at the paranormal. I shook my head. For a second, neither of us moved.

The handle jiggled and the door opened. We both stumbled back. I didn't know what I expected to come through the door, but it wasn't this.

Nik Marson held the doorknob, clearly taken aback by our startled response. "Sorry."

Rage flushed through me and I took a step back. "What are you doing here?"

The only interactions we'd ever had were online. I'd never seen pictures of him in glasses, but now he wore brown square frames a shade darker than his hair, which was short and swept slightly up and over on top. He sported a light scruff of dark facial hair, the length where it's on purpose, not a lack of shaving.

He held both hands up in a sign of surrender. "I came to talk."

Duality raged through me. Let him in or send him off? I felt Carme's eyes on me. What would I tell a client?

He pulled at the navy-and-white knit scarf wrapped loosely around his neck. It gave him the look of a model for some hip, high-end magazine. "Please hear me out."

"We were just leaving." My ears rang so violently, it took everything I had not to scream over the noise they couldn't hear.

"The comment on my blog about your client wasn't me. I thought you might think it was. I've taken it down."

"Thank you," I managed to say. Or I might have yelled it. The ringing in my ears had changed to voices, a lot of them, and their numbers were growing.

*Help us*, they said in unison.

I must've appeared unwell, because Carme grabbed my arm. "We better go," she said.

Nik pointed at our printer, running at higher speeds than I knew it was even capable of. "Do you need to look after that?"

Pages fell out of the tray to the floor. "It's not even plugged in," he added with great surprise.

"No, it's, fine," I put my hand on the doorknob. "Just a glitch."

"Yes, a glitch," Carme repeated.

Nik began to argue the point, but Carme held a hand toward the open door. "Come for coffee," she said, and I shot her a side eye. "We like the cafe," she added to me, and I knew she meant the wards there.

"Thanks, Carme," Nik replied. "It's nice to see you in person." His smile was genuine. They'd never met, but anyone who read my blog knew Carme.

I locked the door behind us. "Carme, could you check that lock? I think something might be wrong with it. She's good with locks," I said to Nik. "Don't want anyone getting in or out either, right?" I laughed like I'd made a joke but lifted my eyebrows at my cousin.

Her eyes widened and she held up a finger. "Right. Don't want that."

"What—" Nik began, but I ushered him toward the stairs.

I held the outside door open for Nik. Maybe I shouldn't have left Carme alone. Only really powerful spirits could physically harm a human, but some could latch on and cause all kinds of problems, mental and emotional.

Carme appeared at the top of the stairs and I let out a breath. Once outside, Carme moved quickly past us and held the cafe door open. Reluctantly, I followed Nik and gave Carme a narrowed glare. She rolled her eyes at me.

"This place is amazing," Nik said.

"It is," Carme answered, far too friendly for my liking. This was the enemy, cousin of mine. Don't be so nice to him. He wasn't supposed to be in my safe haven. As he approached the counter, I pulled Carme aside.

"Is the office okay?"

She nodded with confidence, meaning the door had been warded and those ghosts would stay put for now. We had to do something or I'd be back to meeting clients here in the coffee shop.

Nik smiled at Carme. "I don't have an assistant. She's

very lucky." She smiled back. Clearly, they were sharing a moment, which made me want to kick him out of the cafe and our lives.

The voices had stopped and I didn't smell anything but coffee and living people. What to do about Nik, who was ordering coffee for him and one for Carme? I hung back and sent Aunt Jodene a text.

*Office printer running on its own*

Carme showed Nik to the table by the chalk drawing as I made my order. He had said it wasn't him. Did I believe him? If I was honest with myself, I did. Nothing felt like he was lying. It made no sense for him to go to the trouble of coming to talk to me in person. If his intention was to hurt me by releasing the news about Mary's suicide, why would he be here? Unless he wanted to witness my suffering.

Nik sat and took in the cafe's new chalk wall decor. Carme had always thought I should take my own advice and make amends with Nik. Sometimes, it was easier to give advice than take it.

Throat tight, I waited for Aunt Jodene's reply as Darren made my coffee.

It made sense Mary would use the printer to communicate with me. She had been an administrative assistant, which had led to a few of her unhealthy relationships with bosses. Was she saying I lied? To who? I'd never lied to her.

My phone buzzed. Aunt Jodene.

*Where are you now? If Carme can come watch the shop I'll come to your office*

*We're in the cafe I'll talk to Carme*, I sent back.

I was pretty sure Carme would be fine with heading to her mom's shop so we could clear out the office. Was that what Aunt Jodene intended? She didn't actually say that, did she?

I sat across from Carme, not intentionally ignoring Nik, not really. That would've been immature. "Aunt Jodene wanted you to go cover at the shop so she could help with the office." I figured it was vague enough for Nik but also clear enough for Carme.

Carme gave an enthusiastic nod. She picked up her coffee. "I better do that. Get this to go." She pushed her chair back and got to her feet. "Nice to see you," she said to Nik.

He gave her a big smile. "You, too. Have a great afternoon. Sounds like you're in high demand."

She gave a small giggle, then gave us both a good-bye wave, leaving me alone with Nik. I wanted to be anywhere but where I was.

At least he wasn't staring at me or forcing conversation. He sipped his espresso and took in the coffee shop. I tried hard not to visualize throwing my hot coffee in his face. That would be a waste of coffee. If he started coming here regularly, I'd have to get Ethan to put laxatives in his coffee or something. It cheered me up, slightly, though I told myself I should really work on my revengeful side. Time to deal with this like an adult.

"So, it wasn't you who put the comment on your blog."

"No," he said firmly. "I knew you'd think it was me, which is why I came to see you in person."

"I believe you," I had to admit. "Which means I don't know who did it or why." That was worse than thinking it was Nik. At least I'd had somewhere to target my anger. Maybe it had been Mary's father or a family member.

"I'll post a rebuttal, if that helps," he replied.

"It's okay. I don't need another online battle. The one with you was enough." I took another sip while he shook his head.

"I left one comment on your blog about the benefits of meditation and..." He spread his fingers out and made a noise like an explosion.

"You left it in response to my post addressing people who, for whatever reason, couldn't get a grasp on meditation."

I'd never tell him I couldn't meditate because it was like an invitation for the dead to talk to me. "I wrote it to let them know it was okay. That you didn't have to meditate to make your life complete. Your post basically told them it wasn't okay."

"Not true," he replied. "Go back and look. But I'm not here to rehash all that."

I took a breath and gave him a small, cynical smile. "Two clients left me after that."

He let out a short laugh and shook his head. "I don't think I had anything to do with that."

It had bothered me back then, but I'd learned they left for their own reasons, not the feud.

I filled the awkward silence with more sips of coffee. He finished his espresso and pushed the cup forward. "I just wanted to let you know it wasn't me. That there's no hard feelings. I respect you and what you do."

"Thanks," I replied, feeling like this had shifted from a business fight to some sort of date. I cleared my throat. "I appreciate it."

He motioned his head toward the door. "I better go. I have a few classes today."

"Of course," I replied. He still had his business. What was I going to do? Hopefully, Aunt Jodene could help clear the office of dead people so I could have living people in it again.

Nik got to his feet. "I guess I'll see you around."

"Sure. See you." I gave him an awkward wave, doubting we'd ever see each other again.

I sank back in my chair, body tired, brain a little numb. I'd missed a text from Liam asking if I wanted to do lunch. He'd lose his mind when I told him I'd been having coffee with Nik instead.

Ethan came over and picked up Nik's empty cup. "You okay?"

"I'm fine," I lied. Nothing was fine.

"Need a refill?" He pointed at my mug.

I really didn't. I could feel the caffeine affecting me, my heart, my breathing, my body tingling. "Sure," I said anyway.

He gave me a smile and took my mug. Carme's infatuation with him was well deserved, really.

My phone buzzed. Margaret, a long-time client, emailed to say she was sick and couldn't come in this week. It could have been an excuse because she'd seen the news about Mary. Or maybe she really was sick. Either way, I would use the time to focus on how to continue to increase my client base with all of this going on.

I moved to one of the smaller tables to leave the larger table by the chalk wall for others to enjoy and started brainstorming a new blog series. Maybe it should be about dealing with stress which would certainly be appropriate. Or something lighter, perhaps about the holiday season approaching and everything that comes with it? Ethan came by and set down my refill.

"Thanks."

With a nod and small smile, he moved on. I was a bit surprised Aunt Jodene hadn't come in yet. Maybe she'd had some things to go over with Carme before she left. Halfway through my coffee refill, I started to feel uneasy.

I called the shop. It went to voice mail, which was not entirely unusual. If there was a reading being done or Aunt Jodene was busy with customers, she'd let the phone go to voice mail. Right now, Carme should have been there with her. Shouldn't one of them been able to answer? I called Carme's cell number.

"Amy?" Carme answered. Something crashed in the background.

"Carme? What's going on? Are you okay?" Ethan glanced over from where he talked to customers at a nearby table.

"We're fine." Another sound like something falling. "Well, we've got a visitor."

She didn't mean a living one. "Carme?" Another crash. Carme didn't answer, because we'd gotten cut off. My heart pounded as I got up and left the cafe.

# Chapter 4

I'd been thirteen when my stepfather, Henry, had died. When he and my mom were dating, he gave us both expensive gifts and cards with cash in them. They got married when I was ten, and the gifts kept coming. I was happy accepting it all.

My mom started her own cleaning business when he died. At the time, I'd thought it was demeaning, going into other people's homes to clean up after them and scrub their toilets. Foolishly, I'd held Henry up as the savvy, successful businessman I'd thought he was.

After he died of an overdose of pills, we'd discovered his business had failed shortly before they got married. He'd been spending money he didn't have. He owed hundreds of thousands when he died. His estate didn't have much in it, but it all went to cover those debts.

The devastating part was he had a joint loan and mortgage with my mother. He'd told her he had paid it off and she'd believed him. He had not. They also had a joint bank account my mother thought had been closed, but was in overdraft. Since all of these things were joint debt, it went to my mom when he died.

To say I was furious would be an understatement.

I refused to go to his funeral. I yelled every curse word I could at his ashes my mother kept for no reason I could understand.

He died in September. By Halloween, he made his first appearance.

Up to that point, I'd always talked to the dead. They talked to me in single words or broken sentences and I would talk back. I never saw them, but talking to them had been a normal part of my life until I was old enough to realize not everyone did it. My mom told me it was our secret. Ours and Aunt Jodene's. The spirits never got aggressive, until my stepfather.

Henry's spirit was full of fury and rage. At first, he moved things around in my bedroom. Then doors and cupboards slammed around the house wherever I was. He got stronger and stronger. Eventually, he became able to physically affect me. He knocked me down, tripped me and shoved me. He even pushed me down the stairs once, and I broke my wrist. All were attributed to accidents, by anyone besides my mom and my aunt. I must've been the clumsiest kid in my school

It horrified me.

I thought he was after me because I'd cursed at his ashes. Aunt Jodene told me it was because of how powerful I was. He wanted to weaken me out of jealousy or perhaps steal my powers somehow.

Despite all of Aunt Jodene's sent instructions on how to deal with Henry, things got worse. Much worse.

Two of my best friends died that year. Accidents, the police said. These girls had been my friends since kindergarten, bonded and inseparable. One went off by herself and stepped in front of a train. The other slit her own throat with her father's hunting knife.

After that, my mom got really sick. She couldn't keep any food or liquid in her. She ended up in the hospital, having tests while barely holding on to life.

That was when Aunt Jodene flew across the country from British Columbia to Ontario to help us. She thought my stepfather had entered my mother's body and was causing it as much damage as he could.

Getting rid of him hadn't been easy. Aunt Jodene used a black-candle spell. It left her hospitalized for two weeks recovering from exhaustion, but it had worked. Henry's hauntings stopped. Mom got better and was able to come home, but she was never quite the same.

After high school, I moved to go to college out west with her blessing and encouragement. A few years later, she passed away. There wasn't anything specifically wrong with her when she died, but I knew. The time Henry had spent hurting my mom had taken too much out of her. My mom had been my rock. A solid attachment to the normal world.

Aunt Jodene had saved my life. I had no doubt when my stepfather had finished hurting those I loved, I would've been his final target. Whether he wanted to torture me to weaken me or kill me to steal my powers, he would've succeeded.

I was done with the dead and swore to never allow anything from the world of the dead to make contact with me again. No one would ever be hurt because of me.

Begrudgingly, Aunt Jodene taught me wards, gave me amulets, herbs to burn, crystals and chants to keep the dead from reaching me ever since.

It was only a few blocks down Commercial Drive to my aunt's shop. My heart pounded from the caffeine, adrenaline and fear of what I might find.

Lavender hit me as I dodged people on the sidewalk. It could've been a passerby or one of the shops, but it also could've been Mary. The smell clung to me like a nauseating cloud of perfume. Traffic on the Drive was mostly considerate of jaywalking pedestrians. Once I spotted an opening, I rushed across the street.

Wedged between a sushi restaurant and a women's consignment clothing store was my aunt's shop, the Feathered Serpent. The GONE FOR A SPELL sign hung facing out the glass door. As soon as I knocked, Carme hurried over. She rested a broom against the wall and unlocked the door to let me in.

"We're okay." She closed the door and locked it behind me.

My aunt's beautiful shop was a mess. Aunt Jodene crouched by the glass display counter. The usually packed surface now had nothing on it. Gem necklaces, bracelets, incense sticks, tarot cards and vials of essential oils lay scattered around the floor.

The round table display in the centre of the front part of the shop had been almost completely cleared off.

"What did this?" I asked as I carefully picked up a pile of items from off a small table near the front door.

Aunt Jodene stood and threw her long grey hair over her shoulder. Today she wore a green scarf covered in pink flowers, held together by a pewter clip with a dangling pentagram pendant. It went with the pentagram ring she always wore, along with a rotation of other rings she wore on every finger. My aunt didn't just own a metaphysical shop; she lived and breathed it.

She wiped her hands on her long, floral green dress and smiled. "It would seem we had a visitor." She pulled me

DEATH COACH

in for a hug. "Your printer was running on its own. Did a message come through?"

I took a breath. "It said *lies*, over and over."

"Interesting," Aunt Jodene mused. "Who is lying?"

"We don't know," Carme said as she walked by with the broom.

Coloured sand, herbs and some dark powder covered the floor in front of the black shelving display. The bookshelves on the opposite side had been partially emptied, but the back area where Aunt Jodene did her readings remained undisturbed. I took off my coat, laid it over the counter and crouched to help my aunt. "How could this happen here? The store is warded up the wazoo, right?" It wasn't a technical term, but it seemed to fit.

Carme paused sweeping and gave a sheepish shrug.

Aunt Jodene shook her head. "Actually, no. If I did, it would scare off a lot of customers. They wouldn't know why, but it would keep them away."

An excellent point, but I still didn't like it. "Wouldn't it be a good idea, maybe, to do it now?"

Aunt Jodene sighed, pushed up from one knee and threw a handful of broken incense sticks into the garbage. "I really can't afford that. Especially now we've lost some inventory."

We both paused to take in the store. The stuff Carme swept into the dustpan was garbage, as were some counter display items. The books could go back on the shelves; items from the front display could be put back. "You have insurance, right?" I asked her.

Aunt Jodene gave a small smile. "And just how would we explain this to the insurance man? We can't call the police and tell them a ghost did it, can we?" She must have seen my concern. "It's okay," she said. "It's not that bad. Halloween

33

will make up for it."

I worried about Aunt Jodene and her shop. This was her entire livelihood, for her and Carme. I'd told her lots of times she should move her shop downtown. The overhead would be higher, but she could charge a lot more. She'd have tourist traffic and would end up with a lot more profit. She always refused, saying she loved the Drive and business was just fine. This was definitely not the time to bring it up again. It would be a bit hypocritical of me since I hadn't moved my office yet either.

"Is there anything we can do to protect you and Carme?"

She touched my arm. "I've been doing it," she said. "We're fine."

"It's not fine. A spirit attacked your shop." My chest started to tighten and breathing became difficult. "Crap."

"Come." Aunt Jodene took me by the elbow and led me to the red plush chair in the reading area.

She sat across from me in the tan wicker chair. "Breathe."

We'd been through this often after we'd gotten rid of Henry. I never felt safe again. I'd get panic attacks at anything I thought was related to the dead.

Focusing on deep breaths, I reminded myself I was not that teenager anymore. With practiced determination, I went through the list of vlog episode ideas I'd just written into my phone at the coffee shop. By the time I'd gone through it twice, I could breathe better and had some new ideas for my list. "Thanks," I said to my aunt.

"We can go cleanse the office now, if you'd like."

"Do you think it's Mary?" I asked. "I've been so careful not to let any voices in since Henry."

Aunt Jodene nodded solemnly. "I know."

Despite the horrors of my stepfather, Aunt Jodene still

wished I hadn't stopped communicating with the dead. I reminded myself to breathe. "Mary blames me for her death. Maybe she's out to scare me, get revenge."

Aunt Jodene narrowed her eyes. "I don't know about that. It's confusing for displaced spirits. They're thrown into a realm they don't know, often not knowing what's even happening to them. What we need to do is help her communicate with you."

"Oh, no, we don't." Part of me wanted to help Mary, if it was her, but the risks were too great.

Aunt Jodene gave me the look of disappointment I always got when I refused to want anything to do with the dead. "She could be trying to send you a message."

"Yes. A message she wants me dead right along with her." I shoved down the memories of Henry to keep from falling into a severe anxiety attack.

"Not all spirits are like your stepfather," she said with a sigh. "Any smells now?"

I nodded. "Strong lavender."

"How're your ears?"

"Ranging from bad to really terrible."

"That's them, trying to get through. If it's Mary and she has something to tell you, I think you should listen."

"In that we disagree," I replied.

"Let's see." My aunt rubbed her hands together then moved around the shop, collecting items. First, a mortar, pestle and a tiny jar. Then came two tiny vials filled with oil, a burner shaped like a serpent, some incense, a white candle, a gemstone-encrusted pen and a small notebook. Finally, a small handheld mirror which she placed reflective side down.

She opened the jar and sprinkled whatever dried herbs

were inside it into the mortar, then added drops from both vials. She crushed the mixture, a comforting sound of granite grinding herbs. Satisfied with her work, she sat and lit the incense stick. An earthy, wooden smell rose with the smoke.

She flicked her hand between us. "We will deal with this together."

Arguing with my aunt was not something I took pleasure in. She was the coolest, kindest, biggest-hearted person I knew. So much like Carme, whom she'd raised on her own. Aunt Jodene's husband decided he couldn't deal with a baby with Down syndrome and left them. My aunt deserved nothing but the best in life.

At the same time, the last thing I wanted was to communicate with anything not living. Death followed the dead.

"Sometimes"—my aunt lit the candle then wiggled her fingers at me to take her hand—"the best way to get rid of the dead is to listen. When they've had their say, they go."

I took her hand. "If this goes wrong, I want you to use the black candle." She flicked her other hand at me, rings clicking.

"That is only a last resort. That gets rid of everything. The bad and the good. You know that."

Aunt Jodene believed I no longer had guardian angels or spirit guides. When we banished Henry, it had banished everything. She thought I could have regained some since, but I didn't want them.

I sighed. "You're enjoying this."

Her smile widened and she squeezed my hand. "It's not every day I get to talk to an actual ghost. Oh, I get feelings, images or, once in a while, a voice, just a word or two.

Nothing like what you have the ability to experience. I know you don't want to hear this, but you have a great gift. You are so rare. So many people would love to be like you, to speak to those passed on, but they can't."

I glanced at Carme, who hovered close by. It wasn't the first time I'd heard her and Carme call it a gift. I knew it was not. Carme had done everything she could her entire life to communicate with the dead, without success. I wouldn't wish it on Carme or Aunt Jodene. Despite what they thought, it would be like passing on a curse.

"What are we doing?" I asked.

"Watch the flame." She pointed at the candle. "We didn't do this before because we didn't need to. It's a subtle way of communicating with those passed on. One that doesn't require their presence to be too strong."

"Right." We definitely hadn't needed it with my stepfather.

"You see how straight the flame is now? We'll ask a few yes-or-no questions. If the answer is yes, the flame will grow vertically. If the answer is no, the flame will move from side to side."

My chest tightened. Aunt Jodene squeezed my hand. "It will be okay, I promise."

With a deep inhale, I nodded again. I wanted this to be over.

"Ready?" She flicked her hand through the air at me with great drama. "Never mind. Don't answer that. Let's begin with a protection incantation."

She closed her eyes and deepened her breathing.

"This is a bad idea," I muttered, but joined in with the familiar words. "Save us from harm, guard us from evil. Protect us from unwanted connections."

We repeated it several times, until my aunt raised her

hand, eyes still closed. "We wish to speak to the entity here with us."

Every instinct wanted to make her stop. This was the last thing I ever thought I would be doing. My hands shot to cover my ears as the ringing reached painful levels.

Aunt Jodene took one of my wrists and pushed up my sleeve. She slipped a bracelet on me, cool and smooth against my skin. It had a dozen stones of different shapes and sizes in shades of red, pink, green, blue and black.

She held her hand over the bracelet, pressing it firmly to my wrist. "This will help." The ringing eased to tolerable levels.

"Thanks." I tapped my nose. "Lavender." It was everywhere now, like a flowery cloud.

Aunt Jodene placed both hands on her lap. "Is there a presence here that wishes to speak to us?"

The flame rose straight up in a positive reply before returning back to normal.

My aunt winked. "That was an easy one."

"Please, can we be quick about this?"

"Of course, honey." She had far too much excitement in her voice. She cleared her throat and sat taller. "Are we speaking to Mary—" She paused and leaned over to me. "What's her last name?"

"Brunning." My reply came out choked, the enormity of it hitting me. Mary Brunning, who I'd sat with so many times talking about her life, was now dead.

The flame on the candle grew larger and lowered again.

"Are you trying to scare or harm Amy?" my aunt asked and I held my breath.

The candle flickered with no direction until I couldn't hold my breath any longer.

"What does that mean?" I asked.

"Could be she's having trouble communicating. She's a brand-new spirit, after all. Is it hard for you to move the flame?" she asked the air.

The candle stopped flickering, then shot straight up before shrinking back down.

"Okay." My aunt sighed. "We've got that established. It must be easier for her to simply make it grow bigger."

The candle flame grew once again, momentarily.

"I don't think she means you any harm, honey. I believe she is struggling a bit." The flame grew again. "Are you trying to get a message to Amy?" The flame showed another yes.

I took a breath and sat up straighter. "Mary. Please just leave." The candle began to bounce, like someone jiggled the table, then it flew off the table and hit the wall.

# Chapter 5

The candle had gone out by the time I got to it, and my ears felt better. Palms sweaty, I picked up the candle and set it back on the table.

My aunt stared at the candle. "We were supposed to leave that burning for another twenty-four hours." She stood, but sat again. "I think she got upset when you asked her to leave."

An upset ghost was not a good thing, but at least it was gone.

"Do you know why her preceding scent is lavender?" Aunt Jodene asked.

"She liked lavender oils," I told her. Henry's scent had been moldy leather. He'd been buried in his favourite four-thousand-dollar jacket.

"If Mary killed herself because of you and was out for revenge, she wouldn't just leave because you asked her to. I suppose we can never completely know the ways of the dead or the undead." Aunt Jodene's tone held both sadness and admiration. "I'm pretty sure we had a vampire here the other day, looking for books."

"Vampire?"

She waggled a finger at me. "Lots of them around here; just no one knows it. They keep to themselves. As powerful as they are, they're not keen on getting staked."

"Vampires exist and one came here. During the day?"

She dismissed me with a flick of her hand. "Don't believe everything from the movies."

I ran a hand through my hair. "Don't go poking vampires, please. If they want to stay hidden, let them. I worry about you enough as it is."

Aunt Jodene laughed. "Werewolves, witches, warlocks, goblins, fairies, we just have so much to learn."

A book rattled, then fell off the centre table display.

"I smell lavender." I watched the shop nervously. "Wait." There was something else. Another smell. I got up and moved to the middle of the shop. "It smells like urine," I realized with disgust. "The lavender here. The urine at the front."

Something pulled at my wrist. The lavender smell became so strong, I could taste it. There was another tug at my wrist and I pulled my arm away. My bracelet snapped and fell to the ground. My ears rang so much it hurt.

"Do you have a printer?" I yelled.

"In the back," my aunt replied. "It's not working."

"I don't think it will matter." I went to the back room.

It was a small space with sets of shelves along the walls packed with various inventory and a little break area.

Carme poked her head in behind me. "Over there." She pointed to the bottom shelf on the right. "Under the tarot books."

I found it, a clunky old beast of a printer, and dug it out. Carme held the door for me as I carried it out and set it on the glass counter. Next to the printer was a flyer printed on light blue paper, inviting people to a meditation circle on Halloween. Horrible idea.

I flipped it over and stuck it in the printer. Maybe Mary could tell us who the other spirit was and we could do something about it.

"Mary?" I asked the air. "Are you here?" My chest felt heavy.

We stared at the printer. The circular clock with a black cat laying on a stack of books ticked above us. Metal and wooden chimes in the front window display began a clacking, clanging, menacing symphony.

Carme started to head toward the front, but I put a hand on her arm and shook my head. I didn't want her anywhere near the urine-smelling entity.

The chimes got more violent and frenzied like they were caught in a tornado. The printer vibrated, drawing our attention back to it. I found myself rooting for it to print.

"Come on, Mary," I yelled. "Shed some light on this."

The blue paper shook as the printer came to life and dragged it inside. It printed for a few seconds then spit the page out. I grabbed it before it could slide onto the floor. Aunt Jodene and Carme peeked over the counter. There were only four words.

*Lies Murdered Help Me*

A blast of air moved through the shop, shaking things, then crashed into us. My hand slid along the top edge of the counter as I tried to keep from falling, but I hit the ground, hard.

Aunt Jodene and Carme fell together in a heap. My aunt groaned and I hoped the crack I'd heard was incense sticks and not bone.

It was like a windstorm had overtaken the shop.

"You two all right?" I yelled.

"Yes," came their staggered replies.

I crawled around to the front of the counter to join them. We sat with our backs against the counter.

"We should go," I shouted.

The back of the store became victim to the rush of wind. Candles and trinkets flew off the shelves.

Then things went quiet. I forced myself to breathe, because I wasn't sure if I had been.

Aunt Jodene reached out for my hand and Carme's. She closed her eyes and began to chant, loudly, in what I thought was Hebrew. My hand tingled and I felt my aunt's strength, reassuring and comforting. Her voice grew stronger and louder. I tried to lend her all the energy I could, even though I didn't know if it helped.

The bookcase tilted and then crashed down hard. I got my feet under me but stayed crouched as I held my aunt's hand. She was deep in her chant, under a kind of trance.

"Come on," I urged her. "We've got to go."

Carme grabbed Aunt Jodene's other elbow and we tried to get her up. The smell of urine mixed with the lavender and made me nauseous. The wind whipped in circles, then rushed down on us. Aunt Jodene's eyes went wide and she gasped for air. Her entire body flexed in one giant cramp. She squeezed my hand, then went completely limp.

# Chapter 6

Carme shook Aunt Jodene's shoulders. "Mom?"

For a few, excruciating seconds, Aunt Jodene didn't breathe, but then her chest heaved up and down with big gulps of air. Tears rippled down Carme's face as she cradled her mom's upper body.

"Aunt Jodene?" I leaned in closer. "Can you hear me?"

Her eyes shot open so fast, I fell back. They were completely black and I wasn't sure if she saw anything. Aunt Jodene's mouth moved a little, like she was trying to speak.

I grabbed her hand. "Aunt Jodene?" Silence. "Carme, get her other hand."

Carme sniffled and reached down for her mom's hand. "Mom?"

Aunt Jodene's mouth moved, but nothing came out. Her eyes began to clear, the black disappearing like clouds blown away by the wind.

"Aunt Jodene, we're here. Keep fighting it." Whatever it was.

Her mouth stopped moving and she closed her eyes again, going limp in Carme's arms.

Carme started to panic, but I touched her arm. "I think she's resting now," I told her, which I believed. "She is strong." Also true. "She'll be okay." I wasn't sure about that last one, but I had to believe it, and right now, so did Carme.

"What do we do?" Carme's tears continued to flow.

My first thought was the coffee shop. It always felt safe there and I knew it was well protected. But what if she stopped breathing again?

"Hospital," I replied. "Then we'll figure out how to help her."

My coat had flown off the counter at some point. I grabbed it and dug out my phone but hesitated. Should I call 911? There would be a lot of questions we didn't have answers for: the state of the shop, what happened to Aunt Jodene. The police might get involved. This wasn't the kind of thing you could take to the police. I'd learned years ago when I had tried to convince them my dead stepfather had killed my two best friends. I'd also heard too many stories about people with disabilities being accused of things they didn't do. What if they thought Carme had something to do with this? Would they listen to me? They might assume I was covering for my cousin.

The only person close by I knew with a car who could take us to the hospital was Charles. We wouldn't be able to tell him about what happened, either, but at least he wouldn't question us.

I called the cafe. Ethan answered. "The Artful Cup; how can I help you?"

I swallowed hard. "Ethan, this is Amy. Is Charles there?"

"No, Dad went home sick. Is there anything I can do?"

My brain did acrobatics. "Sorry to hear Charles is sick. I'm at my aunt's shop. There's been an accident and we need to get her to the hospital." I tried not to sound too panicked, but I think I failed.

"Oh, no," came his reply. "What happened? Never mind; details later. I've got my car. Darren?" The call for his brother was muffled, like he'd held the phone away. "Can you watch things if I call in someone to cover me?" There was a pause where I couldn't hear anything, then Ethan's voice came through clearly again.

"I'll call someone to come in to help Darren. Can you wait a few minutes or should you call 911?"

"We're okay to wait," I said, which was true. My aunt had fallen into an easy slumber, her head on Carme's lap.

"Okay," Ethan replied in crisis-management mode. "As soon as I know someone is coming, I'll come get you. At your aunt's shop?"

"Yes," I answered. "And thank you."

"No problem," he answered. We ended the call.

Carme stared at me. I nodded. "Ethan is coming to get us soon." She nodded back and stroked her mother's grey hair.

I set to cleaning what I could before Ethan arrived. The shelving unit could be explained as part of the accident. The scattered books, the scattered inventory made it look like the shop had been attacked. Which it had.

But by what? Mary? The smell of lavender had disappeared. I searched for the blue flyer I'd put in the printer and picked it up.

*Lies Murdered Please Help Me*

Lies. The suicide had been a lie. That's what she'd been trying to tell me. There'd been a note naming me as the cause of the suicide, though. What kind of a note had it been? A handwritten one? Or something printed that anyone could have done?

"Carme. Mary didn't kill herself. I think someone murdered her."

Carme's eyes widened. "Who?"

"I don't know. Who would want to kill Mary? One of her ex-boyfriends?"

They had almost all been controlling, self-centred jerks, but murderers? Maybe one had wanted to hurt us both because I'd helped Mary find herself and get rid of them.

Carme shrugged at me. "But, like, wouldn't the police know if she was murdered?"

"Good point." Her observation threw my hypothesis into doubt. Of course, I wanted to believe Mary hadn't killed herself. It would mean I hadn't driven her to suicide. Then again, it didn't leave me without responsibility for her death. If it had been murder and someone tried to make it look like she'd killed herself because of me, I had either been the motivation or an added bonus. I didn't like the idea of either of those.

What about this other spirit? The one I suspected was now inside Aunt Jodene? How was it connected? Had it been haunting Mary's ghost? Hurting her? The person who might know these things began to stir in Carme's lap.

Aunt Jodene's eyelids fluttered. I crashed down to my knees beside her and Carme. Aunt Jodene's chest heaved as though she were building strength. She was a fighter, my aunt. Eyes still closed, her mouth moved.

Carme folded down over her mom. "Mom?"

"What did she say?" I asked.

"Apparition chamber," Carme said with a small gasp.

"What's an apparition chamber?"

"I'm not sure," Carme said, slowly. "But I've heard of it."

I touched Aunt Jodene's shoulder. She had gone back to easy breathing. "Okay," I said quietly. "We'll figure it out."

Ethan knocked and I let him in. His eyes widened as he took in the shop. My efforts at cleaning up hadn't improved it very much.

"It's a long story," I said, and hoped the cliche would work for now.

He stepped around the scattered items to Aunt Jodene and knelt beside her. "What happened to her?"

"She fell," Carme said, and peered at me.

"Fell?" he echoed.

I stepped over piles of scattered incense to get to them. "She was cleaning the top of that shelf unit." I pointed over at it. "And it fell. She fell. It all fell."

He studied the shelf, several feet away from where Carme and Aunt Jodene were on the floor. "Then," I went on, "she sort of staggered over here, knocking over things, and Carme got her to the ground."

I was not a good liar, never had been. If I had, I might not have spent so many years in therapy talking about the terrifying ghost of my stepfather. I could've lied and gotten out of seeing therapists, since it never helped.

Carme smiled to corroborate the story but Ethan still appeared to have a lot of questions.

He gave my aunt a once-over. "Is it okay to move her?"

"Yes," I replied. "I'm sure it is."

Ethan scooped my aunt up in both arms and did a power squat to stand up, grunting with the effort. I rushed ahead to open the door.

"My car is out front." He nodded toward a mid-sized dark blue SUV parked on the street.

We got my aunt into the back seat and Carme sat with

her. We had a silent fifteen-minute ride to the hospital.

Being the day before Halloween, the hospital swarmed with costumed patients and staff. I focused on admitting Aunt Jodene.

Ethan politely stayed until they called us in. "Do you want me to wait? Take you home?"

"No, you get back to Darren and the cafe. We can take transit or call a cab," I said.

Carme and I both thanked him as many times as we could fit in before he finally waved and walked away.

It took time to get Aunt Jodene settled into a room after her initial examination. They set her up for overnight monitoring, needles and tubes running out of her.

Carme and I hovered over Aunt Jodene, surrounded by buzzing monitors.

"What now?" Carme asked.

I wasn't really sure. "Do you want to stay here? I'll stay with you, if you want." I didn't like hospitals much. People passed away there, and being around recently dead people was the last thing I wanted. But I'd do it for Carme.

Carme shook her head and flopped a hand toward her mom's bed. "I think she's going to stay like this."

Unfortunately, I had to agree. Whatever had gotten inside her would keep her this way until we figured out how to get rid of it. We needed to fix this, fast.

Carme put her hand on my shoulder. "Tomorrow is Halloween."

"I know."

"We can't be closed on Halloween."

"You want to open the shop?"

She nodded. "Mom needs Halloween. And I can find out what an apparition chamber is."

"But, Carme"—I lowered my voice, not knowing if Aunt Jodene could hear us—"it's a mess. It would take hours to clean it."

"So, we clean it," Carme said.

A lot of things had been destroyed, stock lost. Aunt Jodene had said she couldn't get insurance to cover it, so she and the shop would take a loss. If the Feathered Serpent wasn't open on Halloween, it would be another huge hit to Aunt Jodene's business. Thank goodness for Canadian healthcare. Aunt Jodene's time in the hospital wouldn't add to the financial burden.

"But there are no wards there." I pointed at Aunt Jodene in her hospital bed. "What if this happens to us?"

Carme spread her arms wide with an overly exaggerated grin. "What if we get hit by a bus?"

"Not funny," I said, though it was a little. The shop had all my aunt's contacts. We might be able to get help from one of her connections. Or anything we couldn't find on the internet, Carme should be able to locate in a book.

"It has to be safe," I said. "I'm not letting this happen to you or anyone else."

Carme nodded, and I could see the gears work in her head. "I bet I could find something. Temporary. Make it creepy for Halloween."

"Are you sure?"

Carme frowned. "You don't trust me?"

I held both hands up. "No, it's definitely not that. I'm just worried about someone getting hurt. You, most of all."

"Worry about yourself." She pointed at her mom. "Look." My aunt was smiling.

I never booked clients on Halloween. My Halloween plan had been the same as always, to hide with my cats until morning.

"Okay," I said with a sigh. "We open the shop and you get it protected. We find out how to help Aunt Jodene and what an apparition chamber is. I could try to contact Mary."

Carme's eyes went wide. "Yes, you could."

My chest tightened, but I knew I had to do it. "Aunt Jodene," I said toward the bed. "We need you. Please keep fighting."

Aunt Jodene didn't smile again, but her face softened. Carme shooed us out the door. "Let her rest," she whispered to me.

By the time we got to the shop, it was dark. We had four hours till midnight and Halloween, when it would be easier for the dead to talk to me. The fact I wasn't shutting them out with everything I could terrified me.

The shop cleanup appeared manageable. Maybe. The bookcase was still intact, a lot of the books undamaged. The cash counter had lost its surface contents again, but at least the glass and the things inside the case were okay.

There was no scent of lavender. Mary wasn't around anymore. Ghost smell wasn't like a lingering perfume that would hang around after the dead left. It was an entry sign, a signal they were around.

In the reading area, I returned the two chairs and table to their upright position. "After midnight, I'm going to try to talk to Mary."

Carme's eyes widened. "She's a ghost, you know," she said with a smirk.

My insides froze at the thought. "If Mary can help your mom, I have to talk to her."

Carme clapped twice. "Yes. You can do this."

We went to work. Carme focused on the biggest mess at the back of the store. I put back anything not broken, crushed or bent. Or at least I put them where I thought they went. Aunt Jodene would probably rearrange everything if she came back. When she came back. We'd find a way to get her out of this. We had to.

At midnight on the dot, Carme pointed at me. "Ready?"

First, I nodded, but then shook my head. My vision spun a bit and I forced myself to breathe. Mary had shown no aggression or ill intent. No other ghosts. Just her. I could do this for Aunt Jodene.

My cousin studied me. "You okay? I will light a candle." She moved fast, like I might change my mind. She put a candle on the table and lit it. We each sat.

I closed my eyes and took a deep breath. "Mary?" After waiting for what felt like an extremely long time, I sighed and opened my eyes.

"Nothing?" Carme asked.

"No smells, no voices, nothing. Maybe she got scared off by whoever the urine-smelling spirit was."

"Gross." Carme wrinkled her nose.

"Mary?" I repeated. Still nothing.

Carme scooted her chair around to settle across from me. She leaned forward and held both my hands in hers and closed her eyes.

"Again," she said.

I took a big breath through my nose and blew it out my mouth, slowly. "Mary? We'd like to talk to you."

"The printer," I said.

Carme jumped to her feet, grabbed a piece of paper and put it in. She circled a hand at me expectantly.

"Mary?" I asked again. "Can you talk to us?"

We stared at the printer but nothing happened.

My phone buzzed and made me jump. It was a text from Liam.

*Hey! I'm on the Drive, you around?*

I started to type a reply, then deleted it a couple of times because I didn't know what to say.

"I'll get my notebooks. Might help," Carme said.

Before I settled on a lie to keep Liam away from the shop, he sent me another text.

*I see you! Let me in.*

He waved at me from outside, a little goofy like he'd probably been somewhere for a few drinks. I tried to think of excuses to keep him out but hadn't thought of a good one by the time I got to the door.

"Hi," I said, door only partly open.

"What's going on?" He pushed his way in, swearing in Spanish. "What the hell happened here?" He turned back to me.

My brain spun. I hated lying to him but I didn't want him to be in danger, ever. His expectant, raised eyebrows made it worse. Like he knew I was about to lie to him.

"Aunt Jodene fell. She was cleaning those shelves," I lied. "It hit her, she staggered around, knocking things over. Carme knocked this table over, getting to her. We took her to the hospital."

Liam appeared ready to challenge my lies until I got to the hospital part. "Is she all right?"

I nodded, lying again. "She is fine. We left her sleeping." That part was sort of true, at least.

The door to the back room opened. Carme had a small wire notebook in her hands as she came out. "I found Mom's list of people. Maybe we can find help." She stopped when she saw Liam. "Oh. Hi." She lowered the book.

Liam's eyebrows lifted. "You need Jodene's people to help you? As in"—he spread his arms wide and twisted to indicate the shop—"these kinds of people?"

Carme and I exchanged glances. I didn't know what to say.

Liam's arms dropped with loud smacks to his legs. "You don't trust me enough to tell me the truth?"

I started to argue but realized he had a point. Who did I trust more than Carme and Liam? Aunt Jodene. It was a short list. But I couldn't get him involved. "I trust you. I'm just trying to protect you."

He started pacing. "Okay, now I'm even more concerned. What is this? Do you have some sort of stalker or something? Someone bothering you? Is it Nik?"

I waved him off. "No, nothing like that." Not really.

He let out a strong breath. "If you tell me you're not in danger, I will trust you. That's how friendship works," he added with a sarcastic raise of the eyebrows.

"I'm not in danger," I said, which, at the moment was pretty true.

He gave me a bit of side-eye. "Fine. I gotta go meet some friends. Please message me if you need anything."

"I will, I promise." I hoped I didn't need to ever keep that promise.

He stepped over a couple of books as he walked to the door, unlocked it and let himself out.

"Sorry," Carme said quietly from behind me as we watched Liam walk past the shop and out of sight.

I shook my head. "It's okay."

"I found something else." Carme left me for the back

room again, then came out with a large leather-bound book open in her hands. She placed it on the counter and tapped the page like an excited explorer on a new map.

"Something to ward the shop?" I asked.

"No. The apparition chamber." She moved her finger, carefully and slowly reading each word. "It's used to arrange encounters between the living and the dead."

"Aunt Jodene wants me to use one of those to talk to Mary?" My chest tightened.

"I guess so. There's a few tricky things." She squinted at me in apology.

"Of course there is. What?"

"You have to give up dairy." She said it hesitantly, like there was more coming.

"And?" I prompted.

"You have to give up caffeine."

My head hurt at the mere thought. "Please tell me you're joking?"

"Sorry. That's what it says. Also." She took in a deep breath like she really didn't want to say the next part.

"What is it, Carme?"

She gave me a tiny, apologetic smile. "We need Mary's skull."

# Chapter 7

According to Carme's book, an apparition chamber was used by the ancient Greeks to communicate with spirits. To reach it, one had to first make their way through a darkened maze of corridors and rooms. The chamber would be bathed in candlelight and in the centre would stand a large, highly polished metal cauldron. With guidance from priests, the person wishing to speak to the dead would then gaze at the shiny surface of the cauldron until the spirit appeared.

There were preparation rules. A list of protocols for the most clarity, like no dairy and no caffeine.

"You know what else this book says about apparition chambers?" I yelled to Carme in the back room.

She poked her head out the door. "The meditation part?"

"Yes, which you didn't bring up."

She came through the door and propped a hand on her hip. "Didn't seem as important as needing a person's skull." It came out with an impressive amount of snark. She tapped her chin in mock thought. "If only we knew someone good at meditating." She pointed at the paper Mary had printed on. "Look at the other side."

I grabbed the light blue flyer I'd used for Mary's message and flipped it over. It was about a meditation circle, and the name of the person running appeared at the bottom. "Nik Marson? No, way." I turned the flyer facedown again. I'd do it on my own.

"So stubborn," my cousin chided, then disappeared into the back again.

Asking Nik for help with meditation after our history would be almost as bad as giving up caffeine. If it had to be mediation, then I'd figure it out. Aunt Jodene had dozens of books on it here. I'd be fine. Carme did have a point about the skull, though. It kind of made all the rest null and void.

"Do you think there's anything that would substitute for the skull?" I yelled back at Carme.

She poked her head out again. "Kinda busy here." She gave a scoffing noise and closed the door again.

Eventually, Carme came out with another stack of books and plopped them on the counter. She grabbed her mom's contact book and opened it. Almost immediately, she smiled at me. "I found someone to help."

"Good," I answered, glad for some positive news. "Who?"

She held the book open to me. "Your mom."

"Carme, no." Memories of trying to reach my mother after she died rushed back at me. The fear at trying, the disappointment when I couldn't make contact. For whatever reason, I'd never received any messages from my mother.

Carme stared at me.

"What good would it do, anyway?" I asked. "Mom didn't have any abilities with the dead."

Carme tapped the book. "This is Mom's emergency list. Aunt Alicia's name is right here. At the top."

"Sure." I flicked my hand at the list. "Mom was an

emergency contact. If something happened to you or Aunt Jodene."

"You mean like now?" Carme was full of snark tonight. Having her mother in the hospital brought it out in full force.

"You know what I mean. Non-paranormal emergencies."

She shoved the book at me. "It's not that kind of list."

It didn't make any sense. If Mom had had any sort of abilities, she would've told me.

Below my mom's name in Aunt Jodene's book were a few people I recognized from the Vancouver area, other shop owners.

"You have to contact your mom," Carme said.

Maybe my wards had kept her from sending me messages. Still, I thought if our bond had been strong enough, if she'd loved me enough, she would've been able to reach me. It still hurt to think about.

Carme had also tried to contact my mom. She had hoped she might have better luck contacting the dead if it was a family member. Aunt Jodene had tried. No one had ever been able to contact my mother.

"Try," Carme said, clearly annoyed with me. "I will do a ward."

"You found one; fabulous." As usual, I was impressed with her efficiency and skill.

Her head bobbed as she went to the back again. "It's simple but will help. Plus"—she held up her pointer finger as she walked away—"it's Halloween. People like feeling creepy."

Before tackling something challenging, I would tell a client to think of the worst that could happen. In most cases, the worst thing wasn't actually so bad. In some cases, the worst thing was so outrageous and silly, it eased some of the pressure. In this case, the worst thing would be contacting something not my mom, something evil that would hurt those I loved. Like Henry had. My own coaching was not helping.

Holding on to Aunt Jodene's emergency-contact book like a talisman, I went to the reading corner and sat down in the wicker chair. Maybe instead of the candle, I'd simply go with my gut and start talking. Maybe with her sister in danger, my mom would respond.

"Mom? Hey. So, we have some things happening here, paranormal things." The words spilled out. "They say my client killed herself, but I think she's trying to tell me she was actually murdered. Aunt Jodene was helping, but then some other spirit showed up, went inside her and now she's in the hospital. She's doing okay. She's fighting." I stopped, breath held, wanting to hear back, hoping for a smell or signal Mom was there. Nothing.

"Mom, Aunt Jodene has you in her contact book for emergencies. For regular emergencies, right? I mean, I would've known if you were the same as me, wouldn't I? But Carme thought I should contact you. If you can help us, in any way, we really need it."

A strong peppermint scent flooded over me and a woman clearly said, "Where am I?"

It was not my mother's voice.

# Chapter 8

My hands trembled uncontrollably. Carme put an armful of items on the counter. "Your mom?"

I shook my head. It sounded nothing like my mom. "It was a different woman."

Her eyes lit up. "Someone to help us?"

The scent of peppermint, like freshly brewed mint tea, surrounded me. "Excuse me," the voice said. "Can you tell me where I am?"

She spoke clearly, pronounced each letter succinctly with a hint of an accent but not one I could place. My ears weren't ringing. This was a clear, strong voice, as though she stood right next to me. I hadn't heard a spirit this clear since I'd been quite young. Maybe not even then.

Fear clenched my chest. "Carme, we're not safe here."

"Don't worry." She picked up an herb wand, a smaller one I hadn't seen before. "We'll do a cleansing. And personal wards. I'll draw symbols with water around the shop." Carme didn't hide her excitement. She set the stick down again, then picked up two tiny jars and nodded at two more on the counter. "I will fill these with gems and herbs and put them in the four corners of the shop. Get rid of nasty spirits. Keep any good ones. Nobody will even know."

"Excuse me, can anyone hear me?" The voice again.

Carme surveyed her mom's shop approvingly. "Okay. I'll get to it."

Carme didn't ask for help and I didn't offer because we both knew she could do it better. She performed her elaborate movements with the herbal stick while I fought an internal war. Ever since Henry's spirit had tormented me and killed my friends, I'd vowed never to speak to the dead again. Was it possible a spirit could help us in ways no one in the human world could?

The woman started coughing. "Must you? Really?"

"Ready for wards?" Carme grabbed some incense and a burner plus a couple of gemstones from a basket.

"I trust you, you know," I told her.

Carme sat in the red armchair. "You should." She lit three candles on the small table between our chairs, then lit two sticks of incense.

Carme waved her incense stick like a conductor and quietly whispered her own warding words. She repeated the process for me, then placed a round gemstone in her hand and gave one to me. Mine was light green; hers was pink.

"Now hold the stone in your hand. Like this." She sounded every bit like a schoolteacher. She placed her pink stone in the centre of her right palm. "Good. Close your eyes. Take my hand."

I did as I was told and sensed my cousin sit taller. She took a deep breath. "Put your energy in the stone. Then picture, like, a bubble coming out from it."

After several seconds, my hand with the gem began to tingle. It intensified until I swore my hand must've been glowing. The tingling moved up my arms, into my shoulders and chest, then stretched from the top of my head all the way down to my feet.

Carme might not have been able to communicate with the dead, but the energy I felt her put into my ward was incredibly strong. Much stronger than mine, no question. Even stronger than Aunt Jodene's.

"Now create the bubble," Carme said softly.

Feeling more alive, invigorated and positive than I had in a long time, I imagined a bubble around my entire body. In my mind it had a green tint, like the stone. I tried to make it as thick and strong as I could.

"That tickles," the woman's voice said. "Whatever are you silly women doing?"

My eyes popped open. "Carme." It came out in a whisper. "The woman is talking to me again. Full sentences. Like I've never experienced before."

Carme's eyes popped open wide. "What does she want?"

"Could you just help me, please? I'm not sure where I am." The woman's tone had turned anxious, which made me nervous.

"She doesn't know where she is."

Carme sat straighter. "You're in the Feathered Serpent, Vancouver, British Columbia, Canada." She spoke slowly, clearly and loudly to the air.

"The Feathered Serpent?" the voice replied, only to me. "What sort of place is that? At any rate, thank you."

"Did she say anything?" Carme asked.

Reluctantly, I answered my cousin. "She said thank you."

Carme grinned like it was her birthday. "You're welcome," she said to the shop, louder than necessary.

"Why am I here?" the woman asked. "What's this?" I didn't know what she meant, but the peppermint smell vanished.

"I think she's gone," I said. My cousin's face drooped, so I changed the subject. "Should we look at more apparition-chamber books?" We both knew I wasn't going to try to contact my mom again. Not now, at least.

"I'll have to dig around a bit." Carme went to the back and I followed. She held the door open, exposing the cramped room.

"We can do it," I told her.

We moved boxes and piles of stock. Carme pointed at a stack of books on the top shelf. "I think there, maybe."

They certainly appeared old and worn enough. Maybe we could find one that said I didn't have to give up caffeine or, better yet, wouldn't need me to use meditation.

"Can we take these back to my place?" I asked her. "We can just catch the last SkyTrain."

"If I get cat cuddles." She stacked the books into my arms.

"Oh, right," I replied. "As if you wouldn't."

My cats loved Carme. She had recently lost her cat, Fidget. He had been a stray, a bruiser of a cat, with one good eye and a hatred of humans. All humans except for Carme. She had fed Fidget in an alley every night, and after a few weeks he'd led her to a litter of homeless kittens. Carme took them to the shelter. Then they did it again. And again.

Eventually, Fidget had allowed Carme to take him in. He still hated all other humans, including me, till the day he died. Carme wasn't ready for a new cat yet, but she loved my cats. They attached to her like Velcro when she visited.

We used Feathered Serpent bags to carry the books on

the SkyTrain. A little advertising never hurt, especially the night before Halloween.

A group of teenagers around Carme's age made comments among themselves. Some pointed toward my cousin with snickers, and I caught the word *retard* once. Carme pretended not to notice but I saw her flinch.

I'd experienced all the different reactions people had to my cousin. Some older people treated her with pity and talked down to her like she was a small child. I forgave them a little, since they'd grown up with Down syndrome being cause for institutionalization. The amount of research, discoveries and available resources for people with Down syndrome made that archaic thinking. The kids now went to mainstream schools, college, had jobs or owned businesses. They led rich lives.

Kids loved Carme. If they noticed she was different or not, they certainly didn't care. Many people treated her with respect, but there were still small-minded bullies like these jerks.

Would saying something to them accomplish anything? Unlikely. The way she ignored them while having fun with the friendlier transit-goers, I knew this was one to let go. She was capable of standing up for herself. I'd seen it many times, and it often left people cowering, which was awesome to watch. I decided to take her lead and joined in the conversation she was having with two little girls across from us.

Despite all the other smells on the train, I caught the strong scent of peppermint. It didn't overwhelm me but was more like something familiar. Comfortable.

One of the jerks lurched forward like he'd lost his balance because of the train. He fell into the laps of two of the other young men. They pushed him off with indignant expressions while much of the train laughed. They were so busy trying to regain their cool composure when we reached our stop, they didn't even notice us leave.

"So disrespectful," the woman's voice said beside me as we walked toward my apartment.

"Carme." I sped up, not that it would help. If she'd pushed the boy on the train, not only had she been with us, she was strong enough to affect our world. We would have to be careful.

"What?" Carme asked.

"The woman is back."

My cousin smiled. "She is?" She waved in all directions into the air above us. "Hello again, mystery lady," Carme called out. People stared at us, and this time, I didn't blame them.

As expected, the cats were extremely unhappy with me, but once I fed them, they settled down. Wookiee, the leaner, smarter of my cats, howled at Carme, clearly displeased with how long it had been since her last visit. He stuck to her like glue when she sat on the couch. Midnight, Wookiee's brother, was a big brute and also a cuddle bug. He came to join me.

There was a good reason I had cats, besides the company and love of animals. It was strange they didn't react to the woman's presence, but I knew she was there, because I still smelled peppermint.

Carme reached over and gave my sleeve a tug. "Is she still here?"

"Nothing seems to keep her away."

"Well, why would it?" the woman said.

"What's her name?" Carme asked, then scowled at me

when I shrugged. "What's your name?"

"I don't know," the woman said.

I cleared my throat. "She doesn't know."

Carme stopped petting Wookie. "She doesn't know? You don't know who you are?" she asked the air.

"I—no. I guess I don't." The woman sounded sad and a little scared.

"She doesn't," I said, this time with more sympathy. Alive or dead, not knowing who you were or where you were would be pretty awful.

Carme tapped her finger on her chin. "You're a mystery. We could call you Myst."

"I don't know if that's a good—" The woman cut me off.

"Oh, yes. Myst. Tell her I like that."

"She said she likes it." I, however, didn't like how easily this spirit worked her way into our lives. We didn't know if she meant us harm. The sooner we got answers, the sooner this could stop.

"Do you know anything about Mary Brunning?" I asked Myst. "Recently killed?"

Silence. Carme switched between staring at me and scanning the air.

"I'm sorry, who?" Myst replied. I shook my head at Carme and her posture deflated.

Maybe a different approach. "Do you know anything about Jodene Cameron? What's happened to her?"

Myst sighed, loudly. "I'm not some crystal ball. I don't know what you are talking about." She sounded like she was almost on my shoulder.

"Sorry, Carme," I said. "She doesn't know anything."

"Well, I wouldn't say that," Myst snapped. "I'm sure I know plenty. I just...can't seem to remember..." Her voice trailed off.

Carme handed me one of the books, then opened one over top of Wookiee. "So, we keep digging."

"We can't stay up all night doing this." I flipped open the old text. "We have to get up to open the shop." Being home, so close to my bed, I felt exhausted.

"Uh-huh." She had her nose in her book, finger trailing the lines.

With a tired sigh, I began to read. Almost everything on apparition chambers said to avoid caffeine for at least two days before. Most said no dairy, either. The meditation was in every single one.

"Any mention of meditation in yours?"

Carme snickered. "You know someone who is, like, really good at meditation."

"That's it." I went and got blankets and a pillow for the couch. "I'll sleep here; you go take my bed."

Carme tucked her book under her arm, grabbed two more, then headed to my room, Wookiee at her heels. "Good night." Her smile faded. "We're going to help my mom, right?"

"Of course," I said. "It's all going to work out."

She gave a firm nod, hugged the books and went into my bedroom. After getting comfortable on the couch, I tried to sleep, but a thought nagged at me.

Midnight plopped himself down on my chest. "Am I being selfish, not going to Nik for help?" I asked him.

"Obviously, you are," Myst said.

"I didn't ask you," I replied, a little too loud.

Carme rushed out of the bedroom. "Are you okay?"

"Yes. I think I better call Nik in the morning."

Carme gave a fist-pump. "Yes! I'll make notes for the

chamber. Good night."

"Good night." I pulled the blanket up over my head.

# Chapter 9

We opened the shop before the usual time of ten AM but didn't stop at the cafe on our way. I already felt the effects. My brain and body dragged with exhaustion. My head hurt.

Carme appeared unaffected by the lack of caffeine, which she graciously denied herself so I wouldn't have to smell it or see her drinking it. She placed a welcome charm on the outside of the shop door and waved to early-morning sidewalk occupants while I suffered in silence.

Myst hadn't talked to me this morning, but I got consistent hints of peppermint, so I knew she never stayed away long.

Last night before I slept, I went back to the infamous blow-up Nik and I had had online. Years later, despite not wanting to see it, I knew he was right. He'd left a polite and helpful comment about his experience with meditation and I'd blown up. I came across as defensive and wounded. It was because I had deeper issues going on, but it didn't matter. It hadn't been my finest moment online.

While I'd been having a personal-growth moment in the middle of the night, Carme had taken notes. An apparition chamber started with a trip through a dark maze in order to cut out any outside stimuli. Traditionally, the reflective surface was a cauldron with water or oils, but a mirror could also be used. It was similar to scrying—people gazed into water, a mirror or a crystal ball to tell the future—but we wanted to speak to the dead.

"A mirror would be easier than a cauldron," I said to Carme.

"Like Harry Potter," she replied.

"Comfortable attire," I read Carme's handwriting. "That's easy." Today I'd gone true to Feathered Serpent style with black leggings, ankle-high flat boots and a long-sleeved mini dress my aunt had given me. It was a beautiful dark purple with tiny silver galaxies all over. I thought it would make Aunt Jodene happy. We'd called the hospital first thing, and she was still unresponsive.

I focused back on the list. "Cut out dairy and caffeine, okay, started that." I gave it an invisible check with my finger.

Carme pointed at the next one, *meditation*. "You said you'd call."

"I'd rather try to get Mary's skull," I answered.

"Amy," Carme scolded.

I held up a hand in defeat. "I'll call him."

"Now," she ordered.

Excuses popped into my head, but none of them were worth Aunt Jodene's health. Carme greeted two women and some teenagers as they entered the shop.

Cool peppermint preceded the voice close to my head. "Why am I here?"

That was not a question I had expected. My brain tumbled a bit as I listened to the phone ring, wondering if Nik would answer. "I don't know why, I'm sorry."

"I'd ask that lovely Carme, but no matter what I do, she can't hear me," Myst said. "I've figured that much out." The last dripped with snark.

"Leave her alone."

"Seems I am stuck with you."

Was that what she'd been off doing, trying to find someone else to talk to? I found myself with mixed feelings of relief and jealousy. "I'm sorry," I began, but Nik answered.

"Hello?"

"Hi, Nik." I cleared my throat, then pushed forward. "I was wondering if I could hire you to help me with meditation." The apparition-chamber instructions said to meditate regularly before, so I had to get at it. "Soon, if possible."

I picked at my starry sleeves. Carme's laugh filtered back to me as she showed the customers around. After what felt like an eternity, Nik spoke again. "You want me to help you?"

The lack of caffeine in my system made me edgy. "Yes."

Another small silence. "Right. You could come to the meditation circle this afternoon if you'd like. We could talk after."

"I'm not sure about a meditation circle," I admitted. The thought of a whole room of people meditating freaked me out. Who knew what sorts of spirits might show up?

"Okay." He went silent, perhaps judging me or in thought. "What if we meet somewhere after? How about the coffee shop, since I'll be on the Drive for the meditation circle?"

My head throbbed. Of course the coffee shop would be the ideal spot, except for the fact it would be absolute torture for me.

"I would rather not. I've given up caffeine." Since I was a terrible liar, I thought going with the truth was the best option.

"Wow." He sucked in a breath. "That's impressive. What about your office? Or will the smell bother you there?"

I kind of hated how considerate he was being. He was right about the smell, but that wasn't why we couldn't go to the office. If Carme's wards still worked, it was full of ghosts. "I think the smell of coffee would distract me," I answered.

The only other places I felt safe were my apartment and my aunt's shop. My apartment was inappropriate on so many levels. "How about the Feathered Serpent? It closes at seven. Would you be able to come by then? I know it's Halloween and you probably have plans."

"I do," he said.

My brain did this weird thing of being relieved not to have to see him, to being upset he had plans. "That's okay." I hoped I didn't sound like I cared what he was doing.

"But I could meet you there tomorrow morning before opening," he said quickly. "My plans won't keep me out too late."

"Thanks. I'll text you in the morning."

"Great," he said. "See you then."

"That was awkward," Myst sniped.

I flicked a hand through the air in an attempt to dismiss her. "Of course it was awkward."

A couple of days ago I'd hated Nik. Now we were going to get together to meditate so I could try and communicate with the dead. Three things I had never wanted to do.

Carme lifted her eyebrows at me as she went behind the counter to ring up purchases. I saluted her with my phone.

The customers had books, bracelets, candles, incense and a seance kit. They also bought one of the chimes from the front display that had been rattled by the spirit now residing in Aunt Jodene. It gave me the shivers to think of what they'd be doing with all of it, but it wasn't for me to caution them. Most times, it was all for nothing, a little fun and no harm done. Unless they were like me. I hoped, for their sakes, they weren't.

I hadn't been in the shop on Halloween, due to my usual habit of hiding. I'd never seen it so busy.

By midday, Carme and I both started to drag. "Go, get yourself a coffee," I told her.

"Oh, thank you," she said, like I'd just given her permission to open her Christmas presents early.

She grabbed her coat with a guilty grin. "I'll get us food. I'll get you a decaf." She paused in the doorway. "You'll be okay?"

"Of course." I made a shooing motion. "Go on."

She waved as she held the door for a young woman with a pink nose stud and dark red hair under a black hoodie.

"Be right back," Carme called, and scooted off down the sidewalk out of sight. I let out a sigh of longing for the dark goodness she was about to consume. What would she order?

The new customer snapped me out of my coffee daydream as she and another person bumped into each other. They both offered apologies, and I was moving out from behind the counter to see if I could help either of them when I spotted Liam at the door. He had two coffees. Of course he did.

I got the door for him. Despite the mouthwatering aroma of the coffees, I gave him a hug. He kept his arms wide to make sure I didn't knock over the coffees, which would have been a good idea if I'd thought of it.

After the hug, he held out one of the coffees to me. I tried not to clutch the warm cup to my chest like a lost puppy while I walked to the counter.

Liam followed me in. "I thought you might be here. How's your aunt?"

"She's okay," I said, which was sort of the truth. "She's getting a lot of rest." That was less true. She appeared like she rested quietly, but inside I was pretty sure she fought the battle of her life.

"Good to hear. I've always liked her. You, I'm not so sure about. I think you're full of crap." He took a sip of his coffee and surveyed the shop.

"Oh," Myst's voice chimed in my head. "I like her."

"Him," I snapped back instinctively. "And stay away from him," I hissed, hoping Liam hadn't heard me.

"Testy," she replied.

Liam leaned his elbows on the counter. "The shop looks better."

"We were here pretty late." We watched the two customers browsing books.

Liam cupped his coffee with both hands and nodded at the other one in front of me. "You better drink that while it's hot, or I might get in trouble for not delivering it in peak condition. Ethan said to say hello."

I stared at the cup, wanting to drink it so badly, it hurt from my brain down to my toes. Luckily, I wanted to save Aunt Jodene more. I pushed the cup farther away. "I'm good. Thanks for bringing it, though."

He sighed. "Okay, now I really know something is going on. You've never refused a coffee. Even with a coffee already in front of you."

Once again, truth wasn't an option. "I'm thinking about cutting back on caffeine. I thought maybe it would be something I could help clients with."

He held one hand up. "Stop. Whatever you do, stop lying to me. You're terrible at it and it's insulting."

Myst *tsk*ed. I could almost hear her eyes roll. "Oh, just tell her. I mean him. He can handle it."

I almost responded to her but stopped myself. Liam stared at me.

"Saved by the bell?" I quipped as a customer approached with a couple of books. Liam moved out of the way, then stuck his tongue out at me from behind their back while I completed the transaction.

We both watched the customer head back out to the Drive. The young woman still at the bookcase slid her hood off. She had thick, red hair to die for without dyeing it. She scrutinized the books carefully.

"I should go help her," I said to Liam.

"I'll be here, waiting for you not to lie to me."

"It's complicated," I said. He drummed his fingers on the counter with impatience.

I let out a breath. "It's not just complicated. It's dangerous."

"Dangerous?" he echoed, but I didn't get a chance to reply. The redhaired woman grabbed at the bookshelf as her legs gave out from under her. We rushed over, unable to stop her before she crashed to the floor.

"Are you okay?" I asked. Her eyes were closed and she didn't respond.

Liam said something in Spanish I didn't understand as I sat next to the fallen woman. Her chest moved up and down rapidly. My heart started to rev as much as hers. Liam pulled out his phone.

The woman's entire body went stiff. Her eyes opened, then rolled back. I lifted her head onto my lap and tried to get her comfortable. This reminded me too much of my aunt.

"Get out of her," I yelled at whatever spirit it was.

"Amy, what?" Liam asked. "Do you want me to call 911?"

Myst scoffed. "It's not me, if that's what you mean." She sounded insulted.

"Another dead," the young woman on the floor whispered. "Another dead." Her eyes closed again. My heart pounded. I tried to think.

Her eyes popped wide open. She scrambled away from me and held her head as she took us both in.

"What the hell," she whispered. She got herself to her feet and wobbled. Liam went to help her but she pushed him aside.

"Are you okay?" I asked her.

She rushed out the door and pulled her hood back up over her head as she disappeared down the sidewalk.

Liam stared down at me, thumb hovered over his phone. "Okay, what the fuck?"

My heart pounded as I leaned back against the bookcase. *Another dead?* What did that mean? Who had said it? Not the young woman; she hadn't even known what had happened. Was it a spirit speaking through her? I couldn't tell Liam that.

"Maybe she had a seizure or something." I moved toward the counter and the coffee calling my name, not literally, thank goodness.

"Again with the bad lying." Liam followed me. "I know what's going on here."

I stared at the coffee cup. "You do?" Part of me of really did want him to know, but I also didn't want him put in harm's way. I picked up the coffee.

"I really don't think you're supposed to drink that," Myst said.

Great, now I had a verbal conscience? Unfortunately, she was right. In order to help Aunt Jodene, I had to succeed at the apparition chamber.

Liam leaned on the counter across from me. "Your aunt. This shop. Your avoidance of all things Halloween. That woman just now whispering about dead people? It's kind of obvious."

"It is?" I tried to sound innocent. *Another dead*? Maybe it had nothing to do with us. Maybe it was coincidence the woman blurted it here.

He stood straight. "Are you kidding me?" He jabbed both thumbs onto his chest. "Day of the Dead? Día de Muertos? That's ours, you know that, right? My abuela swears she talks to my grandfather every breakfast, and he's been dead for three years. My uncle puts rainbow sprinkles on his windowsills to keep the fairies happy. My sister-in-law bought a sound machine to keep the fantasmas out of the baby's room. Come on. You can't fool me. Something is up with you, all your life, I'd guess. I'd also bet my next paycheck your aunt had a bad run-in with something not from our world. Am I close?"

Relief washed over me. Still, I wasn't willing to risk his safety. "I don't want anyone close to me getting hurt, ever again. Definitely not my best friend."

He playfully punched my shoulder. "You're lucky I'm still your best friend. Pretty sure I can handle myself. Plus, hey, maybe my grandfather is looking out for me." Grief flashed across his face, and I knew Liam worried his grandfather hated him for coming out.

"Promise me." I pointed at him with as much sternness

as I could. "If anything weird starts happening, you will tell me right away."

He held up one hand and placed the other over his heart. "I promise."

I told him everything. I'd finished when Carme got back from the cafe. She gave us a tentative glance as she put a tasty-smelling paper bag on the counter.

"I told him," I said.

She smiled and gave Liam an enthusiastic hug. "I'm so glad." Her smile faded when they separated again. "Have you checked the news?" My heart froze at the concern on her face.

"No." My head pounded. "Why?"

Liam pulled out his phone. Carme directed him to the right news feed.

"There," she said.

Liam shrugged and handed me the phone. It was an article about a businesswoman, killed in a freak SkyTrain accident. They showed a photo of her, a professional with flattering makeup and carefully curled dark hair.

It was Heidi. She had been to see me yesterday and now she was dead.

# Chapter 10

According to the article, the SkyTrain's doors had opened, inexplicably, between stations. Heidi Franklin, business entrepreneur and mother of one, had been standing next to the doors. She fell out to be crushed against the cement and metal fencing.

My legs gave out from under me.

Liam grabbed my elbow. "Whoa, hold on." He helped me stay upright, but my chest heaved.

"I need to get out. I need air."

Carme said something from behind me but I didn't register it. My brain couldn't focus on anything but getting out. *Get out. Move.* My legs didn't want to move, like in a dream where you run but go nowhere. My vision tunneled. The door was too far away. I think I ran. I might have cried out. Cool air and rain hit my face, and I started to walk away from the shop but collapsed onto the sidewalk.

Three sharp claps blasted my ears. "Come on now, buck up." It was Myst.

"Go the hell away!" I yelled at the woman I couldn't see.

"Fine," she replied. The smell of peppermint vanished.

Hands grabbed my arms and hauled me to my feet. "Let's get you back inside," Liam said.

I wasn't sure if I acknowledged him or not, but I allowed him to lead me back inside, through the shop and into the red plush chair.

Carme put something in my hand. "Breathe."

It was small, smooth and round. As I rubbed it with my thumb, I focused on my breathing. It registered in my brain I was having an anxiety attack. I tried to bring to mind the list of menu items at the Artful Cup. At first it didn't work; I couldn't think past the Americano. After a few slower breaths, I started reciting the entire thing. My chest loosened and it didn't feel like the walls were closing in on me anymore.

"You okay?" Liam asked.

I nodded, still focused on taking deep, slow breaths. "Anxiety attack. I used to have them a lot when I was younger." I let out a big breath. "I doubt Heidi's death was an accident, which means something is killing my clients." I rubbed the green stone Carme had given me. "I have to call all my clients. Present and past. Make sure they're okay. Carme, can you do a personal ward for Liam?"

Carme took Liam's arm. "I sure can."

Liam gave me a worried glance over his shoulder but went with Carme.

A little shaky, I went through my client list. Most were surprised to get a call from me, since we mostly used email and text, especially the ones I wasn't even working with at the moment, but I wasn't taking any chances. I wanted to check on all of them.

Everyone I spoke to was okay. Those I couldn't reach I left messages and sent emails. It hurt to cancel so many appointments, emotionally and financially, but I had to do it to try and keep them safe. I used the excuse my aunt was in the hospital. All of them gave their sympathies and support. I let them know I'd reschedule as soon as I could. Again, sticking close to the truth. Canceling and checking in on them didn't guarantee they would be safe. I had to find out who or what was doing this and stop it.

I managed to help some customers while Carme worked on Liam's wards. It boosted business to have them in the back corner, holding hands with their eyes closed as Carme quietly whispered her wards. People browsed, took a few peeks at my cousin and best friend, then came to the front with armloads of stuff. Aunt Jodene would be pleased when we got her back. Which we would.

Liam disappeared into the back room for what I assumed was a bathroom break, and Carme joined me at the counter.

"Thanks for doing that," I said to her. "These deaths, Mary, Heidi, do you think it could be my stepfather? Back again, somehow?"

Carme shrugged one shoulder. "Do you think it's him?"

"Honestly, no. I think I would know. He wasn't exactly stealthy about it before." There was no smell, no feeling like when he'd been around.

"Who's your stepfather?" asked Myst.

I winced. "Long story."

Liam came out of the back and joined us. "Are you sure you're okay?"

I sighed. "I have to be. Something is killing my clients and something has Aunt Jodene fighting for her life in the hospital. It's all connected to me. I have to figure it out and stop it."

He gave me a strong nod and a smile. "Then I'm with

you. Except on the cutting-caffeine thing. You're on your own with that."

"Thanks," I replied with a small smile, still worried about my best friend now mixed up in all this. "We have to find a place to work as an apparition chamber."

"What about here?" Liam held his hand out to indicate the shop.

"Won't work," Carme said.

"Too much interference." I wiggled my fingers at all the bric-a-brac, gems and other paraphernalia. "We need somewhere fairly small, safe, where we could set up a mirror and where we can do a maze."

"What about the cafe?" Liam piped up. "I'm sure they'd let you. We could do a maze with chairs and tables, blindfold you, it's perfect."

"No," I said, at the same time Carme said yes. I met her gaze and shook my head. "Ethan, Darren, Charles. We can't. It's because we love it; we can't. I'd hate for something horrible to happen there."

Carme scowled, then sighed. Liam folded his arms and leaned on the counter. "Fine. What about your apartment?"

"I'd have to displace my cats, which would not be pleasant. But most of all, I don't want to have to sleep in the same place after."

"What about my place?" he asked.

"Same thing applies. I'm not unleashing the dead in your home." Who knew what I would awaken or if they'd just go away when we were done?

"Okay," Liam said, a little defeated. "We'll think on it some more. There has to be a place."

I called the hospital to check on Aunt Jodene. There wasn't anything new. My aunt was stable; they were doing tests but got nothing conclusive. Not surprising.

As afternoon turned to evening, many customers came in, lots of them in costume.

It was so busy, we stayed open later than we normally would, which was great for Aunt Jodene's business, but my body and brain dragged more and more. Every cell in my body begged for coffee. Liam kept me fueled with food and herbal tea, but it wasn't the same.

Once the foot traffic outside the shop was more interested in heading to the restaurants than in shopping, Carme stretched. "I think we can close up now."

"Agreed," I said, and helped her with the till.

"Do you want to come stay at my place?" Liam asked.

"No, thanks. Carme's staying with me while Aunt Jodene is in the hospital. I have to take care of the cats and try to get some sleep."

"She's got a date in the morning," Carme said with a grin.

"What?" Liam turned to me with a playfully curious smile.

"It's not a date."

"Who is it?" Liam asked.

Before I could answer, Carme said, "Nik Marson."

Liam's face contorted with surprise and disgust. "You have a date with Nik Marson?"

"Are we in high school? It's not a date. To do the apparition chamber, I'm supposed to be meditating, which I have a lot of issues with. Frankly, I can't really do it. I asked him to help."

Liam crossed his arms over his chest. "I guess I can accept that. Is there anything else I can do?"

Carme and I shared a glance. He was involved now; we might as well get his help. "You could research how to get a hold of someone's skull," I said.

"Creepy, huh?" Carme said with excitement I thought was uncalled-for.

He widened his eyes in agreement as he grabbed his coat. "Definitely. But I'm on it."

"We need to do this apparition chamber," I told them both. "Whatever it takes."

I got to the shop the next morning with time to spare and found myself daydreaming about a cup of hot, dark coffee. The calm surprised me. No spirits attacking, no customers collapsing, not even the smell of peppermint. It felt like I was alone for the first time in a long time.

I took off my coat and hung it on the hooks in the back room. I'd taken too long to decide what to wear, mad at myself for it the whole time. I'd finally settled on navy blue leggings and a comfortable white-and-navy striped sweater dress with my brown boots. It was Carme's fault for getting into my head about this being a date.

The scent of peppermint floated around me. "Just be yourself," Myst said.

"Don't give me dating advice. This isn't a date."

"If you insist," she replied. "But you might want to check your makeup."

"What?" I went to one of the small mirrors on the counter for people to try on jewelry. Sure enough, my mascara had smeared under my eye. "I shouldn't even have worn makeup," I muttered as I wiped it off.

I spun at a knock on the glass front door. Nik waved to me from outside. He was early, of course, which kind of annoyed me. I really had to stop being so petty.

I opened the door for him. "Hi." I didn't like how awkward I sounded and felt.

"Morning," he replied. "Good to see you again."

"You, too," I replied automatically, not sure I meant it.

"Oh, he is cute," Myst said. It took great resolve not to hush her.

Nik unwound his black knit scarf and took it off. He caught me noticing the grey paint on his hands.

He flipped his hands over a couple of times. "Helped my brother last night to paint the suite he's putting into his house flip. Turns out I'm really bad at painting." He gave a little chuckle. Was that nervous laughter from him?

"I'm sure you're good at it, like everything else," I replied. "You didn't go out for Halloween?"

"Careful," Myst said. "You don't want to sound too eager." If she hadn't already been dead, I would've killed her.

"We did the Halloween thing," Nik replied. "We took my niece out trick-or-treating first, which I think was more exhausting than the painting but far cuter." He held up his scarf with a questioning expression.

"Just on the counter is fine."

He put down the scarf and took off his long coat to reveal a beige loose-knit sweater and dark jeans with holes in the knees. I wondered for a second if he'd put any thought into his outfit, like I had.

"We could sit there." I waved a hand toward the back corner. "If that's okay."

"Whatever you're comfortable with. That's the important thing," he replied. Right now, comfort was the last thing I felt.

"Okay, let's sit." With a deep breath, I resolved to overcome my personal issues with meditation.

In hopes it would help me relax, I lit the candle on the table. The flame crackled to life. It could also serve to signal a presence that didn't belong. If the candle flame flared or bounced around, the meditation session was over.

Nik waited for me to sit. After I chose the white wicker chair, he sat in the red plush one.

"Okay." He said it with some hesitation like he didn't really know what to make of me, which was fair. "Let's start simple. I'll lead you through a relaxation meditation. Ready?"

"As I'll ever be," I joked, then inwardly rolled my eyes for being such a dork.

"I thought this wasn't a date," Myst said. "You're rather nervous for a not-date."

Though I had no idea what she looked like, I could imagine a grin as she said it.

"Get comfortable," Nik instructed. "Close your eyes."

I squeezed my eyes shut. I would do this for Aunt Jodene and my clients.

"Easy," Nik said. "Less effort is actually better in this situation."

My eyes popped open. "Right." I closed my eyes, not so hard this time.

"Take a deep breath in and let it out. Just relax. Now breathe in through your nose for a count of four, then breathe out through your mouth to the count of six."

I nodded. I could do this. I could breathe. I could count.

"Good," Nik said softly. "Do that a few times."

"He is quite nice to look at, isn't he," Myst said in my ear.

I let out a hard breath to tell her to be quiet.

"Easy," Nik said again. "Feel the cool darkness behind your eyes."

That did it. My instincts kicked in. Panic welled up. This was a bad idea. I opened my eyes and met Nik's gaze.

"This doesn't seem to be working," he said. "Do you want to try sitting on the floor?"

Truthfully, I didn't really want to try at all. I wanted to stop. "Sure," I replied.

We moved down to the floor. There wasn't a lot of space on the rug. We sat cross-legged, facing each other. Our knees almost touched.

"Let's relax our entire bodies." Nik placed the back of his hands on his knees, fingers curled easily in an open position. I copied him, trying not to think about how intimate this had become.

"Close your eyes again; focus on your breathing. Don't force it. Just easy, natural breathing."

With my eyes closed, I could still sense him. He had a strong presence, confident and in control without a need to be overbearing.

"Now, this is getting interesting," Myst said.

"Good," Nik said, his voice far too calm and sexy. "Imagine a white pillar of light at the top of your head. Visualize it cascading down, relaxing your entire body. Your eyes relax, your jaw, your lips, your neck."

It worked. He was good at this. I could actually feel myself letting go and relaxing for the first time in longer than I could remember.

"Excellent," Nik said softly. "The white light continues moving down, over your shoulders."

My shoulders dropped and I felt the rest of me follow suit, giving in, letting go. My ears started to ring.

"I think something is here," Myst said.

My eyes popped open. I smelled vanilla. This close to

Nik, I knew it wasn't him.

"Nik, you have to go," I said.

Nik opened his eyes. "What?"

I got to my feet and reached out for his hand. He gave it to me with a confused expression. I pulled him to his feet. "I just remembered"—I paused, trying to think of an excuse—"I have to do a ton of stuff before the store opens." I shoved him toward his coat on the counter.

"What is going on?" He spun to face me.

"This is not anything to do with you. It's—" Why did I have to be so bad at lying? I took a breath. "I appreciate your help; I just need you to leave now."

"Definitely something here," Myst said, curious but cautious. I believed her; the ringing in my ears had increased.

Something crashed behind us. I flinched. My chest tightened, panic threatening to take hold. The table with the candle on it had fallen over, but the flame was out. Thankfully, the rug hadn't caught on fire.

Nik walked over, picked up the table up and set it back up. "That was weird. Maybe someone doesn't want us meditating."

"What?" For one, brief instant I thought he might know something about the world of the dead, but saw from his expression he was joking. "Right." I tried to sound lighthearted as I put the candle back on the table. "You really need to go now."

"Are you okay?" he asked. No, I really wasn't. The dead wanted to take over my life and something was killing my clients, but I couldn't tell him those details.

"I'm fine," I said instead. "Sorry, but I need to ask you to leave." It came out sterner then intended, but whatever it took to get him out. I was not about to put someone else in danger.

I picked up his coat, a black insulated Columbia, probably from Mountain Equipment Co-op. It smelled like rain and a hint of aftershave. I grabbed his scarf with the other hand and shoved both at him.

Someone knocked on the shop door, and it startled us both. Nik gave a small laugh. "Now I'm jumpy."

Liam stood outside, waving me over. No, not now. I didn't want to let him in while something was in the shop. He knocked on the door repeatedly, then pointed at me.

Nik also stared at me. "Aren't you going to let him in?"

Trying to act casual, I went and opened the door. Liam gave Nik an obvious once-over as he moved past him.

"I wanted to show you something before I headed to work. I think," he added with emphasis, "you'll want to see it." I heard the subtext. Nik did too.

"No problem. I'm leaving." Nik put on his coat and scarf. "Text me if you need me."

"Thanks. Yes, I will text you." I must have meant it, because it didn't come out as awkward as one of my lies.

He gave me a small smile, like he figured he wouldn't hear from me. "Good luck with whatever it is you're dealing with." He pulled the door closed behind him.

I wanted to disappear through the floor. That hadn't gone well at all. The shop felt emptier without him.

"The other spirit is gone," Myst said. I relaxed as I realized the ringing in my ears had stopped. A faint hint of Liam's cologne was the only thing I could smell. The vanilla scent had gone.

My breath caught. "Oh, crap," I said. "I think it left with Nik."

# Chapter 11

Liam shrugged. "So what if a spirit followed Nik? What's it going to do?"

"It depends on the strength of the spirit. If it's strong, it could cause him physical harm. Trust me on that." I let out a quick breath. "I'm going to talk to a spirit like I'm talking to the air. Just don't think I'm too weird."

"We were way past that even before I knew about your ghostly talents, my friend." He smiled and I couldn't help giving him one back.

I paused, then directed my voice to the room around us. "Myst?"

"Now you want to talk to me?" she replied. Peppermint assaulted my nostrils like she'd amplified it on purpose.

"Is it possible whatever was in here went with Nik?" Silence. "Myst?"

"Oh, I'm sorry. I just wanted to see what it felt like to ignore someone trying to speak to me."

I held back my eye roll. "Could you just answer my question, please?"

She gave a loud sigh. "It's possible, I suppose. Wait."

The smell of peppermint faded. I pulled out my phone to call Carme as Liam watched.

He leaned back against the counter, arms crossed over his chest. "Life has seriously gotten strange."

Carme picked up my call. "Amy?"

"Hi, Carme. Is there something in the shop I can give Nik to keep him safe? In case something is following him?"

"What happened?" she asked.

"A ghost showed up while we were meditating, and I think it left with him."

"Okay," she said in a thoughtful tone. "Can't be obvious, right?"

"That would be preferred," I answered. It would be awkward enough to give him anything.

"And for a guy." She gave a hum as though thinking it through.

The smell of peppermint returned. "I have no idea who it is, but they're definitely following him," Myst said.

"You don't know who it is?"

"We're not a club," she snapped back.

"Myst says he's being followed," I told Carme.

"Okay. There's a pendant," Carme said. "On a black cord. A silver flame. Should protect him. Not from anything too strong, though."

Well, it would have to do. I searched the necklaces hung on display. "Carme, there's a lot here."

Liam came over to help me look. "A silver flame on a black cord," I told him, and he started going through another rack of necklaces.

"It's shaped kind of like a sword," Carme said.

"Like a sword. With flames," I repeated to Liam as we both searched.

"This?" Liam held up a silver pendant. It did look a bit like a hilt and sword, but with curves like flames.

I grabbed it from him. "Got it, Carme. Thanks. See you soon."

"Let me know how it goes," she said, and hung up.

I grabbed the only other necklace like the one we'd found for Nik and held it out to Liam. "Here. It'd make me feel better."

"Me, too." He put it over his neck.

I sent Nik a text to ask him where he was and I'd forgotten to give him something. How was I going to convince him to wear it? We weren't exactly on gift-giving terms.

*The Artful Cup,* he texted back.

"Dammit, he's at the cafe." Of course he was.

"Want me to take it to him?" Liam asked. "I gotta catch the SkyTrain."

Relief rushed over me at the thought of having Liam take it to Nik instead, but the feeling didn't last. If Liam gave it to him, Nik might ignore it altogether and it could end up in a drawer somewhere. "I should do it. How am I going to get him to wear it?"

"Ask him to go steady?" He winked.

"Very funny. And not helpful."

"But funny." He grinned at his own wit.

I sent a text back to Nik. *I'll be right there.*

I'd figure out what to say on the walk over. "What did you want to show me?"

"Oh, right," Liam patted his coat pockets, then brought out his phone. "I almost forgot with all this flirting stuff you have going on."

"Stop it."

"No way; this is too fun." He held his phone for me to

see. "You asked me to look up stuff on getting someone's skull and this popped up."

"*How to Ethically Purchase a Human Skull*," I read out.

He scrolled down. "Recognize anyone?"

I grabbed his phone to get a better look. "That's the woman who collapsed here yesterday." It was definitely her. Dark red hair, tiny nose ring. Her stunning dark blue eyes stared solemnly out at me, but that wasn't the most noticeable thing. In one hand she held a human skull.

"Holy crap," I whispered.

"Indeed." Liam took his phone back. "Turns out she lives around the Drive. Doesn't say exactly where, but I bet we could find out."

"That definitely sounds like a place to start. I better get to the cafe before Nik leaves. Can you come back after your shift? Maybe we can figure this out then."

"You got it. I bet I can sneak out a bit early today. I like this sleuthing thing. Better than HR any day."

"Just be careful," I said.

We parted ways at the cafe. Before I even opened the door, I could smell the coffee. Wondering if I could hold my breath the entire time I was inside, I pulled the door open.

Nik sat at one of the small tables, an espresso in front of him, an e-reader in his hand. I waved at Darren behind the counter as I went over to Nik and sat across from him. The smell of vanilla hit me hard, and it wasn't anything Ethan was baking.

Maybe Nik would make this easy on me. "Hi."

He slowly raised his gaze. "That was quick. It's not often I get dismissed and recalled so quickly."

"Sorry about all that. I have something for you." I grabbed the pendant from my coat pocket and held it awkwardly by the cord in front of him. "To thank you for trying to help me. I know it didn't go very well. And also to say sorry for kicking you out of the store." I knew I was rambling and stopped.

He studied me for several seconds, which was fair. This was weird from any point of view let alone from his. He was only getting a fraction of the story.

"You don't have to do that." There was a bit of edge to his voice.

I held the necklace a heartbeat more. I grabbed his wrist, turned his arm over and put the pendant in his hand. I pulled away quickly. "Please, take it." His eyebrows raised slightly, but he closed his hand over the pendant. I pointed at his hand. "And you have to wear it. It's important."

He took a closer look at it, turning it over, then met my eyes. Maybe he saw my desperation there. He took off his scarf to put the pendant on.

"Thank you." I got to my feet and started for the door but turned back. "Wear it all the time. It's, um, it's good luck." I stumbled over the lie.

"Thanks." He let it flop onto his chest.

My stomach sank. He was going to take it off the minute I left the coffee shop. I went over and sat back down, all pretense gone. "Listen. I know I don't sound like the most stable person right now, but it's really important you wear it. Important to me, you and possibly those you love."

He blinked, hard, several times. His expression went from confused to concerned. He reached across and touched my wrist. "I got it," he said. "I'll wear it."

I believed him, and by now he'd definitely think there was something wrong with me. "Thank you."

I got up to make a quick exit, but Charles caught me on

my way out. He was pale. His eyes drooped along with his shoulders, like maybe he should still be at home sick.

"How you doing?" he asked.

"I'm fine," came my auto reply.

"Carme told me about you ladies wanting to use the coffee shop after hours for recording your blog video show thing."

"She did?" Dammit. Carme went behind my back to ask Charles about using the cafe for an apparition chamber? The vlog idea was an excellent cover, I had to admit, but we couldn't risk it.

"Just wanted to let you know that's fine with me," Charles said. "Some nice exposure for us. We could use it." He gave me his warm smile, but I could see the worry behind it.

"I'll let you know," I answered. "See you soon."

"Take care," he called after me. I dared not look back at Nik as I left the cafe.

Liam sent me the link to the article with our mysterious bone collector. When I got back to the shop, I did some reading. It was an interview but didn't include her name. It went into great detail about her passion for human bone collecting. She explained how common it was and methods for obtaining them both legally and illegally. She claimed she personally wanted nothing to do with stolen remains. I had to admire her candor about the whole thing. Plus, her resolve to do it ethically, as she put it, was also admirable. Still creepy and nothing I wanted anything to do with, but admirable.

Checking laws in your area was important since they could vary from country to country. It was never legal to buy the bones of indigenous cultures, almost never legal to buy human tissue. Grave robbing was illegal. There was a black market, of course, but she warned people off it for various reasons. To my surprise and slight disgust, you could buy human bones on eBay and other e-commerce sites. Even Etsy sold human teeth and hair.

Hair and teeth were the easier things to purchase, according to our expert, and could substitute for a skull for many reasons. Would Mary's teeth be enough? Her hair? Could we get either? It all made my stomach turn.

Carme appeared at the door, used her key and worked her way through the shop toward me.

"Hey," I said. "I saw Charles this morning. He said you asked if we could use the cafe."

She let out a sigh, like she knew this would be a battle. "We don't have anywhere else."

"We'll think of somewhere," I said.

"Fine." She stuck her tongue out at me. "Did you get the pendant to Nik?"

"I did. Not sure he's going to keep wearing it, but I'll check in on him. How's your mom?"

"The same. I can talk to the doctor later today." She gave a little shrug, implying what we both knew. It didn't matter what the doctor said; nothing they tried would help her. We had to take care of it ourselves.

I filled Carme in on Liam's discovery of our bone collector.

"That's creepy." Carme scrolled through some of the photos in the interview.

"I thought I'd send the bone collector a message she will want to answer."

Carme's eyes widened. "How? I think we should give her

a better name."

I grinned at my cousin. "She recommends in her blog for people to go to their local oddities shop for leads for collecting." I held my arms out wide. "We're a metaphysical shop. She came here before. I'll post a comment on the article that we at the Feathered Serpent may have something of interest to her. Should do it. Unless she's too freaked out about collapsing here."

"Tell her we can help with that," Carme said.

"Brilliant."

Carme scrunched her face in disgust. "Do you think the bones she has made her talk?"

"She doesn't believe bones carry ghosts or spirits, but she does say they bring a magical energy." I shuddered involuntarily. "I, on the other hand, think the bones absolutely have something to do with her speaking in the shop."

I'd had no ear-ringing; there'd been no scent. Whatever she had inside her, she'd carried in with her. But why did it feel the need to tell us about Heidi's death? It felt like a warning.

Carme unlocked the door for customers and I posted my comment, hoping the bone collector would see it soon.

"How did it go with Nik?" Carme asked later when the store was void of customers.

"Not well, considering it let in something and then it followed Nik."

Carme's face tensed with stress. "But you have to meditate," she said. "My mom." Her words got choked a little and her eyes began to tear.

"I know. I promise I will be ready."

"You should do some now," she said, her voice firm.

"You're right," I replied. "But I can't let anything in again. What if they decided to start following you?"

Carme leaned in to me, her face as angry as I'd ever seen it. "You know what I'd do?" She jabbed a finger to her chest. "I'd talk to them. Ask them to be good. You ignore them."

"It's not that simple," I tried, but she shook her head.

"How do you know?" She stared at me and I could see my aunt's face so clearly in hers, like she channeled some of her mom to get her point across.

"Okay. I'll do it." If I felt anything, smelled anything, if Myst gave me any clues, I'd stop. I checked to see if our bone collector had responded. Nothing yet.

How much meditating did it take to prepare oneself for an apparition chamber? Everything we'd found was a little vague.

I sat in the wicker chair but that didn't seem right, so I moved to the red chair. I sat tall with my feet flat on the floor, hands on my knees, and closed my eyes. I tried the breathing exercise Nik had done with me, in through my nose for the count of four, out for the count of six. The memory of him close to me on the floor disrupted my counting, and I started again. He probably thought I was completely unstable. Most likely wouldn't want anything to do with me again. Why did that make me feel a little empty?

"You probably should stop thinking about him," Myst said.

"You're not helping," I whispered, and opened my eyes to catch a customer gawking at me.

The shop door opened and another customer walked in, ending my attempts at meditation. It was our red-headed bone collector.

# Chapter 12

Our bone collector wore the same hoodie as before, pulled up over her head even though the rain had stopped. I felt like a bird watcher spotting a skittish fledgling. If I moved or made a sound, she would flutter out of sight.

While Carme finished with the other customer in the store, our bone collector hung back near the bookshelves. Our eyes met. Her passion for bone collecting must have been strong for her to come back. Or she wanted our help. I gave her a nod I hoped came across as conspiratorial, then slowly went over to the counter. After the other customer left the store our bone collector stepped up to the counter.

"Someone sent me a message," she said. "You might have something I'd be interested in."

Carme leaned forward over the counter. "We can help each other." Our bone collector backed up a step.

"We wanted to talk to you because we need your help," I said. "We got you here to ask you some questions. Please."

Her eyes narrowed, shoulders tensed. "You've got to be kidding me. I'm out of here."

"Did you know you spoke when you collapsed?" I asked

before she made it to the door. She hesitated, so I kept going. "It wasn't actually you. It was someone else, telling us something had happened we didn't know about yet."

She stopped and turned back to us. "What do you mean? What did I say?"

How much to tell her? I didn't want to scare her away. "You told us someone had died in an accident. After you left, we found out it was true."

"What the fuck?" she whispered, and walked back over to us.

"We might be able to help you. If something is, you know"—I waved my hand in a circle—"communicating through you."

She appeared understandably disturbed by this information. "You're telling me I've been possessed."

Carme held up her hands. "Maybe not," she said. "Maybe somebody talked through you."

To her credit, our bone collector listened to Carme as an equal. "Right. How is that better?" She paced a bit in front of the counter. Carme and I let the young woman process.

"Fine," she said. "Ask your questions. Then help me never have that happen again."

"Deal." I took a deep breath. "Is it possible to get the skull of someone who's recently passed away? Like, as in, they died less than a week ago?"

Her dark blue eyes widened. "Not unless you have their body and haven't reported it." She leaned in over the counter. "You don't, do you?"

"No," I said, and her shoulders dropped. "Nothing like that. We don't have the body. We..." I paused and looked at Carme. "We don't know what's happened to her body."

Carme's face scrunched. I dug out my phone and

searched for information about a wake or funeral for Mary.

"Shit. I mean, shoot." I turned my phone around to show Carme. "She's been cremated."

Our bone collector laughed and tapped the top of the counter. "Well. I'd say that's a bit of karma for you."

"What if, let's just say, someone wanted to talk to a person who had died and you needed their skull—"

"Someone who's been cremated," she interrupted, and laughed again.

"Someone who died"—I tried to stay positive—"and you needed their skull to communicate with them but couldn't get it. Would anything else work?"

The bone collector put a hand on her chest. "I'm not an expert in communing with the dead; I just like to own their bits. Though I'm questioning that now, too. However"—she tapped a finger on her cheek—"I'd see if scalp tissue or hair would work. Those might be obtained from her belongings."

"Right. Thanks." We didn't have a choice, anyway. There was no skull.

"Okay. Now help me," the bone collector said. "What are you going to do?"

That was a good question. Carme gave me a tiny shrug. The apparition chamber would be the answer to freeing Aunt Jodene from her imprisoned state, and she would know how to help our bone collector.

I cleared my throat. "Come back in a few days and we'll have some answers for you."

"A few days?" She threw her hands up and let them slap against her legs. "Great. What if it happens again before that?"

"Call us," Carme said with such assurance, even I felt better. She handed the young woman one of the shop's cards. "I'm Carme. This is Amy." I gave a small wave when she looked at me.

"Right." She shook her head but took the card. "A few days. I guess I'll see you then."

The door closed behind her with a sad thud. Carme leaned on the table, chin propped in her hands. "We're no closer."

"Yes, we are," I told her. "I hadn't thought of Mary's belongings. That they'd have, you know, parts of her on them." We both cringed, but it was true.

"Pretty sure her family won't give us anything," Carme said.

I moved out from behind the counter. "They don't have to. I have something. Mary left a hat, a knit one, at one of our sessions."

Carme straightened. "You still have it?"

I let out a hard breath. "It's in the office. I tucked it in a desk drawer."

"I'll get it," Carme said.

"No," I said firmly. She tilted her head at me and threw a hand on her hip like she was about to argue.

"I have to do it," I told her. "I'll be fast, in and out. If I don't come back soon, don't try and come in after me. Call 911. Make something up for them to come in." I got my coat.

"Be careful," she said as I headed out the door. I nodded back at her.

What was I doing? Days ago I'd beaten a path out of my office at the first sign of a haunting. Now I'd started talking to a spirit we'd named Myst and I was actively trying to communicate with Mary's ghost. I couldn't pause to think about it too much or I might freak out. Best to keep moving forward, one step at a time. The next step, get into the office.

The smell from the Artful Cup beckoned me to go in for a coffee. My head ached, my mouth watered and my brain longed for a caffeine hit. Tempted as I was, I couldn't. Just like I couldn't avoid going into a room full of ghosts to get a gift from my dead client. For Aunt Jodene, Carme and everyone I cared about.

As I stood at the office door, I imagined I could see the wards Carme put on it to keep the spirits inside. I took a deep breath and let it out slowly. The last thing I needed was to go in there already tense.

As soon as I entered, my ears filled with loud static. It almost knocked me to my knees. Smells assaulted me and made me so dizzy, I dry-heaved. It was a mix of florals, tobacco, earth and something wet, possibly moldy. Hand over my nose, I made a rush for the desk. The curtains flapped as if struck by a strong wind, though there was none.

The top of my desk had been cleared off. Anything that had been on it now lay scattered on the floor. Something brushed my shoulder as I opened the top drawer. I dug through old notebooks, papers, business cards but found nothing. I moved to the next drawer.

Mixed into the ringing in my ears, someone asked for help. My heart pounded faster as my frantic search continued. I found Mary's hat, and something pushed me from behind. I fell against the desk.

Everything in me screamed to get out. The macramé wall hanging from my aunt's shop swung, then flew off the wall straight at me. My mind registered it but my body couldn't react fast enough. It hit me in the side of the head. My feet caught up with my brain and I raced for the door.

Like some nightmare, the air thickened as I approached the exit. It felt like walking through chest-high Jell-O, if that

Jell-O also clung to you and didn't want to let you go.

"Come on," I yelled at myself. I was steps from the door, but the air had turned to cement. Every movement was a strain.

*Help us.*

It was one voice, soft and feminine.

"I can't," I said, unable to move my arms or legs.

*Help us.*

This time it was more voices.

*Help us.*

More voices together, dozens at least, men, women and children.

*You're helping Mary. Help us.*

My heart pounded in my ears along with their requests for help. Breathing became painful. I started to feel faint.

"Breathe, sweeting, breathe." It was Myst. Her voice was clear and crisp next to me despite the cacophony of voices around me.

Breathe, she'd said. Yes, I had to breathe, dammit. In, then out. I went to my list of items at the cafe. Americano, mocha, cappuccino, macchiato, caramel macchiato, espresso. Now I wanted a coffee, but at least my head had cleared enough to focus on getting my breath under control.

"Can you do something?" I asked Myst.

"Sadly, no. They don't seem to hear me."

My jaw clenched. "I have to get out of here."

"Well, do it, then," she shot back.

I pictured Carme back at the shop, worried for me, desperate to help her mom, then calling 911 because I hadn't returned.

"You have to let me out," I screamed at the ghosts around me. "There are living people who need my help." Nothing changed. As hard as I tried, I couldn't move.

*Help us*, they chanted.

"Fine," I yelled at them. "I'll help you. After I help my aunt and find out what's killing the people in my life."

The voices stopped. I nearly fell face-first as I was freed, then lunged for the open doorway and slammed the door shut behind me.

Hands shaking, I stared at the pink knit hat in my hand. "It's okay. I got it."

"You are going to help them, right?" Myst asked as I raced down the stairs.

Out on the street, the smells from the cafe helped me calm down as I took big gulps of air. "If I help those ghosts, more will come."

"You said you would help them."

"I know; I had to get out. Just let me help the living people first."

The smell of peppermint vanished.

# Chapter 13

Liam was at the shop when I got back. He and Carme both tried to hide coffees behind their backs when I walked in.

"You did it." Carme shoved her coffee at Liam so she could give me a hug.

I held up Mary's hat. "Let's hope it works."

"Have you figured out where to do it yet?" Liam asked.

Carme said yes at the same time I said no. She gave me a frustrated sigh. "We could use the cafe."

I envisioned the cafe overtaken like my office, and I shook my head. There was no way I would let that happen. It would endanger Charles, Ethan, Darren and their customers. It could destroy the whole place if things went wrong. "There must be somewhere else," I said.

The door chimed and Nik walked into the shop. Liam and Carme suddenly became scarce, taking their coffees to the back reading area. Nik didn't have his scarf on this time, and I could see the titanium pendant around his neck. I tried not to make it obvious as I sniffed the air around him for spirits. He held the pendant off his chest toward me.

Vanilla filled my nostrils.

"So, I have a friend," he began. "She's pretty up on all things metaphysical. She told me this is supposed to ward off spirits." He paused and I tried to keep my expression blank, like a poker player, but probably failed. He leaned a hand on the counter. "Why would I need that?"

I scoffed and waved him off, trying to diffuse the vanilla smell as well. "Just a quirk to a great-looking pendant," I lied. He still had a spirit with him but seemed unaffected by it. For now.

"I might believe that," he said. "Except for how insistent you were that I wear it."

"Just supporting my aunt's business," I tried.

"So, I could take it off now." He eyed me as he started to lift it over his head.

"No." I pushed his arm back down. "It's better if you wear it."

His narrowed eyes said he wasn't buying it, but he didn't try to take it off again.

"How's the meditating going?" he asked.

"Okay," I replied.

"Good; let me know if you want any more help. I should probably go. Just wanted to thank you again for the pendant." He held it up again, a sarcastic crinkle to his face. Fresh speckles of paint decorated his hands.

I pointed at the spots. "More painting?"

He flipped his hands over and laughed. "Pretty, isn't it? We're getting both the upper and lower suites ready for renting. It's a lot of painting."

My brain nudged me as I walked him to the door. If they were preparing it for renting, it didn't have anyone living in it. No furniture, likely. Being newly renovated, it might have less residual energy in it. I couldn't ask him to borrow the space, could I? My brain poked harder.

"I have a weird question," I said as we got to the door.

"Why am I not surprised?" He gave me a warm smile that had me wishing circumstances were different.

I cleared my throat, bringing my focus back. "Your brother's renovation, how long will it be until anyone moves in?"

"Why, do you need a place to live?"

I shook my head. "Not me; I'm just, um, wondering."

He tilted his head as if viewing me from another angle. "It won't be ready until the summer, probably."

The summer. More than six months away. Plenty of time to figure out a way to get rid of any ghosts who might show up. I held one finger up. "I have a follow-up weird question."

He laughed. "Go ahead."

"Could I borrow the basement suite?"

His expression froze in a half smile. "You want to use the suite? For what? It's not finished yet; it's just an empty space."

"That's why," I said. "It would just be me. No weird parties or anything." Unless you counted the dead. "For an experiment in meditation," I added, which was kind of true.

"There's no furniture," he said.

"That's okay."

"It's quite small."

"That's okay, too."

"It stinks of paint."

"That's fine."

He must've realized I wasn't about to give up, because he shrugged one shoulder. "I'll talk to my brother and let you know."

"Thanks. I appreciate it."

I closed the door behind him and went to join Liam and Carme. Both of them stared at me like I'd just let out the family's indoor cat.

"What?" I asked.

"I cannot believe you did that," Carme said in a hushed voice, either with admiration or disbelief.

"We needed a place. I may have found one."

"He's never going to date you," Liam said, and Carme laughed.

"Not concerned about that right now," I replied.

Liam held a finger up. "So, you're saying it's something that does concern you, just not right now."

"Stop it," I said, and they both laughed.

"What about the maze part of it?" Liam asked. "Aren't you supposed to wander through a maze to get sensory deprivation?"

"Right," I said. "I'll search the address online, see what's around there. Maybe I could wear a blindfold and earplugs and walk around outside."

Liam lifted his eyebrows. "Right. Because that wouldn't be weird at all."

My phone rang. It was one of my clients.

"Hi, Margaret," I answered.

"Hi, Amy. I know you're having a family emergency right now, but I needed to call." Desperation resonated through her words.

"What's going on?" I kept my voice calm while my insides tightened.

"I don't know, exactly. I've been feeling really odd." She said the words slowly, as if afraid of the reaction they'd receive.

"Do you need to see a doctor?" I asked, with only a faint hope it was a medical issue and not a paranormal one.

"I don't think they could help. I'm pretty sure it's all in my head. But I haven't been able to shake it."

My grip on my phone tightened. "I'm at my aunt's shop on Commercial Drive; could you come here?" Maybe I could tell if anything haunted her, give her a pendant or protect her.

"Your aunt who's in the hospital? You're working there for her? I'm sorry for bothering you." Margaret's voice crumbled. "You must be so busy; this isn't a good time."

"No, it's fine," I said, probably too loud and too fast. "Please. Come see me as soon as you can." There was a brief pause where I held my breath.

"I'll drop my daughter off at my mom's and then be there," Margaret said.

"Terrific." I gave her the address of the shop.

Margaret sounded relieved at the end, but I would still worry about her until she got to the shop.

Once she arrived at the Feathered Serpent, she appeared exhausted, stressed and a little panicked all at once.

I gave her a hug. "Come, sit." I needed to hold her up a bit as we walked to the back of the shop. She was usually so strong, so outgoing. Seeing her like this made my heart pound with worry.

"I think there's something with her," Myst said in my ear, and I responded with a small nod.

Margaret sat and clasped her hands hard in her lap, then took in the entirety of the shop. "This is pretty amazing," she said.

I sat and surveyed the shop as if through her eyes. I'd

been so focused on putting the place back together, I'd forgotten how warm, complex and beautiful it all was.

"It is," I replied, proud of what my aunt had created here. Now I needed to save her and it. "What's going on?" I asked, trying not to sound as worried as I was.

Margaret stared at the floor in uncharacteristic sadness. "I can't really explain it. I've had strange thoughts." She met my eyes. "Weird thoughts I've never had before. Of suicide."

"Are you hearing voices?" I asked.

She sat back and let out a frustrated sigh. "No, I mean, they're my own voices, right? I've just had the worst depression. I've never had anything like this before. I would've told you." I nodded. She'd always been extremely open. Something like severe depression would've come up.

"My daughter," Margaret went on. "Even the thought of her usually makes the worst stuff come out rainbows and sunshine. But now, it's like I'm..." She hesitated and I waited.

When she didn't go on, I sat forward a bit. "You can tell me. Trust me, I know about weird." I waved my hand to indicate the shop around us.

"That's an understatement," Myst put in, and I resisted shushing her.

Margaret took a deep breath. "It's like I'm forgetting who I am but I don't care. I don't care if I live or die."

"We can't let that happen," I told her. "Who you are is damn awesome. I'm going to help you. First, I would like to give you something. Wait one second."

Carme watched me closely as I went over to the counter. I lowered my voice. "I think she's in danger. Can you ward her without her knowing?"

Carme's eyes widened, then narrowed in thought. "I think so."

I searched for another pendant like the ones I'd given Nik and Liam. Maybe there was something similar?

Carme grabbed my wrist as I went to pull off a necklace. "Not that one. This is different." She fingered through the hanging necklaces like a harp. With a little noise of triumph, she pulled off a necklace and handed it to me. "This will help."

It was a tiny vial on a chain. Both ends of the vial had metal lids with leaves reaching down toward the middle. The glass tube held something amber-coloured and a tiny scroll. I took it from her and felt a slight buzzing.

"Why didn't you give one of these to the bone collector?" I asked.

Carme shrugged. "She wasn't very nice."

Myst laughed as I did a double take at my cousin. "Remind me never to piss you off," I said.

She threw one hand on her hip and snapped with the other. "Believe it." She grabbed some incense. "You're going to pay for all this, right?"

"Right. Yes, of course," I replied. "Add it to my tab." I'd have to get some new clients after this to pay for all the things I needed to keep my current ones alive.

I gave the necklace to Margaret. "Please wear this. Carme tells me it will help. I always believe her about these things."

Margaret nodded and put it over her neck. She gave a little sigh as though it eased her.

Carme came over with her incense. "Don't mind me." She waved the incense around, trying to appear casual, but I knew she was warding Margaret. After a minute or so, Margaret pointed at the incense.

"Are you doing something to me?" she asked.

"Me?" Carme placed one hand over her heart with

an overly innocent expression which made her appear completely guilty.

Being a bad liar must run in our family. Margaret-snort laughed and I was glad to see a bit of her old self back again. "Just go ahead," Margaret said. "Do what you need to do."

My cousin gave us both a little smile, then stopped trying to be stealthy. After waving the incense over Margaret, Carme handed it to me.

"Hold my hands," she told Margaret. She knelt on the floor in front of my client. I watched them, willing Margaret to be all right. No one else could die because of me.

Carme finished and Margaret thanked her. "I feel a bit better," she said. I thought I saw a little more colour in her cheeks.

"I don't suppose you can stay here with us?" I asked Margaret as she pulled her coat on.

"I have to go get my daughter; she has a doctor's appointment."

"Right." Was there anything else we could do for her? Protect her any more? "Please call me any time. If you have any bad thoughts, if things start to spiral downward, call me."

"I will," she said, and I believed her. But would she be able to think clearly if things got bad?

Soon after she left, I got a text from Nik.

*Brother says it's okay.*

It was followed by an address out in Burnaby, the other direction from my place.

"We've got our space," I told Carme. "I can go there after closing."

We spent the rest of the afternoon going over the apparition-chamber details or, rather, our version of it. Liam borrowed his dad's truck to help us move his aunt's standing mirror and a folding chair for me to use. Transporting them on public transit would have proved difficult.

Carme wanted to come but I insisted she go see her mom. Truth was, the farther Carme was from me while I did the apparition chamber, the better. I wasn't going to let anything get to her. Ever.

She wrote out the incantation for me to call Mary and wished me luck. I told her I'd meet her at my place later.

Liam picked me up and we parked on the street outside an older house in a quiet crescent. I'd searched the address online and had seen street views of it. The crescent backed onto a wooded gorge with paths woven through them. Our plan was for Liam to guide me blindfolded for as long as we thought necessary, then bring me to the suite.

The house had stacks of tiles under tarps in the driveway as well as big piles of paving stones. It was quiet, getting dark and a little creepy, but maybe my mind made it that way.

Nik said he'd meet me there to let me in. He even agreed to give me a key to lock up when I was done.

"You sure about doing this by yourself?" Liam asked.

"I don't have a choice. I'm supposed to do it alone."

"Yeah." Liam leaned over the steering wheel to get a better look at the house. "But it doesn't mean someone can't be just outside the door. Or I could stay here in the truck until you're done, instead of coming back to get you."

I shook my head. "Nope. I can't risk it. I don't want some rogue, pissed-off ghost latching on to you. No way."

Liam grinned. "You plan on pissing off some ghosts?"

The way he said it made me smile despite my growing anxiety. "I have a feeling I might have to. You go; come back when I call you."

Liam rolled his eyes, but reached for the door. "Feeling a bit like hired help, Miss Amy." He brought out his Spanish accent he usually only used when quoting his grandmother.

"He's funny," Myst said.

"I'm sorry for keeping you out of it," I said to Liam. "I'll make it up to you with coffee, baked goods, wine, whatever it takes."

He grunted like I better keep that promise, got out of the truck and went to the back. I caught up to him. "Maybe let's wait on that." I pointed at the giant mirror. "I don't want to explain to Nik why I need it."

"You made it."

I jumped at the sound of Nik's voice behind me. He'd come up the driveway but I hadn't seen him.

"Shit." I grabbed my pounding chest.

"Sorry," Nik said with a laugh. "Didn't mean to scare you. Though it is oddly quiet tonight, isn't it?" He took in the trees and the clear sky above, a rarity in November.

"He still has someone with him," Myst said. The vanilla scent confirmed it. Was he a little pale?

"Thanks again for this," I said.

He nodded. "This way, around back."

Liam leaned against the driver-side door. "I'll just be here. You come say bye when you're ready."

Nik paused, maybe to ask why we didn't just say good-bye now, but he waved me onward without comment.

I followed him along a path of old, wobbly cement slabs, to a door with no window. The doorknob gave him a bit of trouble. He had to jiggle the doorknob up and down a few times before it released. "There's a lot to do around here. It just takes a special touch." He pushed the door open.

It looked like most of the suites in Vancouver's Lower Mainland. We entered into what would be the kitchen when it was finished. It opened into a living area, with a few doors off to other rooms.

"The bathroom isn't functional yet; sorry about that," he said. I hadn't really thought of that but hoped I wouldn't be there long enough to have to worry about it. "No running water, either." He stuck his hands in his pockets and rocked back on his heels. "Are you sure about this? I mean"—he took one hand out to wave it in an arc—"you want to do meditation here?"

I nodded. "I do."

He gave a little shrug. "Okay. I've got to go; some clients have arranged a get-together to thank me for my last meditation course." He paused, maybe waiting to see if I'd change my mind.

"Great," I said. "Have fun."

"Good luck." Nik moved out the door. "Call me if you need me."

"I will. Bye."

I stood in the smell of fresh paint and new plaster until his car left the crescent. Liam already had the wooden folding chair out of the truck by the time I walked out to him. He hooked it over one arm, carried it to the door then came back. Together we got the mirror out and carried it. It was taller than me, oval, framed in brass and had two brass legs.

I helped him get it through the door.

"Careful with this," Liam said. "Mom would be out for my blood if it broke. Been in our family for generations."

"You're telling me that now? I'm pretty sure you just jinxed it."

"Don't be ridiculous," he said. "I did not."

I put my side of the mirror down. "You don't believe in jinxes?"

Liam laughed, tilting the mirror upright. "Oh, hell, yes. Jinxes are totally a thing. You just can't acknowledge it like that or you make it happen." He stared down at me expectantly.

"Okay, then I take it back."

"Good. Again, you're sure about this?" He checked out the unfinished suite.

"I am," I said.

"Then shall we get on with the deprivation of your senses?"

I pulled out the earplugs and eye mask from my pockets. "We shall."

The streetlights and house lights didn't reach the paths. Liam had a little flashlight on his key chain and we found the beginning of the path.

"This is insane," Liam said. "Even with me leading you, you're still going to trip and break your neck."

"Thanks for that," I answered, then put in the earplugs. "I know it's weird, but so is this whole thing. Let's just do it." My voice sounded muffled, sort of like when ghosts tried to talk to me. Except Myst. She was crystal clear. Was she nearby? I found myself wanting her to be. I put on the eye mask and reached out my hand. Liam took it and put it through the crook of his arm.

I stumbled along in the dark, not able to hear much but muffled smooshing of damp leaves underfoot and the occasional rush of water. Would this be good enough for the apparition chamber to work? After only a few minutes, I wanted to rip the mask off and pull the damn earplugs out.

It wasn't just awkward and tricky going; it was downright scary. It kept me in my head far too much and I didn't like it. For the same reason I didn't like meditating.

"You're doing just fine," Myst said.

Eventually, focusing on not falling on my face kept me from agonizing over what was at stake. Maybe that was the point.

We moved from earth to pavement and I almost tripped up the curb. We made it to what I was pretty sure was the stone path to the back of the house. We stopped and I gave Liam the key. After a lot of rattling, he swore. I felt my way to the doorknob and tried what Nik had done. I felt it click and give way. This certainly wasn't complete sensory deprivation, but it was as good as it was going to get. With Liam's help, I stumbled inside.

His hand patted my shoulder, then a breath later the door closed. I took off the mask and removed the earplugs. I was alone, but knew I wouldn't be for long.

# Chapter 14

My ears started ringing before I even had time to open the folding chair. I took the candle from my pack, placed it on the floor in front of the mirror and lit it. I put the fire blanket next to it. There was nothing flammable in the suite except possibly the fresh paint, but I had an awful image of the entire house burning to the ground.

I sat in the slightly wobbly chair, gazed into the mirror at my own reflection and took a deep breath. I could do this. I had to do this.

Eyes closed, I counted out my breath, four in, six out. The ringing in my ears got louder. Panic rose within me. Without wards, I felt too vulnerable, like I'd been when Henry had made my life hell and killed my friends.

This was not the same, I reminded myself, then recited the words from Carme's incantation to summon Mary. The ringing in my ears got louder. A tornado of scents whirled around me and made me want to vomit. A few whispers got through. I was certain there were at least five or six ghosts with me.

"Please," I tried. "I'm trying to reach someone. It's

urgent." I had no idea if that would work, but the ringing eased off.

"Mary?"

A sharp smell like blue cheese overpowered my thoughts, and my stomach churned threateningly.

"Hello there," a man said, deep and jovial. It wasn't just a voice.

An elderly gentleman with a cowboy hat, black coat and black rubber boots stared out at me from the mirror. He brushed his thick grey moustache with his thumb.

My chest tightened and I felt hot, like I couldn't breathe. "It's just a reflection," I said aloud. That didn't help much, but I had to do this. It was just the apparition chamber doing this, letting me see him; that was all.

"I'm trying to find Mary Brunning," I said, and looked away from him.

"Don't know any Mary Brunning," said the man. "But since I have you here, do you mind me asking you a question?" He didn't give me a chance to reply. "Do you know how I could reach my daughter? Her lazy-ass husband is cheating on her, and I really want to tell her. None of her friends seem up to the task, even though it's plain as the nose on his face."

I refused to look at him because then I'd need to acknowledge I could see him. I held up a hand to get him to stop talking because it really seemed he didn't intend to any time soon. "Hold on. Are you sure she doesn't already know? Maybe she just isn't dealing with it at the moment?" The coach took over before I could stop myself.

The room went silent, as if all of the ghosts present waited to hear his response. "Why on earth would she do that?"

Despite his friendly demeanor, I still didn't want to piss him off. He was a ghost and I didn't trust them. "Well, it could be," I replied calmly, "she needs time to make an escape plan. She might need time to get her finances prepared. Maybe get proof of his infidelity." There were some ghostly murmured agreements.

"So, you're suggesting I do nothing?" he asked.

"For a bit," I replied. "Sit back and watch. If she needs you, you'll know."

"Fine," he said after a short silence. "But I'm not above haunting his cheating ass."

"Be my guest." I felt a difference in the air, a void. He had gone. The ringing in my ears increased once again and the whispers came back.

"Everyone else, unless your name is Mary Brunning, be quiet!" I yelled. The buzz in the room lowered to tolerable levels.

I clutched Mary's hat to my chest and refocused on the mirror. "Mary, I need you to talk to me."

"I think she's here," Myst said.

Slowly, like watching an artist apply brush strokes, Mary's image appeared in the mirror. She floated behind me, looking the same as when she'd been alive. Perhaps the red dress she wore was what she'd died in. Her hair and makeup were done, too, like she'd been going out for the night.

"Amy?" Her voice was soft, distant and sounded like she wasn't sure where she was.

"It's me." I registered mixed emotions at reaching her, anxiety, fear and a little excitement. I didn't look away. "Mary, can you tell me who killed you?"

"Can't," came her whispered reply. "Danger."

"What danger?" I wanted to jump into the mirror and get the information out of her. "From your killer?"

She nodded. Someone killed her and was still a threat to her in the afterlife?

A cold draft crept down the back of my neck. I gripped the sides of the chair and forced myself to stay put.

As calm as I could, I said the words Aunt Jodene gave me when I was a teen. "If you're not here with peaceful intent, you're not welcome here."

A laugh echoed, low and at the farthest end of friendly.

"Careful," Myst warned.

"Mary." It came out as a whisper. Familiar signs of a panic attack threatened to take over my mind and body. "No," Mary cried.

The weight of my anxiety fell heavy on my chest. I froze, unable to speak or move.

"Weak," said a low, raspy voice.

Mary's image began to fade. She reached out a finger. Letters began to appear on the mirror. They were backwards to me, but after a second of getting my brain around it, I could follow her. She finished and disappeared completely. She'd written, *dybbuk not safe*. The words faded soon after she did. I didn't know what it meant, but I wasn't about to forget it, either.

My image began to run, like crayons left in the sun. It reached the bottom of the mirror, spilled out and pooled into a puddle on the floor in front of me. The room went meat-freezer cold.

"Look out," Myst yelled.

The mirror shattered as if hit by a dozen bricks at once. Pieces blew from it with frightful force. I threw my arms over my face and braced for pain.

It never came. I peeked out from under my arm. The mirror stood as it had when Liam and I brought it in.

Now it showed dozens of people, young, old, men, women, and children. They all talked at once. The walls closed in as their smells overwhelmed me.

I ran the cafe menu list. Americano, mocha, cappuccino, macchiato, caramel macchiato, white chocolate mocha, latte, espresso, hot chocolate. I'm not sure how long I crouched as I fought to breathe, the presence of the ghosts pressing down on me. Their scents filled my body and my mind.

Over the pounding of my heart, the whispers and cries of the ghosts, it was Myst's voice that reached me loud and clear. "All right, sweeting. Time to get up."

I'd fallen to the ground at some point. I reached out and grabbed the chair. It wasn't very stable, but it served as a solid, tangible reminder of the real world.

"You can do it," Myst said. "Just get right up and out of here."

I forced myself to stand. The dead people in the mirror started to walk out toward me.

"Run. Now," Myst said. So I did.

I rushed to the door, swung it open and slammed it behind me. I backed away from the door and bumped into something, someone, solid. I spun to face Liam. My body shook and I couldn't stop it.

An older gentleman hovered behind Liam's right shoulder. He wasn't solid, but I couldn't exactly see through him, either. His wrinkled skin was the same colour as Liam's. He had sparse grey hair and a familiar depth to his dark eyes. I had no doubt it was Liam's grandfather.

I'd never seen a spirit before, only felt them or heard

them. Now I felt the urge to throw up, scream or run, but I didn't because I couldn't even move.

"Thought you might get yourself into trouble and need help." Liam tilted his head at me. "What?"

I shook my head, eyes squeezed tight, and hoped the old man would go away. "Nothing. I'm okay." When I opened my eyes, his grandfather still hovered there. "It worked, sort of. I have some new information."

"Okay, great." Liam went to go past me to the door, but I blocked his way. His grandfather frowned at me as he moved with him.

"You can't go in there," I told him.

"I have to get that mirror. Mom will have my head."

I put my back up against the door. "You can't go in there."

His eyes widened. "You didn't break it, did you?"

"No." Not in this world, thank goodness. "I can't let you in there. You need to trust me on this."

He threw his hands up, then walked in a little circle. His grandfather stayed still. He didn't watch Liam. He watched me. I wrapped my arms around myself against the cold night air and wished to be back at my place, smothered in cats, not seeing any ghosts.

Liam pushed past me and grabbed the doorknob. It wouldn't turn for him and he swore. His grandfather swooped down between him and the door, then glared back at me.

Grateful for the faulty doorknob, I put my hand over Liam's. "Stop. You can't go in. There are too many ghosts in there. I can't let you."

Liam let go of the doorknob. "What about when Nik comes back? What's going to happen to him when he goes in? Or anybody else, for that matter?"

"I don't know." Yet it was my responsibility. I had to do something.

"What do they want?" Liam asked.

"They've all got stuff they want." I choked back tears of overwhelm. "Things they say they need help with."

Liam's eyebrows shot up. "The dead have problems? Interesting. So, help them."

I shook my head. "No way."

He pointed at the door. "Go in there; tell them you'll help. Not right now. Not all at once. Tell them to book a time with you." He laughed at the last bit but then got serious again and jabbed his finger toward the door. "Do it."

His grandfather raised his arm and pointed at the door. It was clearly two against one. I held up one finger. "One second." I walked away a few steps. "Myst?"

"Yes?" she answered. I heard her like she stood next to me, but unlike Liam's grandfather, I still couldn't see her.

"What do you think?" I asked.

"I think you should help me before you help all these strangers."

"You know you're a stranger to me, too, right?"

"Not my fault," she snorted. "You already said you would help the ones in your office, so I'd say they're in line first."

"But do you think if I said I'd help them, they'd leave? Not bother anyone else?"

"It is likely," she said.

"Right." I held up my hand to keep Liam back. "I'm going in."

With a deep inhale, I used the jiggle technique on the doorknob and went inside. The ghosts gathered as close as they could to me, smaller ones floated up higher over the taller ones. My breath caught in my throat and the room spun. They continued to throw their questions and complaints at me.

"Listen," I yelled over the raucous voices and my own brain panic. "If you want me to help you, I will. Just not here, not right now. I need you to leave this place."

Then what? Have them call Carme and make an appointment? What the hell was I doing? The voices hushed, presumably waiting for more from me. It felt too hot. I couldn't breathe.

"There has to be some sort of order to it." I couldn't believe what I was saying. "I can't deal with all of you at once." Every breath felt like a battle. Breathe in, breathe out.

There was movement among the crowd of ghosts. A tall woman in a professional, dark blue dress suit appeared at the front of the crowd. She radiated stress even as a ghost. "Who gets to go first?"

"I don't know," I replied honestly. Every instinct in me wanted to run but I had to make this work. "We will come up with some sort of system. Tomorrow. Come to me tomorrow. That's the only way this will work. Do we have a deal?"

The ghosts all talked at once, some in anger, some in agreement, some with yet more questions.

Liam's grandfather appeared through the door and faced the throng of ghosts. "Out." His voice was deep and commanding. "Now." The words didn't match the movements from his mouth. "You want help, you'll get help. Later," he said.

Most of the ghosts now looked at him; some still stared at me.

"Fine," said the anxious woman in the blue dress. "I'm first in line." With that, she disappeared. Others made departing comments of how much they needed my help. Soon, I was left alone with Liam's grandfather. Without acknowledging me, he drifted back through the closed door.

I followed, tired and shaky. "It's okay; you can come in now. Your grandfather, he helped me."

Liam's eyes widened. "What? He was here?"

"He's still here." I pointed over Liam's right shoulder where his grandfather now hovered. "He's definitely watching out for you."

Liam swallowed hard and his eyes teared. "Guess he's okay with me, then?" He pinched the bridge of his nose, then waved me off when I tried to move in to comfort him. "I'm good; I'm good."

I went in for the hug. "He is here and clearly loves you. Unconditionally."

Liam gave a quick hug back then gave me a gentle shove. "Right. That's enough. Let's get the mirror."

Liam's grandfather stuck close as we got the mirror out of the suite and carried it back to the truck. All the way home, Liam's grandfather studied me, and I was pretty sure he didn't like what he saw. I wasn't thrilled about being able to see him, so we were even.

# Chapter 15

Carme wanted us all at the Feathered Serpent to go over everything. We got there just before ten o'clock.

Carme let us in. "Was Mary Jewish?" She closed and locked the door behind us.

To my relief, there were no scents or signs of ghosts in the shop. "Yes. She didn't talk about it much, just a bit about her parents. How's your mom?"

"Sleeping." Tears welled in Carme's eyes. "She woke up for a minute. I thought you got it out of her."

My determination to end all of this and return her mom to her flared through my entire body. "Sorry, Carme. Maybe we're getting closer, though."

"Mom talked to me."

My knees gave out a little. "What did she say?"

"Well, I told her you were trying to get the spirit out of her. She said not to. Then she said she wanted water but she didn't get it. She, you know, fell asleep again." She clutched her necklace pendant.

"That doesn't make any sense. She doesn't want us to get rid of the spirit inside her?"

"That's what she said. So, it can't be bad."

I rubbed the back of my neck to try and ease the building headache. "Why would she not want us to get rid of the spirit inside of her? We're missing something." Or was it so bad, she didn't want it out?

I shrugged off my coat. Liam took his off, too, and I didn't like the way his grandfather's spirit scowled at me.

"You don't have to stay," I said, afraid to meet his grandfather's eyes and see the anger there.

"Shut it. Of course I'm staying," Liam answered.

Carme took both our coats and threw them over the counter. She already had books spread out. "Jewish." She jabbed at one of the pages. "That's why Mary said *dybbuk*."

Liam shrugged at me, but I knew to let her run with it.

"Mom told me about dybbuks before," Carme said, excited. "There's a lot of different stuff on them. Movies have it wrong." She flicked her hand through the air with disapproval. "Listen." She put her finger on the page, reading slowly and clearly.

"*In Jewish mythology, dybbuks are believed to be displaced spirits that possess the body of a living being. They are unable to pass because of their terrible sins or unfinished business or sometimes possess someone as an escape from punishment after death. It often leaves the person after it has accomplished its goal or if it is helped.*"

I moved next to Carme. "Is Mary a dybbuk, then? Or did one possess her when she was alive? Made her kill herself?" My head hurt and I really wanted a coffee. Could I have coffee now? "How do they possess someone? Do they just pick randomly?"

"Can be anyone." She flipped a page. "Someone they knew or didn't like. Or someone can send it."

Liam leaned on the counter with both elbows. "That's a pretty wide range."

Carme scanned the page. "Someone with a dybbuk can—"

She stopped as Liam pulled one of her other books toward him.

I put my hand on Carme's arm. "It's okay. He'll be careful."

Liam smiled at Carme and drew an X on his chest. "I promise."

Carme relaxed only slightly but went back to her text. "Someone with a dybbuk can act really weird. Like, not themselves."

I took a deep breath to try to clear my head, but that proved difficult with Liam's grandfather glaring at me. "So, let's say a dybbuk possessed Mary. It made her kill herself. She was trying to tell us she didn't do it. Not by choice."

"Adds up," Liam said, then focused back on the book in front of him.

"How do we get rid of it?" In an effort to get my brain functioning better, I paced and worked through it out loud. "The day Aunt Jodene went to the hospital, we assumed it was the bad spirit after Mary that went inside her. Mary was so scared when I spoke to her tonight. Like, as though something is after her still." I spun to face Carme. "You said your mom woke up briefly. What if it was while I was talking to Mary?"

Carme studied me for a bit, and I waited to see if she had the same thought as me. Her eyes widened. "It's not the bad spirit inside Mom," she said. "It's Mary!"

"Hiding from the other spirit," I agreed. "At least we know Mary isn't purposely trying to harm your mom. That's better than whatever Mary is afraid of."

Carme smiled. "It is better."

Liam cleared his throat. "A pious man has to exorcise it."

"Excuse me?" Carme threw a hand on her hip. "Sexist much?"

Liam gave a shrug in solidarity. "Sure as shit I'm not going to pay attention to what gender someone is supposed to be. So, ignoring that, it says you have to interview the dybbuk along with an angel." He held up his hand when I started to interrupt. "The purpose is to determine why the spirit hasn't moved on. Boy, that's a cliche, isn't it?" He snorted a little laugh. When we didn't join in, he cleared his throat and continued. "Anyway, finding out is supposed to help you convince it to leave. You need to know its name so you can command it. Then you hold out a flask." He leaned in and squinted a little at the text, then nodded. "Which will glow red when the dybbuk goes into it."

Carme ran her finger along the lines of her book. "The dybbuk needs a living host. If it leaves one person, if the person dies, for example, it goes to another and another and another."

"And," Liam added, "a dybbuk can be commanded by someone else. Someone living."

"I think I need to sit down." I headed for the chairs at the back, plunked down and rested my head back. This wasn't an anxiety attack. I knew the difference. This was exhaustion and overwhelm.

Carme came and sat in the other chair. Liam hung back and watched, reminding me of his grandfather, who still glared at me.

"We can do this," Carme said, her words strong but pleading at the same time.

I took a deep breath and sat upright. Right. I coached people how to overcome adversity all the time, how to beat whatever challenges they faced. "You're right. We can do this. Myst? We could use some help." Peppermint filled my nostrils, but she didn't say anything.

Carme and Liam stared at me, but I had to shrug. I pointed at my cousin. "You ask. She likes you."

Carme cleared her throat, like she was about to address someone extremely important. "Hello, Myst." She gave a little wave to the air. "We could use some help. If that's all right with you."

"This one, I will help," Myst said with tremendous snark.

"She says she'll help," I answered, but left out the attitude.

Carme nodded and wiped her hands on her pants. "Is there a dybbuk in Amy's client, Margaret?"

My jaw dropped in a small gasp. Carme had jumped straight to a connection to my Margaret, which I hadn't even thought of. Margaret, who had been having uncharacteristic suicidal thoughts.

"I'm sorry, tell her I don't know," Myst replied.

"Who's Margaret?" Liam asked.

"A client." I grabbed my phone. It was late, especially for someone with a toddler, but I didn't care. "She wasn't feeling herself, said she had weird, depressing thoughts. Hi, Margaret?" Relief washed over me when she answered her phone.

"Amy, hi." She didn't sound good.

"Is everything okay? Are you all right?"

"Much better, actually. I feel weak, exhausted, like I could sleep for a week. But mentally better."

What did that mean? Was the dybbuk gone? Or was it still in her but she was fighting it? If it had left her, would it come back?

"Do you have someone who can be with you?" I hoped I didn't sound like I was treating her like a child but I would feel better if someone was with her.

"It's just me and the kiddo." She sounded truly exhausted. I looked up at Liam's grandfather.

"If I do this," he growled at me, "you leave him alone." He nodded toward Liam.

My heart squeezed as his terms sank in. If he went to watch over Margaret, I had to keep Liam out of this. How could I do that, after just letting him into this side of my life? How was I supposed to push my best friend away?

I couldn't risk Margaret's life. Maybe keeping Liam away from me would save him, too. I nodded at Liam's grandfather and he disappeared.

"Margaret," I said into my phone, "I want you to stay focused on your daughter. She needs you. I'll get back to you as soon as I can." She promised me she would keep in touch.

After the call, I let out a long breath. "I'm not sure if the dybbuk is in Margaret anymore. She says she's mentally better but is exhausted. She did sound more like herself."

Liam went back to the books on the counter. "That's a good thing, isn't it?"

"Yes, but then, where is the dybbuk now?"

Carme sat taller. "Myst, do you know?"

We waited. Liam and Carme watched me intently.

"Maybe she's checking," Liam said with a shrug.

"Not checking," Myst said, "just thinking."

I tapped a finger to my temple to let Carme and Liam know.

"Did it kill Mary?" Carme asked.

"Can't say," Myst said, and I repeated it.

"So, can we get rid of it like the books say?" I asked her.

"Can't say on that, either," she replied. "Sounds like you should try it."

I let out a heavy breath. "She's not sure but thinks we should do it."

Carme got to her feet and clapped her hands twice. "Thank you, Myst." She went back to her books.

I rubbed my forehead to make the headache go away, then stood. "Fine. Let's find this damn dybbuk as fast as we can, then. What's the first step?"

We gathered around Carme's books once again; the familiar woodsy scent prickled my nose and gave me courage. Outside the shop, several figures peered in. None of them were living.

"Carme, how are the wards on the shop?" I watched more ghosts gather. Some I recognized from earlier in the suite. "We've got visitors." I pointed at the front windows.

Carme squinted hard, as though trying to see what I saw. "The wards are good." She patted a different book, and I knew she enjoyed this research stuff. "You need an angel or"—she paused, took a deep breath and read—"beneficent spirit." She peered at us. "What's that?"

Liam got his phone. "I don't know what the hell that means, either." He typed and then scrolled. "Generous or doing good, given to acts that are kind, charitable." He chewed his lip. "So, you need an angel or a spirit that's in contact with angels?"

"Maybe Myst?" Carme asked.

Myst laughed close to my ear. "I don't remember who I was, but I know I was no goody-two-shoes."

"I don't think she can help us," I loosely interpreted.

"How do you get an angel?" Liam asked.

"We all have them." Carme gave me a sideways glance. "Most of us." Liam's eyebrows shot up.

I stretched my tense neck. "She means not me. When we got rid of Henry, it meant we got rid of every spirit around me, including any guardian angels."

Carme's eyes brightened. "Do I have angels? Can you see them?"

"I'm positive you do. Many, many of them. But I don't see anything, probably because of your wards. Or maybe they like to lay low, focus on protecting you."

She smiled, but it was halfhearted. "Meditation can get you in touch with angels," she said. I knew exactly where she was going with this.

"Are you saying that to get Nik back here? Remember when you accused me of trying to set you up with Darren?"

Her smile brightened. "This is different. You really like him." Liam chuckled.

"I can't believe you two. No. We're not asking any more of Nik. I can't."

"Carme's got a good point. Again." Liam scrolled on his phone as Carme beamed. "I mean, look at his bio. He coaches breathwork, he leads meditation groups, he hosts his own charity events for kids. I don't think you could find anyone better to help with the dybbuk. Why you're not all over this guy, I have no idea."

I clenched my jaw, then let out a breath. "I'm going to ignore that last comment because we need to focus. If you both think we need Nik, figure out a way I could ask him without putting him in any danger. For now, let's focus on the dybbuk. It started out in Mary, as far as we know, made her kill herself, then went to Heidi, made her fall out of the SkyTrain."

Liam gave a giant sigh. "Seems so."

"Why is this dybbuk after my clients?"

"We better find out," Liam said. "Maybe we could ask my grandfather?" He must have seen my anguish. "What?"

"Your grandfather went to watch over Margaret."

Liam pointed up. "Good on ya, Abuelo," he called out.

"But he would only do it if I agreed to keep you out of this."

Liam's smile disappeared and he shook his head. "No way."

"I don't think we have a choice," I told him. "Ghosts, especially family ones, can be extremely vengeful. We can't ignore his wishes."

Liam crossed his arms on his chest. "There never should have been a deal without talking to me first."

I threw up a hand. "There wasn't time; I had Margaret on the phone. I had to make sure she was safe."

He shook his head. "Not just you. Same goes for my grandfather. You two can't make a deal involving me without my say. I don't have to go along with it."

"It's not a good idea to piss off a ghost. Especially your grandfather, I'm pretty sure. You have to go. You have to stop coming around and you have to try to forget about all this stuff."

Liam slapped the counter with both hands. "Really? You think I'm going to do that? Not a chance. I'm staying. You and my grandfather can both kiss my ass."

Carme giggled. I threw her an angry stare. "You're not helping. Liam really has to go."

My cousin shrugged at me but then gave a sneaky thumbs-up to Liam.

"This is not a joke." My voice came out too loud, too

angry, but maybe that's what it took. "You two think this ghost business is fun and games. Let me tell you, it is not. It is death, death and more death. You both need to take this more seriously." Carme stared down at her books, obviously hurt.

Liam stared at me, then pointed a finger at Carme and then himself. "We know," he said. "You have not let us forget it. But we're still in this. Together. So, stop acting like you're in charge when Carme clearly is."

Like magic, the tension broke. Carme smiled and I let the anger fall away. They wanted to help save Aunt Jodene as much as I did. But I would be damn sure to keep them safe, however I could.

"We will be careful," Carme said, then pointed at Liam. "You probably should go, though. Not make your grandpa mad."

"You know, I didn't say out loud I wanted your grandfather to go be with Margaret, but he knew. Do you think he can hear my thoughts?"

Carme shrugged. "I don't know."

Liam smiled. "Probably he just knew he needed to do it."

"I can't hear your thoughts," Myst said. "But you shine them like a marquee. Don't ever take up poker."

That wasn't surprising to me but brought up something interesting. "No one says *marquee* anymore, do they?" I asked Carme and Liam.

A knock on the front door made us all jump. My first thought was the ghosts, but it wasn't them. It was our bone collector, and she didn't look good.

# Chapter 16

Carme turned to me and I nodded. "Let her in."

She grabbed the keys. Liam flanked her as she opened the door. Worried the ghosts might try to come in, I held my breath, not that they needed an open door. They didn't enter. They hovered outside the shop and stared at me expectantly through the window.

Carme locked the door again and I waved our bone collector over. She wore similar clothes to before, black jeans and a dark hoodie. This time, she had a large black duffel bag. She looked rough, like maybe she hadn't slept or eaten since she'd last been here.

I held a hand out toward the back corner. "Would you like to sit?"

She gave a cautious glance around, then nodded.

Moving slowly and carefully like I might spook her, I made my way to the back. Liam went to follow us, and I pointed at the door, trying to shoo him out. He rolled his eyes at me and stayed with Carme at the counter.

"What's your name?" I asked after we sat. "We've been calling you our bone collector." She gave a snort-laugh and put her bag at her feet.

"I wanted to give you a better name," Carme said, quite serious.

"I'm not sure if that's endearing or not." She held out her hand across the space between us. "Andrea."

"I'm Amy," I replied. Her hand was cold and a bit clammy as we shook. "Welcome back."

"Didn't think I would be, but..." She reached down, unzipped her backpack and pulled out a skull. She shoved it toward me. "Take it. I don't want it."

I tucked my feet up under me and moved back in the chair as far as I could. "We don't want it either."

She put it on the floor by her feet then used both hands to dump her bag out. "None of it." Bones clacked and clattered out onto the rug.

Carme rushed over. "Maybe we want it." She crouched down for a closer look.

"Carme," I snapped.

"What? Might be cool in the shop," she replied. "These all human?" Andrea nodded.

With my feet still tucked up on the chair, I leaned to put a hand between Carme and the pile of bones. "Let's find out why Andrea doesn't want them, first. Don't touch them."

Carme scoffed but sat down on the rug. Liam joined us and stood behind Carme.

I sat back. "So?"

Andrea let out a long breath. "If this is why things are happening to me, I don't want them."

"What is happening to you?"

She chewed her lower lip a couple times. "I've been having blackouts. Before you ask, no, it's not drugs or alcohol. I don't know when the blackouts are going to hit or

SANDRA WICKHAM

why. I just wake up after."

"Have you seen a doctor?" I asked.

"I don't think they can help. When I wake up, I've written things. At first, it was with whatever was lying around, but then I started leaving out paper and a pen."

Carme bounced on her butt. "Automatic writing."

"That would be a good name for it," Andrea said.

"It's a way for the dead to talk," Carme went on. "What do they write?"

Andrea reached inside her black coat and pulled out crumpled sheets of paper. "Mostly, it doesn't make any sense." The pages crackled as she handed them to Carme.

The fact she didn't hesitate to give the pages to my cousin, never questioned her capabilities, raised my opinion of Andrea greatly.

Carme took the pages to the counter, put them down and smoothed them out.

Liam crouched down to see the skull Andrea had tried to give me. "Whose is it?"

Andrea shrugged. "I know where all my other bones came from, who they belonged to. These were an ill-informed purchase; I don't even know why I did it. I've had them tested; they're real. Human. But I haven't identified them."

"Oh, my goodness!" Myst said loudly. "Maybe it's me. Ask her if it's a woman."

Could this all be connected somehow? "Do you know if it's a man or woman?" I asked.

"Man," Andrea replied.

Myst sighed and I gave a sympathetic nod, though no one else knew it was for her.

I pointed at the bones. "You've had them for a long time,

140

then. Why do you think they're causing this now?"

She clasped her hands in her lap. "I don't know; I just feel like it has to be the source."

Liam reached out to touch the skull, and I slapped his hand. He gave me an annoyed glare, then smiled at Andrea.

"Don't touch it," I said. "We don't know anything about it."

"I found something," Carme said from behind the counter. I navigated carefully around the pile of bones as I went to my cousin. Liam followed close behind. Andrea stuffed the skull back in the bag and then joined us.

"What is it?" I asked.

"Automatic writing isn't always words," Carme said. "You're supposed to look for pictures and stuff, too. Look." She pointed at what first appeared to be scribbles. "It's a mirror." She gave a proud smile.

I tilted my head and tried to get my brain to ignore the other scribbles to see what she meant. It was a handheld mirror reflecting an X from in front of it. There were scattered words around the page, but nothing connected. "You think this message is about me and the apparition chamber?"

"Maybe?" Carme answered. "It tried to talk to us before. Through Andrea."

"Wait." Andrea's eyes narrowed at me, then Carme and Liam. She pointed an accusing finger at all three of us. "It's not the skull, is it? It's all of you." Liam stood up taller, like he was proud to be included.

"We don't know why it's happening," I said calmly, hoping she wouldn't run away. "I can't see or hear the spirit that's communicating through you."

Andrea blinked a few times at me and backed up.

"Can we still keep the skull?" Carme asked, and I elbowed her in the side.

Andrea glared at me. "You see ghosts?"

"Well, that part is kind of new." I gave a quick glance at the ghosts outside the shop. Their number had increased. "I used to only hear them. I don't see all of them, apparently. Not sure why."

Andrea clenched her jaw. "All I really want is to make this stop. Can you do that?"

I could definitely relate to that. "We can try."

Liam had his phone out. "What if you do some of that writing on purpose?"

Andrea rubbed her forehead. "It's not much fun blacking out and losing time from your life."

"I don't think you would," Carme said. "Black out, I mean. You black out because it's, like, the only way for them to do it."

Liam nodded. "Right. If you work with them, they wouldn't need to take over your body or whatever it is they're doing."

Andrea leaned all the way over and put her head on the counter. "I don't like this," she said into the glass.

"This is something I know about; trust me. It's the only way to get rid of them." I scanned the ghosts outside and knew I would have to take my own advice and help them.

Andrea stood upright, determination now set on her face. "If this will stop it, fine. Let's do it."

"I'll get paper," Carme said with a flourish. "And a pen."

Liam scrolled on his phone with one hand, pointed at Andrea with the other. "You're going to need to meditate for a bit."

I tried not to cringe as Andrea shrugged. "I can do that."

"Then you're supposed to write down a question," Liam went on. "Something you want answered, but don't ask something you already know; they don't like to be tested, apparently. And don't make it a yes-or-no question." He looked up from his phone. "What are we asking?"

Carme gave the pen to Andrea. "Maybe ask: what do they want to tell us?"

"Sounds good to me," Andrea replied, then pointed the pen to the chairs. "Over there?"

I nodded. "Anything else?" I asked Liam.

"Yeah, it says go with your first thoughts. Don't stop to think or analyze. Just write as fast as possible."

Carme tapped her temple. "Too much thinking can mess it up."

Andrea let out a throaty laugh from the red chair. "I'm too tired to think, so this should be perfect."

Carme grabbed a clipboard from the back and put a piece of paper on it. Andrea gave us a nod and closed her eyes. I waved Liam and Carme to the counter.

"What?" Liam asked, and I put a finger to my lips to hush him.

"Just thinking," I whispered, "the dybbuk needs a live host, not a dead one. So, what is after Mary's ghost? Not the dybbuk. What is so terrible Mary has to hide inside Aunt Jodene?"

Carme's face paled a little. She pointed over at Andrea, pen and clipboard in hand. "Maybe that's what this ghost is trying to tell us?"

Liam swallowed hard. "Or maybe that thing is this ghost."

We watched Andrea scribble fiercely back and forth across the paper. She reached the bottom of the page and showed no signs of stopping.

Carme grabbed another piece of paper and placed it on top, but Andrea didn't notice. Her face scrunched in concentration, but her eyes didn't follow what she wrote. She looked pale. Too pale.

I went to get a bottle of water from the back. When I came back, Andrea had stopped writing. The pen hovered over the page while her eyes stared off into space. I set the water on the table next to her.

"Should we wake her out of it?" I whispered to Carme.

My cousin shook her head. "Let her do it," she said.

We waited. Andrea finally blinked several times and put the pen down. She looked down at the clipboard, then over at us.

"It worked." Her hand shook as she held the pages out.

Carme rushed over and took the pages from her. "You okay?"

Andrea nodded, then leaned back in her chair. Her face had gone deathly pale, for lack of a better description.

I pointed at the bottle on the table beside her. "Drink some water."

She took the bottle and twisted open the lid like it took great effort to do.

Carme ushered me and Liam away. "Give her space."

We followed Carme. She put the pages down so we could see them.

"What the hell," Liam said in a hushed tone.

There was only one sentence repeated on the first page. *Let them out.*

The second page had a different sentence. *Let me in.*

Carme and I looked out the window, but I knew she

didn't see what I saw. Dozens of ghosts now pressed against the glass.

"Let me in?" Carme asked. "Skull?" Of course she named our new ghost.

Liam pointed from Andrea's bag on the floor to the window. "The owner of that skull is outside the shop right now?"

"I don't know," I whispered. "Maybe. It's possible. There's a lot of them."

"*Let them out*, this says." Carme tapped the paper. "From the office?"

I let out a tense breath. "Probably."

Liam shook his head. "Wow. Skull wants you to let them out? Why? They're locked in there for a reason. They were trying to harm you, right?"

"Maybe they didn't mean to," Carme said.

"Guys," Andrea called in a weak voice. "I don't feel so good." Before we could get to her, she slumped down, eyes closed. She slid out of the chair. Liam and I positioned her flat on the floor. She breathed steadily but was still far too pale.

"Should I call 911?" Liam asked.

Andrea went rigid and her eyes popped open. "Let us in." It came out low and monotone.

Liam smacked me in the arm. "It's Skull."

"I get it," I hissed back.

"The others are weak," Skull said through Andrea. "I am respecting your boundaries for now, but you need to let them speak."

Carme and Liam stared at me with wide eyes.

"Help them," Skull continued. "Then they will help you with your problem."

Andrea gasped for breath. Her upper body lurched forward, then she collapsed back to the floor, eyes closed.

"Is she okay?" Carme asked.

Andrea's eyes opened before I could answer. "He's coming in," she said.

# Chapter 17

He came through the front window. There was no sound, no warning.

For one horrible, terror-inducing moment, I thought it was my stepfather. I stepped in front of the others. A strong scent of cigar preceded him and turned my stomach, but I then knew it wasn't Henry.

My heart pounded. "Stay back," I said to the others.

This ghost, in his eighties or so, resembled Henry too much not to be related. He wore an elaborately embroidered dark green waistcoat, matching knee-length pants and long white socks.

"I will not hurt you." His voice rang clear and strong. "You are family."

Liam stepped forward. "Amy, what's going on?"

I held a hand out to keep him back. "Family. As in my stepfather?"

"Still family," he replied with a slight bow.

"Are you the one terrifying Mary?" I asked.

"No." His voice remained steady and he held his gaze firmly on mine. Despite my rising anxiety, I believed him.

"What do you want?" I asked.

"You need help. They need help. So, help them. They have no one else."

"Amy, Andrea doesn't look good," Carme said.

I threw my arms out wide in an attempt to shield Liam, Carme and Andrea. Deep down I knew if he wanted to harm us, there would be nothing I could do. My breath came in short gasps. "Leave the girl alone."

"An unfortunate side effect of using her to reach you," he said.

"You're telling me a bone collector I'd never met just happens to have the skull of Henry's ancestor?"

"The skull is someone from your family?" Liam exclaimed. "That's unbelievable."

In spite of my brain's insistence on seeing the resemblance, I nodded. "He's right. Far too coincidental."

"Not coincidence," the ghost replied. "I influenced the seller of my skull to reach out to this woman who lived close to you. I then brought her to this shop."

I repeated this to the others. Carme smiled, which worried me. Liam gave an exaggerated jaw drop. Andrea struggled to take a sip of water.

"All to get to me?" I fought to keep my emotional intelligence in check. "Why?"

"To help you," he snapped, like I was an insolent child. "I felt I owed it to you, after what he did. He was descended from me, after all."

"Where were you when he was terrorizing me?" My chest tightened. Each breath felt like a chore.

His eyes narrowed. "I was being kept in an airtight box by a small man at the time."

"Careful," Myst said close to me, and I took a breath to

rein in my anger.

"We're not all-knowing or all-powerful," he went on. "Some of us have been around a long time and have learned a thing or two. That's all. These ones are troubled." He twisted to point at the ghosts outside, "They need your help. Give it to them and they will help you. I cannot help you; my strength is limited until my bones are laid to rest."

"Why me?" My brain screamed for this all to stop, now.

"Do you know of any other living humans who can hear them? See them?"

I paused. "My aunt—"

"Is nowhere near as strong as you are."

"There must be others," I tried.

"A few, but none with your vocational skills."

"Perfect." All that time and money spent to become a life coach had literally come back to haunt me. "What about her?" I pointed at Andrea. "Will you leave her alone now?"

"She purchased my dead remains, which have been handed around for centuries. What do you think should happen to her?"

I felt his anger and knew I had to keep him from hurting her. "If I do this, help those ghosts, will you leave her alone?"

He gave a slow nod. "If you agree to help those outside and the ones you've locked away. If she lays my remains to rest. Then I will. If not, things will not go well for her."

I didn't like being blackmailed, but when I explained the situation out loud to Liam and Carme, I knew I didn't have a choice.

"What's his name?" Carme asked.

My ancestor's face twisted. "Names are powerful."

"He won't tell us," I told Carme as I wished for more space. The shop felt smaller every minute.

Carme tapped her chin. "Let's call him Adam."

"What…" my ancestor began, but I held up a hand.

"Don't bother arguing with her," I said.

Myst laughed. "Indeed."

"Why do you care if I help them or not?" My nerves were on the edge of the edge.

"Perhaps I feel for my spirit kindred after what I've been forced to endure. Those ghosts out there deserve help. The other ones you've imprisoned, too."

"We didn't imprison them." I met Carme's eyes, and knew I couldn't deny that's exactly what we'd done. "We kept them from hurting anyone." The walls of the shop began to close in on me. "They'll be more aggressive now, after being locked up."

"Not aggressive," he said with a shake of his head. "Desperate. I'll talk with them first. Do we have a deal?"

"Fine." I turned my attention back to the living people in the room. "I'm going to help the ghosts. All of them. Andrea, he wants you to bury his remains."

She nodded furiously. "Big ol' ceremony to go with it." She fought to sit up, so Carme and I helped her.

Carme's face lit up when I told her everything he'd said, and I didn't like it. I felt both panic and exhaustion at the mere prospect of talking to so many dead people.

Her smile widened and she clasped her hands over her heart. "We're going to help ghosts."

I shook my head. "No. Not us. Me. I don't want you involved."

Her smile didn't let up. "But I am. I'm your secretary."

I gestured a hand toward the window and the ghosts I hated seeing there. "What are you going to do for me? Take their calls? Book their appointments? You can't see or hear them, and I don't trust them."

Her smile dropped, and so did my heart at the sight of it. Liam came over and wrapped one arm around her and gave her a squeeze. "Come on," he said. "Carme knows more about this whole ghost thing than you do."

Myst chuckled. "He has a point there."

My mind searched for reasons Carme shouldn't help me. None of them came up against the pained expression on her face.

"Fine," I said with the opposite of enthusiasm, but it didn't faze Carme. She zipped past me to get her coat. I called out after her. "Grab the black candle, pendants, whatever else you've got."

She didn't turn around, just waved a hand over her head to acknowledge me.

I jabbed a finger at Liam. "You're supposed to be on my side."

He shrugged with fake innocence. "Just telling it like it is. She does know more than you, and she has just as much at stake. She wants to save her mom."

"If anything happens to her, I will never forgive myself."

I held open Andrea's duffel bag so she could put Adam's bones back inside, which she did with far more care and reverence than she had previously. The owner of them stayed silent but kept an eye on all of us.

Andrea pushed off the chair to standing. "I'm feeling better already. You go do your death coaching. I'll be fine."

"I'm not death coaching," I started, then clammed up. My heart filled with rocks and my stomach did acrobatics.

"I can take you home," Liam said to Andrea. She gave him a small smile and a nod. Maybe there was more in the air than ghosts. They'd have a unique story about how they met, that was for sure.

I tried not to reveal how hard my heart pounded or how bad my hands shook as I grabbed my coat.

"Don't worry." Carme wrapped her arm through mine as we headed to the door. "It's going to be great."

No, it most definitely would not. It couldn't be, I wanted to scream at her but I held it in. My inner dialogue spiraled downward into fear and anxiety.

"I do so like Carme," Myst said, still close by. "You're smart to keep these people around you."

Of course she was right, but I worried about their safety. How did I know one of these ghosts wouldn't harm them? Kill them?

Carme unlocked the door and I walked out into a cloud of overpowering scents and impatient ghosts.

As Liam and Andrea walked away into the dark night, the ghosts ignored them, much to my relief.

"Follow me," I told the cloud of spirits without looking at them. I couldn't and I didn't, all the way to the office.

Even though the Artful Cup wasn't open, the scent of coffee hung in the stairwell. If I got through the night, I swore I'd have the largest, strongest cup of coffee Charles could make me.

We reached the door to the office and Carme stepped in front of me.

"The wards," Carme said.

I grabbed her arm. "I don't think I can do this. I don't think we should do this."

She pulled her arm away. "We're doing it."

Her hands wove through the air as she removed the wards. My mind and body panicked. Surely there was another way. The rocks from my heart fell into my stomach, and my legs felt weak, like they couldn't hold me up.

The anxious woman in the blue dress from the apparition chamber zipped over to me, anger all over her face. "You locked them in?" A flowery scent accompanied her, so strong it was like I'd been sprayed all over with perfume.

"Yes," I snapped back. "They tried to hold me captive."

"Ready?" Carme stopped, one hand held up. Adam nodded, so I forced myself to as well. Carme swooped her finger and whispered a few words.

The door flew open. A strong wind twisted our hair and tugged our coats, but it wasn't air. It was spirits.

My breath caught and wouldn't return. I could see them now. Dozens of them. Old, young, all genders, all sizes.

My chest tightened and I let out a gasp as the new spirits filled the hall. Their angry chatter felt like a mob about to explode. Adam moved quickly among them. Whatever he said didn't seem to be doing any good. Smells attacked me from every direction.

I grabbed Carme's arm. "You have to get away from here."

She scowled and pulled away. "Listen up," she said into the air. A few of the spirits looked at her. "You are all going to pay attention to me. Now."

Almost all of them focused on her. I tried to catch my breath.

Carme smiled. "We are going to help all of you. But with order." She jabbed a thumb on her chest and her smile grew. "I am Amy's secretary. You don't see her"—she pointed at me—"unless you go through me. Clear? Or no one gets helped."

She turned with great flair and walked into the office. The last part was a bluff—we had to help them—but she made it believable.

I raced after her. "Carme, this is not a good idea."

The ghosts followed us in. Carme had worked her magic; we had their attention. Some of them discussed how best to try to communicate with Carme to get their appointment with me. Me, their new life coach. Could I really help them? Would it help Aunt Jodene?

"Why should we listen to this mongoloid?" a deep voice yelled.

My entire body stiffened. A ghost flew through the others to come to the front of the group.

It was a middle-aged man, dressed in scholar's robes from the days of Socrates. He smelled horrible, like a combination of wet paper, smoke and mold.

I stood my ground, grateful Carme couldn't hear him. "You need to leave."

He bristled into a pose I imagined worked to intimidate others when he'd been alive. "I shall do no such thing." He swooped his arms in dramatic fashion as he spoke. "That mongoloid has no power here. I should be first."

Carme stared at me, arms held up in question.

There had been times I'd wanted to stand up for Carme but she didn't want me to. I was angry and on edge. My anxiety hid in the depths, ready to take over, like a horror-movie villain everyone thinks is dead but will rise up and kill them all.

"I don't care who you are or were," I yelled at the spirits. "We have zero tolerance for disrespect. I will not speak to anyone who is not on board with that."

The spirit who had insulted Carme rose. Anger emanated from his entire being.

"Carme, remember when I told you to pack those things

in case of angry ghosts?"

Her eyes widened, then she flung the pack from her back onto the ground.

The robed ghost grew in size. "Do you know who I am?" Most of the other ghosts cringed.

I did my best to block Carme. If he had enough strength to attack, I'd be absolutely useless against him. Having Carme there had been a huge mistake. Confronting this ghost had been a horrible idea. What was I thinking? Ghosts couldn't be trusted. They couldn't be helped. They were a danger right now to the person I loved most.

"Carme, we have to leave. Now."

The office went meat-freezer cold. The drawers on both our desks flew out and smashed into the walls. Our chairs zipped off in different directions.

Carme crouched and pulled things out of her pack.

"What is she doing?" the robed ghost yelled.

One second, he was in front of me; the next, a chill pushed through me as he went for Carme. I stumbled back, my body and brain numbed. He grabbed Carme around the throat with both hands.

Carme fell to her side. She clawed at her throat, but it didn't do any good. Her fingers went through his hands and scratched her own neck in ragged red lines.

"Get off her," I screamed, and tried to pull him off her. My hands went right through him.

Adam appeared beside him and punched him in the side of the head.

The impact sounded as real as if they'd been alive; however, the robed ghost barely reacted to the punch. He released his hands from around Carme's throat long enough to shove Adam, who flew across the room and disappeared through the office wall.

My heart pounded too hard in my chest. This couldn't be happening. Not again. Not to Carme. I wouldn't let it.

Carme gasped for air. I tried to drag her away from the robed ghost. He was too fast, on her again in a flash.

His hand closed on her throat. "If she wants us to go through her, then I will make her one of us."

"Fight me, you coward," I yelled at him. His scent churned with the others in the room and made my head spin. Carme fought to breathe, her eyes watered and her face went a darker red every second.

"Hang on, Carme," I said.

Her bag lay open beside her, contents scattered. I grabbed the black candle. Carme's eyes found mine as I struck a match. Those eyes told me to stop but I had to do it. I had to save her. There was no other choice.

I lit the black candle and slowly waved it through the air, then spoke the words ingrained in my brain from Aunt Jodene's expulsion of Henry's spirit.

"The armies of the righteous are mine to command, and I cast you out. Begone and fly to banishment. As smoke is driven away, so are you driven. As wax melts before the fire, so are you melted from this plane. Haunt here no more."

A small figure appeared on the floor beside Carme.

It was her old cat, Fidget. I would have known him anywhere, light brown scruffy hair, a big rip on one ear and one eye completely white with blindness.

Carme squirmed, desperate for breath. Fidget's tiny ghost paw reached up and gently touched her arm. He hissed at the robed figure and crouched, ears back.

The air changed, squeezed with pressure. Ghost screams filled my ears, and then they were all gone.

# Chapter 18

Carme sat up, rubbed her throat and gasped for breath. "What have you done?"

My whole body shook. It took several tries to blow out the candle. "I had to. He was going to kill you." The spell had taken its toll. I felt completely worn out but not as bad as Aunt Jodene had been. She'd spent weeks recovering.

"They're gone, aren't they?" Carme took in the office. "All of them."

I nodded slowly. The quiet and empty office felt wrong. There had been spirits of young children, a mother holding an infant. Carme's cat, Fidget.

"I had to," I repeated.

She shook her head and pushed me away when I went to help her up. "You killed them." She crab-walked back to lean against her desk.

"I didn't kill them, Carme. They were already dead."

"They wanted your help." She used her desk to pull herself up as tears trailed down her cheeks. "They were going to help Mom." She turned away from me, grabbed her coat and staggered to the open door.

"Carme, wait." She didn't stop, didn't look back. I followed her out. "At least come to my place to get some rest."

She stopped at the top of the stairs but didn't turn around. "No. I'm going to the hospital."

"I'll come with you."

"Don't." Her tone left little room for negotiation. She disappeared down the stairs.

I debated whether to meet her there. In the end, I came to the conclusion she meant it. She didn't want me there and I understood why.

"Myst?" I whispered to the empty hall. No answer came.

The smell of the extinguished flame lingered in the office. There were no other scents. I quickly grabbed my coat, locked the office door and made my way down the stairs, more alone than I'd ever felt.

The sun hadn't yet come up and the streets lay almost deserted. The SkyTrain and buses weren't running yet, so I called a cab. I'd go home, feed and hug my cats. I'd text Liam with an update. He'd probably hate me too. I'd had no other choice. That ghost would've killed Carme. The others were collateral damage.

It didn't make me feel any better to think of it that way. After I got some rest and had given Carme some space, I'd head to the hospital. Carme was angry at me, but we had to figure out what to do next.

After a couple hours of restless sleep, I got up and fed the cats again. Before I left for the hospital, I called Margaret. She sounded more like her old self, chipper, despite the early hour. While I was relieved, it left the question of where the dybbuk could be now.

"Thanks for checking in," Margaret said. "Can we set an

appointment for me to come see you soon?"

"Sure, I will let you know," I replied without much conviction. I wasn't sure I'd ever help anyone ever again. Not if I couldn't keep them alive.

My nerves flared as I approached Aunt Jodene's room. Would Carme still be furious with me? What if I'd blown our only chance to help Aunt Jodene? How could I face Carme with her mom lying there?

I walked into the room and almost burst into tears. Carme had squeezed herself into the hospital bed beside her mom and was fast asleep. I stayed where I was, not sure whether to make my presence known or not.

A nurse entered and stepped up beside me. "Are you family?" she asked in a whisper, and I nodded. She motioned me to follow her out of the room, so I did.

"How is she?" I asked.

"Her vitals are slipping. We don't know why. It could just be the length of time she's been this way."

"Thanks," I said. She gave me a caring nod and continued down the hall.

I had to find that damn dybbuk. Now. Which meant I needed help from the dead people I'd banished. Where had I sent them? Another realm? Or had I extinguished them from all existence? The person who might know the answer lay in a hospital bed as her life slowly slipped away from her.

The other person who would know was my stepfather, since Aunt Jodene had done the same thing to him. What had happened to Henry when we vanquished him? If he still remained, somewhere, somehow, if he'd been able to make contact with me, I believed he definitely would have done so already.

I took a snapshot in my brain of Carme curled up with her mom and went straight to the shop. Carme would come in to open in a couple of hours. Maybe by then I'd have a solution and a shop full of ghosts.

Unfortunately, it didn't work out that way. I meditated. I whispered invitations, and when that didn't work, I yelled. Nothing happened. I never thought the absence of ghosts could fill me with such despair.

Where were they all? I'd vanquished the ones in the office, yes, but what about others? Had I marked myself and no other ghosts wanted anything to do with me?

My stomach grumbled and my head hurt. I locked up the shop and went to the Artful Cup. The aroma welcomed me with open arms. So did Charles. He came out from behind the counter and wrapped me in a big hug.

"I thought we'd lost our best customer," he joked, with an undertone of concern.

"Never," I replied.

"How's Jodene?" he asked.

"The same," I lied, not wanting to dampen his spirits with the truth of her decline. He was in a better mood than I'd seen for a while.

He shook his head. "She'll get better. You'll see. She's made of tough stuff."

"That she is," I agreed.

"Let me get your coffee." He patted me on the shoulder and moved back around the counter.

Darren gave me a big smile as I approached. "Morning." His fingers hovered over the till. "Your regular?"

"Yes, please. Your dad's already on it."

Darren nodded and rang it up. "How's Carme?" He kept his eyes on the register, but his cheeks flushed. Maybe it was time for Carme to tell Darren how she felt, let the poor guy off the hook. "Is her mom okay?" he asked.

More guilt blanketed me and I forced myself to smile. "Good; they're both good." All this lying was giving me a serious stomachache. I handed over my card and tried not to meet his eye. He was a lot like Carme in that he could pick up when people weren't being completely honest.

"Your dad looks back to health."

Darren nodded. "Yeah. But now Ethan's sick."

"Sorry to hear that," I replied. "Careful you don't get it."

He nodded and I stepped aside to let the next customer place their order.

I settled myself at a small table near the chalkboard. The bouquet of flowers still remained. Some of it had been smudged, but it was still an impressive piece of artwork. It calmed me. Or maybe it was an effect of finally having my hands around a hot mug of coffee. My phone vibrated with a message from Liam.

*I am ridiculously ill.*

I typed quickly. *Oh no! What's wrong?*

*Everything. Everywhere,* he replied. *Ask Carme if my grandfather could make me sick*

*Why?*

*It started when I tried to leave to come see you*

That was not good. *I'll ask her,* I sent back.

*What next?*

I had to find the dybbuk, but it could be anywhere, inside anyone. Had someone summoned it to kill my clients? Who did I even know that could do that?

*Carme is furious at me, I have no idea if I can undo what I did or how to find the dybbuk*

*She will come around, ask her to help you contact some*

*ghosts*

He was probably right. He sent another text I didn't want to see. *What about Nik? Is he on board?*

*I haven't asked him yet*

*Do it,* came his fast reply. *Message me later too ill to type let me know how it goes with Carme AND Nik*

*I will. Please take care of yourself*

Darren picked up empty dishes off the table next to me. I pointed at the chalk bouquet. "Who did that?" I asked.

He gave a big, proud smile. "Ethan did." The smile quickly disappeared and his gaze fell to the ground as he walked off, hands full of cups and plates.

Ethan? Baking and art? He was definitely multitalented. But why had Darren been sad about it?

I had to admit I felt sad not to be able to talk to Myst. Maybe that's what I should start with when I saw Carme. Also, a coffee and her favourite breakfast bagel couldn't hurt.

The coffee I brought to the shop for Carme didn't get thrown in my face. She even smiled when she saw the bagel, because my cousin was amazing. She was smarter than most of us and knew it didn't serve to hold grudges. Carme was more of a take-action woman. She munched on her bagel and pointed at a new stack of books on the counter.

"I think I found a way to get them back." She gave me a proud grin and took another big bite.

I tilted my head to read one of the spines. *"Travel to the Spirit Realm?"*

"My whole life, I tried everything to talk to ghosts," she said. Her words slurred together a bit as she spoke with speedy excitement. "Know why it didn't work?"

"Why?"

"They just can't with me. If they can't, they can't." Her shoulders shrugged away her disappointment. I felt a pang of guilt for her cat Fidget, who had shown up when she was in danger and I'd banished him along with the others.

"Right now," she went on, "with you, I think they can't. So, they can't. But they could."

"Okay, I think that makes sense." I patted the book stack. "This will let them again?"

"It's our best chance." She wiped her hands repeatedly on the Artful Cup napkin, then picked up the book with her usual reverence. "It's like a seance in reverse," she said. "Except you don't need a bunch of people to do it."

"How is it like a reverse seance, exactly?"

"Someone sends your spirit over there."

"Oh, hell, no."

Carme scowled at me.

I held up a hand to defend myself. "Travel to a spirit realm? To be attacked by any of the ghosts there?" Would my stepfather be there? I took a lap around the counter to think.

"You should read these." Carme tipped the book toward me. "You'll see. It's nothing to be afraid of."

Except Henry might be there waiting to kill me. "Could we even do this?"

"We can."

With a sigh, I held out my hand. "Guess I'm doing some reading."

Her eyes narrowed. "Are your hands clean?"

After close inspection, she gave me a book and I settled into the red chair.

The authors of this book, a collaborated work, all held the same view. It was indeed a safe venture to undertake. Carme had called it a backwards seance, and that was an accurate description. Two or more people gathered, held hands and combined their energies to send one of them into the spirit realm. It required a bit of setup. I took notes and added questions for Carme as I read.

It was suggested to cleanse the room first. Another important element was to make sure everyone involved was on board and supportive. What you didn't want was someone who broke the circle and ran, or who was secretly against the entire process. Could Carme and I do it alone?

Candles, incense and flowers could be placed on the table, all things favoured by spirits. Also, the table could be covered in a light-coloured fabric to calm the living and dead. My stomach twisted into knots. What if I ran into unfriendly spirits in their realm? Wasn't there a pretty good chance of that? What if some nasty ones came through to our world when we attempted this? More questions for Carme.

The book had a chant to send the person's spirit into the other realm. Each step sounded simple enough but together they added up to a lot.

The authors warned of three things. One, there had to be enough energy generated by the people involved. Two, there had to be a strength of conviction to overpower the boundaries between the two worlds. Three, there had to be enough innate ability in the person doing the travelling. That was a lot to ask.

If it worked, if I suddenly found myself in the spirit realm, there wasn't any foolproof way of communicating with me. Having a communication link would be nice, but I was more concerned about getting back.

I wrote down *return* in my notes and circled it several times. After a moment, I also wrote down *HENRY*.

A cat being present could help, I read. My cats hated carriers. It would be a fight from beginning to end.

My heart wrenched again at the thought of Fidget. If Carme knew her beloved cat had appeared at her side only to have me destroy him, she'd be devastated and furious with me again.

The book also said meditation was helpful. Of course. At least there was no mention of cutting out caffeine.

An important element was who led the reverse seance. Not only did they have to know what they were doing, they had to be able to keep their cool no matter what happened. My gaze drifted to Carme near the front of the store. She helped a customer, a teenager near her own age. My cousin smiled at the young woman, who laughed at something Carme had said, and I knew I trusted her with all my heart.

We could do it. The two of us. I could find ghosts who would be able to help find the dybbuk. We could put an end to the murders and save Aunt Jodene. If I ran into my stepfather there, I would have to deal with it.

Once the young woman made her purchase and left the shop, I placed the book gently on the counter. "Let's do it," I said.

Carme smiled.

# Chapter 19

I'd assumed we would do the reverse seance in the shop. Carme had other ideas.

"Has to be the office," she informed me. "That's where it happened." The shop felt safer, but I'd learned to listen to Carme.

We locked up the shop and walked up the Drive.

On the stairs up to the office, I felt dizzy. My chest tightened, shortening my breaths. Carme glanced back over her shoulder at me.

"It's okay." She gave me one her most beautiful, supportive smiles. "We're going to make it better."

"Right." My heart swelled with admiration for my cousin. This had been my fault, but she was the one leading the charge to fix it.

Once inside, I felt the emptiness deep in my soul. Faces of the ghosts I'd banished haunted me, appropriately, with their absence.

Carme did her cleansing routine, completely in her element as she set up for our reverse seance. I stayed out of her way.

"We'll use my desk as the table." She dragged it further to the centre of the room, and I jumped in to help. "My chair, your chair." She pointed directions and I did as I was told.

She laid out a light yellow tablecloth then added several small, white candles and an incense burner. "We don't have any fresh flowers," she said with a shrug. "But not all spirits like flowers, so we should be fine."

My anxiety continued to gather momentum. Carme believed we could do this. Somewhere from deep inside myself, I had to believe it, too.

As Carme fussed over the setup, I shook out my arms then sat and tried to relax. All the doubts rushed into my brain. I couldn't do this, I'd have another anxiety attack, I would put Carme in danger again, I'd never be able to save Aunt Jodene and anyone else targeted because of me. I closed my eyes. My mind swirled. I tried to bring my focus back to the breath, gave up and opened my eyes.

Carme sat across from me now with her eyes closed. A peaceful smile lifted her expression.

She never stopped teaching me lessons. If she could do this, with her mother's life on the line, I could do it. I would do it. My mind still wandered, but I brought it back to the breath. After some time, after my body and mind had relaxed and let go, I opened my eyes again.

Carme now watched me closely. "Ready?"

I forced myself to nod. "I am."

She clapped a few times, then got up and turned the lights out. We held hands across the desk. My cousin gave me a nod of reassurance and we closed our eyes.

"Sorry about the sweaty hands," I whispered, and peeked at her.

She giggled but didn't open her eyes. She started the chant. I steeled myself for whatever was to come. What would it feel like? Would I feel ripped from my body? Or would it feel more like waking up somewhere else?

My heart raced. I fought to breathe as Carme's chant went on. There was no backing out now. I trusted Carme and she trusted me. I could do this. My breath deepened. I was ready.

Nothing happened. Carme continued to chant. I focused all my energy on leaving this world. Maybe I was trying too hard.

Eventually, Carme stopped chanting. She sighed and let go of my hands. "I can't do it."

"It's not your fault," I told her. "I'm sure the blame is on me. I'm the one who's supposed to go over there. I'm probably resisting or something. Let's try again."

She nodded, took a deep breath and we tried again. And again. And again.

Carme let go of me and stood with so much force, her desk chair rolled back and hit the wall behind her. She paced around the desk, examining it. "What is wrong?"

I pointed at myself. "It's probably me. Maybe I don't have the talent everyone thinks I do. Or maybe the fear of running into my stepfather is holding me back."

Carme slumped against the desk, grasping her necklace pendant. "I wish I could ask Mom."

"Me, too."

We stayed in our thoughts for a bit. We needed this to work. "Maybe we double up on things," I said. "Make up for my lack of power or whatever it is."

Carme's face scrunched in thought then she shook her head. "Not things, people."

"Who?" Her eyes lit up and I shook my head. "Please don't say Nik."

"Nik," she said, and giggled. "For real, though."

"What about Liam?"

She shook her head. "You know his grandfather won't let him."

Carme was right. "How do we even know Nik would be okay with all this?"

"I bet we'd find out if we asked." She gave me a sly grin.

I leaned forward. "Why don't I ask Ethan?"

She blushed. "That doesn't even make sense."

"You could ask him."

"He probably doesn't meditate," she said, then turned serious. "Plus, his girlfriend just died. I don't think it would be good."

"Right," I replied in a whisper. "I'd forgotten about that."

Andrea? She'd sworn off anything to do with the dead after her experience. I was definitely in no position to question anyone on that decision.

"Nik, really?"

Carme nodded. "Really."

"If I do this, if I call Nik, you have to let Darren know you don't have feelings for him. I think maybe you like the attention, but it would be better to be honest with him."

Her eyebrows shot up and I thought I was going to get an earful again. She crossed her arms with a huff. "Fine."

My palms were sweaty before but now they threatened to cause a flood as I listened to the phone ring on Nik's line. It was late. Maybe he didn't want to answer his phone or had it turned off. Another ring.

"Amy?"

I took a quick breath. "Hi, Nik. I need to ask another

favour." Carme gave me two thumbs-up.

"What is it?"

"Carme and I need your help."

"Is this related to the pendant you gave me? My brother's suite?"

If he thought I was off my rocker before, this would definitely seal it. "It is exactly related," I replied. "This time, we need to borrow your time and positive energy." He didn't laugh or hang up, which I took as a good sign.

"Why do you keep coming to me?" he asked. I wasn't prepared for that question.

"Because you're an expert at meditating, and for some reason, I trust you."

Silence. Carme widened her eyes at me.

"Well, then," Nik answered. "I can hardly say no to that, can I?"

I let out a relieved breath. "Fantastic. Thank you."

"How can my energy help you?" I thought I noted a flirtatious undertone but told myself to stay focused.

"It's kind of difficult to explain. I'd rather talk in person, if that's okay."

"Where are you now?" he asked.

"At the office, but it doesn't have to be right now. It's late."

Carme stabbed a finger repeatedly at the floor. "Now, now," she said.

"Sounds like Carme would prefer it be now," Nik said.

"If it's not too much trouble." I winced at Carme, who clasped her hands hopefully.

"No trouble at all." I gave Carme a thumbs-up and she did a little happy jump. "Good for me to get out of the apartment"—Nik went on—"get out of my own head for a bit. You'd be doing me a favour."

I found myself wondering about what was going on inside that head but didn't voice it. "We'll be here. Whenever."

"Should I bring you anything?"

My brain screamed, *Yes, bring coffee.* If my recent caffeine consumption had anything to do with our failure here, I really shouldn't have any. "No, thanks," I replied with regret.

"Right, then. I'll see you soon." It sounded like he was smiling.

"He's on his way," I told Carme after I ended the call.

Carme clapped her hands and bounced some more. "Yes. I knew he would. This is going to work."

"When he gets here, you're going to help me explain all this, right?"

"Of course." Beaming, she straightened the tablecloth. I brought the extra chair from my area over to Carme's desk so we'd have three seats. She repositioned the candles and incense several times and I let her. She cleansed the office again, and it wasn't until she went to move the candles once more that I stopped her.

"It's all perfect, Carme. It's going to work."

She sat down and let out a breath. "It has to."

We fell into a long silence until a knock at the door made both of us jump to our feet.

"He's here," she whispered.

"I know," I whispered back. "Stop making me more nervous than I already am." She laughed, which helped.

I opened the door for Nik, who wore black tapered sweat pants and his Columbia jacket. "Hi, come on in."

His gaze drifted over my shoulder to Carme and the desk set for our reverse seance. My heart thudded. Would he see our setup, turn around and walk away?

He smiled down at me. "Hi." He walked in and went to

Carme, hand held out. "Good to see you again," he said. I thought I smelled vanilla, but it disappeared quickly.

Carme shook his hand, head held high. "You, too." She waved her other hand toward the chairs. "Would you sit?"

"I would, thank you," Nik answered.

I plunked down beside him. Carme eagerly sat across from us and rolled her chair in. She slowly and carefully explained what we had planned and the entire backstory of why.

What if Nik wasn't truly over our disagreement? What if he was playing us and wanted to reveal all this wacky stuff I was doing to hurt my career? Or was he somehow behind the dybbuk? Could he have been angry at me from our online interaction, enough to want to kill my clients? Maybe being here was his way of making sure it didn't work. My mind spun out, and part of me knew it was nerves for what we were about to do.

"Amy?" Carme snapped me back to reality. "With us?" She rolled her eyes, but I could see she enjoyed this. "Are you ready?"

I studied Nik. "You're okay with doing this?"

"Your advocate here"—he gave a respectful nod to Carme—"has made an excellent case for why I should help. We need to save Jodene. She's always been incredibly nice to me, unlike some people I know." He gave me an exaggerated side-eye.

"Me. I get it," I said with intentional snark. "Let's do this."

Nik and Carme clasped hands like it was no big deal, like we tried to send me to a spirit realm every day. Nik held his other hand out for me. With a deep breath, I put my hand in his.

The touch of his skin against mine shot beams of heat

through me. I forced myself to focus and reached across to take Carme's hand. Doubt fluttered in my stomach. Now we had dragged Nik into this, could I even do it?

Nik squeezed my hand, then waited for me to look at him. "We've got this."

"Everyone close your eyes," Carme said, her voice steady, calm and in control.

With another squeeze of my hand, Nik closed his eyes. His hand in mine felt solid, strong and warm. This time would be different. It would work. I knew it, which made the urge to flee almost overtake me. I let it go. We had to do this. A heartbeat later, I closed my eyes, ready to travel to the spirit realm.

# Chapter 20

Energy surged through me. I floated upward, even though I still felt their hands in mine, which proved unnerving. Carme's chants faded. I was fairly certain I hadn't fallen asleep, yet I woke up somewhere else.

It was dark, but not like night, more like the dark grey of wet stones, the colour thickly laid in blankets all around me. I wasn't sure I could see ground when I looked down, so I stopped trying. The air felt heavy, which made me wonder if I was breathing here. Somehow, I knew I had to stop focusing on that or it would all be gone, like pulling a fine thread too fast.

I felt like I had my body with me. I tested my voice. "Hello? Is anyone here?"

No reply came, no echo. I almost panicked at the absence of sound. Was this the spirit realm? Or did we send me somewhere else? I thought they'd all be there, talking at me at once.

A blurry blob appeared ahead of me, moving slowly in my direction. The terrified teenager I'd been rose up again, like I'd walked into my own nightmare. What if it was Henry walking toward me now, come to finish me off? I wanted out.

"You can't go, honey." Her voice drifted to me as if through a thick window.

"Aunt Jodene?" No. She couldn't be there.

"It is me. Pretty amazing, right?" My aunt's spirit stood in front of me, light grey hair striking against the darkness around us.

I shook my head. "It can't be." I hoped Carme couldn't hear me and my real eyes weren't also crying.

"I'm not dead, honey. Not yet. But close enough, apparently, to meet you here." She spread her arms, her sleeves flowing as she spun. "It's absolutely incredible, isn't it?"

*Close to death* was not acceptable. I had to save her. "How did you know we were sending me here? And where is here?"

"I didn't know. I had some help from your friend, Mary."

"Mary?" I echoed. "Is she here? Is she out of you?"

Aunt Jodene shrugged. "She's not here and I don't have all the answers for you. I'm sorry."

I wanted to scream. My aunt was dying. I was so close to ending this, yet still so far. "Where are all the other spirits?"

"The ones you're looking for aren't here. Mary told me where to take you. Poor thing. You really need to help her."

Of course my aunt would be more concerned about a spirit inside her than her own health. "I'm working on it. I think. But if this is the spirit realm, shouldn't there be zillions of ghosts zipping around?"

"They'd only choose to appear if they wanted to. You branded yourself unsafe with the black-candle ritual."

"I know I screwed up. I panicked; I didn't know what else to do. But I'm going to fix it." The sympathetic expression on her face worried me. "Aren't I?"

She held out a hand ahead of her. "We need to go this way. It's not going to be as simple as you and Carme might have thought."

"Of course it's not."

I walked with my aunt, though I couldn't see where we were going. The dark grey landscape around us didn't change; we could've been staying on the same spot. "Carme's doing so great," I said. "She's amazing."

My aunt gave a proud nod. "She is." She faced me. "Get me back to her. Soon. Not sure how much longer I have. She still needs her mom."

I nodded and shoved aside the thought of Carme going on without her mom. It was too overwhelming, too painful. I would save Aunt Jodene. Whatever it took.

Aunt Jodene pointed ahead. "Here."

A wall began to take shape, as if coming into being as we approached. At the same time, it felt as though it had always been there. It extended out of sight on both sides and up, like frosted glass swirling slowly. I couldn't see much through it but a few formless shapes.

A pin-sized spot appeared, like a peephole. It grew until it was the size of a person. More specifically, it became my size. Now I could see spirits, hovering or moving slowly as if they paced a jail cell.

They were all there, the anxious woman, the mother with her child and Henry's ancestor, Adam. My nerves rattled at the sight of the robed man who'd tried to kill Carme.

The edges of the opening wobbled slightly. Aunt Jodene tilted her head. "I think I have been here as long as I can.

Great as it is to see you, honey, I have to go."

She opened her arms to hug me and I responded, not caring we didn't actually have bodies. Somehow, I felt her embrace and it made me stronger.

"Mary says you can only bring one ghost out of there," Aunt Jodene said.

"What? I thought I was releasing them all."

Aunt Jodene pointed at her ear, like she had an earpiece connected to Mary. "Just the way it is." With that, Aunt Jodene's spirit disappeared.

One ghost. Would that be enough to help Aunt Jodene, to find the dybbuk? How would I know which one? The spirits inside hadn't looked at me yet. They didn't notice me at all. Perhaps they couldn't see me or the opening. It was there for me to go through and to bring one spirit back out again. How were they going to feel about only one of them getting to leave?

They would have to deal with it, as would I. Carme had my back in the world of the living, and I had to do my part here. I walked through the opening and into the swirling mass of spirits.

The spirits turned as one and rushed toward me.

My hands flew up, but nothing touched me. I peeked through my fingers. The spirits hovered a few feet away.

It was as if I had my own personal protection shield. There were no smells, probably because I was in their world.

The robed man who'd attacked Carme flew straight at me but bounced away. He came back, got as close as he could and glared at me.

Adam also came forward, looking exactly like Henry now, angry and horrifying. The teenage girl in me wanted to turn and run. I held my ground.

The personal shield didn't block their voices. Many shouted. Some cried. Others begged in quieter tones that broke my heart. All of them wanted out.

I held my palms out. "Please, let me speak."

There were murmurs, more shouts. The robed man yelled insults at me, some I'd never even heard before. His words came at me like a firehose of venom.

Some of the spirits, including Adam, tried to pull him away, but he threw them off. Was there anything I could do to calm him?

He cried out in pain. Three bloody slices appeared on his shin. The gaping wounds began to close, but it clearly had hurt him. While we all watched his leg, he cried out again and covered one cheek, then the other.

"Stupid human, listen to me," said a low, gravelly voice. "You will let this one speak or I will end you."

"What in the—" The robed man's fury was cut off with another scream of pain. This time, gashes appeared across his neck. I didn't know how much abuse a ghost could take, but he appeared to be near the end of it.

He stumbled back as the cuts closed slower this time. Now, I had my silence. The spirits moved aside to allow the robed man's retreat.

A brown, scruffy, one-eyed cat materialized in the open space between me and the other spirits. Fidget walked right up to me, unaffected by the shield, and sat beside my right foot, facing the ghosts. He shook a paw before licking it.

"Stop staring," he said, though his mouth didn't move. "Start talking."

I forced my attention back to the other spirits, who all stared down at Fidget too.

Out of habit, I took a deep breath, even though I still wasn't sure whether I was breathing here. "I need help finding a dybbuk. A wayward spirit. It's killing people and I need to stop it."

The anxious business woman appeared at the front of the pack once again. "Take us out of here."

Many of the others echoed her. I tried to answer but it became too loud for me to be heard over them.

"It doesn't work like that, you idiots," Fidget yelled. The voices fell silent. He walked in front of me and brushed up against my legs. He'd never done that when he was alive.

I nodded. "Unfortunately, I can only take one of you."

The expected outcries and despairing wails cut me off. Adam glared at me but gave a firm nod.

"Just for now," I yelled. "After I deal with this dybbuk, I will free all of you." They glared like they didn't believe me, which was fair. I had sent them there in the first place.

Fidget hissed and they fell silent. "Shut up and let her take someone," he said. "And don't act like you can help if you can't."

The anxious woman lifted her head and gave a tiny nod. "We will let you decide." She smiled at me, and it made me ill. How was I supposed to choose?

It had to be someone powerful enough to locate the dybbuk and help me get rid of it. But I also had to trust the spirit to do their best to help and not disappear or, worse, turn against us.

Adam had some strength but, until Andrea buried his bones, not enough to help. The mom with the child had been genuine, seemed powerful, but I could never separate her from her little one.

"Amy?"

I knew that voice. My heart threatened to explode. "Mom?"

The other spirits moved aside.

My mom came toward me. She didn't have on what she was buried in. Instead, she wore her loose black pants with a black-and-white striped cotton top, one of her favourite comfortable outfits. It was what she'd worn to the hospital for the last time.

"Mom?" I repeated. My entire being shook with grief and relief at the sight of her. Tears flooded my eyes, here or in the living world, I didn't know. Both, maybe. She put her arms around me.

"I'm so proud of you," she whispered.

I wanted to lose myself in that hug even though part of my brain told me it wasn't real. "Mom, what are you doing here?" My mind raced in disjointed directions. How could she be there? Who vanquished her? I went from grief to joy to confusion.

Mom pulled back from the hug. "I am not sure, but I think it has to do with your stepfather. You best go soon." Her eyes held exactly what I felt, love, joy and a desire to hold on.

"Mom, I can't leave you here."

She gave a nod, the one of strength and encouragement she'd given me all my life. When I'd said I wanted to go to school for creative arts and media. When I'd said I wanted to start my own business coaching others. When she knew she was going to die. "Yes, you can," she said.

The other spirits moved, restless, as if frightened. A sound rumbled toward us. "What's that?" I asked my mother, but she drifted back away from me.

"Time to go," she said.

I felt it then. Whatever, whoever was coming, it was full of power and evil.

Some of the other weaker spirits zipped away, chosing hiding over being picked to leave.

Chanting filled my ears. Back in the human world, Carme recited the spell to bring me back. Either they had felt my fear or they couldn't keep me here any longer. Either way, I had to go and I had to take one spirit with me.

Somehow, I knew all I had to do was decide and the spirit I chose would come with me. I also knew who I had to take.

# Chapter 21

It felt like waking from a dream that lingers into reality. The atmosphere felt heavier, I could hear Nik breathing beside me before I opened my eyes.

Carme yawned and stretched. "What happened? It's been hours!"

"Hours?" I repeated. "It didn't feel that long to me.

Nik squeezed my hand. "You okay?"

Carme gasped, eyes wide and both hands flew to her face. Fidget sat on the desk, facing her, and she stared right at him.

"You can see him?" She ignored me.

Tears filled her eyes. She picked Fidget up and hugged him.

"How are you doing that?" I asked.

She sat back down and put him on her lap. Fidget didn't appear more solid to me than any other ghost, yet she petted him like he was a living cat. On closer examination, her hand dipped into his body every now and then.

Tears flowed down my cousin's cheeks. "You brought

Fidget back?"

I touched her lightly on the arm. "He was the strongest one there, except one other, but it felt—" I stopped as a shiver ran down my spine. "Evil." I waved a hand toward Fidget. "I don't know why he's so strong, but he is. Probably also knows the most."

He flicked his scruffy brown ears in my general direction. "Obviously," he said.

Carme let out a little gasp. "You can talk?"

"You can hear him?" I asked at the same time.

Fidget gave a snort-laugh.

"In my head, I hear him," Carme said.

I nodded. "Same."

Did this mean Carme could see all spirits now? Or just Fidget? Was he letting her see him?

"What about the others?" Carme asked.

"I could only bring one, found out that tidbit when I got there." I decided not to mention seeing her mom there. Carme didn't need to know how close her mom was to joining those spirits. We had to focus on saving her.

Carme hugged Fidget till he squirmed and pushed against her with one paw to get some space.

Nik, to his credit, remained quiet throughout.

"It worked," I told him. "Sort of. I was only able to bring one spirit back."

He nodded as I spoke. "Got that part. And you brought back a what?" He pointed at Carme, whom he would see petting nothing but air.

"Cat." I grinned.

His eyebrows went up just slightly. "And a cat is going to help you with what you need to do?"

"Who's this dolt?" Fidget flicked his tail. Carme shushed

him.

"This is Nik," I replied to Fidget. "He's helping us. I couldn't have gotten you here without him. And we still need his help." Fidget continued to glare his distaste at Nik. That cat didn't like anyone, so it was par for the course.

"What do you need?" Nik asked.

"It's complicated, but we need an angel to help us get rid of the dybbuk. You're the only person I know who has any connection to angels."

His expression turned worrisome. "You know I don't literally talk to angels, right? It's more of a symbolic sort of thing."

'It's going to have to do," I said. "We've made do with half-assery this far, and you're all we've got."

He laughed. "Wow, thanks. When you put it that way, how could I resist?"

"Sorry." I shrugged and grinned back. "We still need to find the dybbuk, but I don't know how long that will take. Maybe we should all get some rest first."

"No need for rest," Fidget said in my head. Carme and I both stared at him. He gave his paw a slow lick. "I felt it when I was here."

Carme raised her eyebrows at me and I knew I'd have to explain later, but I needed clarification. "You felt it when you were here at the office before?"

His paw hovered. He gave me a look like he was not about to repeat himself and then continued his grooming.

The only living humans here had been Carme and me. Had it somehow gotten inside of Carme? That idea dissipated as she gave me a once-over, obviously thinking the same of me.

"It's not in us," I said to Fidget. "So, who?"

"Below us," the cat said.

My heart squeezed. "The cafe? But there's no one down there."

Fidget gave me a slow blink. "Not right now." He head-butted Carme's arm because she'd stopped petting him. Her face held the same anguished expression my entire body felt.

"Who?" my cousin asked, as she scratched under his chin.

"Not sure." He squeezed his eyes closed in enjoyment.

Carme and I held each other's gaze. It might not be Darren or Charles or Ethan. It might have been a customer. "If we go down there when the cafe opens this morning, will you be able to tell us who?" I checked my phone. "We have a couple of hours till then."

Chin out, eyes shut tight, Fidget didn't answer. Carme stopped scratching him. His eyes popped open and he pulled his head back. "What?"

Carme leaned down to him and pointed at me. "She asked you a question."

Fidget let out an annoyed sigh. "I can feel it but not see it. I can get you close."

Carme went back to scratching his chin. "Then we figure out who it's in."

I filled Nik in on Fidget's side of the conversation.

"Figure it out how?" Nik asked.

"I had hoped Fidget could point it out to us. No offence," I added, though the cat truly didn't seem to care what I thought. "Carme?"

Carme picked up Fidget, plopped him on the desk and stood up. "Back to the shop. To the books." She went for her coat and paused as she put it on. "You coming?" For a second

I thought she meant me, but it was directed at Fidget.

The one-eyed cat bowed his head to her. "Where you go, I follow."

I hadn't seen Carme's smile get so huge for a long time. "Good." She shrugged on her coat and watched us expectantly.

Nik gave her a nod and went for his jacket. I felt something beside him but couldn't see it or hear it.

At the doorway, I touched Nik's arm to stop him. "You don't have to do this." I stared into those dark eyes and knew I didn't want any harm to come to him.

"I know I don't have to, but I'm going to." He flicked a thumb over his shoulder at the office. "All this ghost stuff. Is that why you didn't like meditating? It brings you closer to all this and you didn't want it to?"

Without meaning it to, a sigh rushed out of me. "Yes. I fought a long time not to talk to the dead. Meditating was like opening a gateway. Now I need it. And we need you."

"Don't worry. I'm in. I'll do what I can."

"Thanks," I said, and caught myself admiring the view as he walked away down the hall.

Once inside The Feathered Serpent, Carme and Fidget went into the back room while Nik and I waited. He examined the centre table display.

I stood close to him but not too close. "I want to apologize for being a jerk online."

He glanced up from the book he'd picked up. "Go on." His grin told me I was already forgiven, but I didn't mind paying my dues.

"I went back and looked. You were right. I took things

the wrong way because of all this stuff. My emotions, my anxiety, made it impossible for me to see clearly."

He gave a little laugh. "Said as well as a life coach could say it. Apology accepted." He flipped the book over to read the back.

"You don't seem rattled by any of this," I said.

"That's not true." He pointed the book at me. "But I trust you and Carme."

Cheeks hot, I pointed over my shoulder. "I'll just go see if Carme needs any help." I felt his eyes on me as I walked away, and was glad I wore good butt pants today.

I pushed the back room door open. "Need any help?"

Carme sat on the floor, surrounded by books. Fidget sat in her lap. Tears streamed down her face. I scrambled over the books to sit next to her as she wiped the tears away.

"I'm okay." She dug in her pocket for a tissue.

"No, you're not. I'm not, either. It's all a bit much, isn't it?" She nodded, then blew her nose.

I waved a hand at the books on the floor. "Do we need all these?"

She flicked her fingers. "Not those. These."

I helped her pick up the ones she wanted. We carried them out of the back and put them on the counter, in what now felt like a regular routine.

Carme filled Nik in. "Amy has to talk to the dybbuk," she explained. "Find out why it is here. Then get it into a flask."

"A flask?" Nik's face scrunched in surprise.

I laughed. "That's what you're questioning in all this?"

He shrugged and gave me a little grin. "Seems a bit odd. I would have thought a genie bottle or something."

"Fair enough," I replied.

"Do you have a flask?" Nik asked.

"Well, no." I hadn't thought that far ahead. "But we can get one—"

Carme cut me off with a raised finger. "I have a flask."

Nik laughed. "Make sure you empty it first."

She grinned and gave him a sharp nod. "I will."

I waggled a finger at Carme. "You're not nineteen yet, young lady. But I'll be the fun cousin. Let your mom worry about that." The jovial atmosphere extinguished and I swallowed hard. "I've been thinking about how a dybbuk can be controlled by someone living. I feel like that might be what's going on."

Nik ran a hand through his hair. "Someone has been ordering this dybbuk into your clients to kill them? And Jodene?"

"She's collateral damage," Carme said. She narrowed her eyes at him when he gave her a double take. "What?" she asked. "I watch movies."

"My client Mary hid herself inside Aunt Jodene," I said.

"Hid from what?" he asked.

"We're not sure."

"Is Liam in on all this?" Nik asked.

"Kind of a long story. He is now, but the spirit of his grandfather doesn't want him around me."

Nik held his hands up in surrender. "Okay, not asking any more about that."

I missed Liam so much, but his grandfather had the right idea. People had died because of me. Now I'd brought Nik into it, and I felt a pang of guilt, but we needed him.

Carme scribbled notes, pen sliding across her notepad intensely. I moved over to take a look. "Find something?"

She kept writing, then tapped the book she was taking notes from. "It would find someone weak."

I slid the book over to read the part she'd indicated. It said a dybbuk tended to enter someone susceptible, weak, or weakened by an emotion like grief.

Thoughts I didn't want to voice out loud rushed through my mind. Charles's wife had left him. Had it grieved him enough to make him susceptible to a dybbuk? What about Darren? Did having his mom so far away hurt him more than he let on? Ethan had recently lost his girlfriend. Everyone had their stories.

The other page held more details about getting rid of the dybbuk. "The dybbuk must be cooperative," I read out, "or the host may be hurt. Potentially fatally."

"I don't think it's in Ethan," Carme said, as if reassuring herself. "He was fine when he was here."

"Ethan was here?" I asked.

Carme nodded and her cheeks flushed. "After we took Mom to the hospital. He came in, asked some questions, got a few books."

"What kinds of questions?"

"About contacting the dead. He liked how much I knew." She smiled, but my heart twisted in my chest. "He asked about what happened to Mom." She rolled her eyes when I started to jump in. "I didn't tell him. He was worried about her." She smiled again, then went back to her notes.

My head spun. A hand touched my arm, and I looked up at Nik, who tilted his head at me. My anguish must've been all over my face, but I didn't want Carme to see.

"I think I need a little air," I said.

Nik grabbed our coats. "I'll come with you."

"Be right back," I called to Carme over my shoulder. She gave me a thumbs-up and a wink when Nik wasn't looking.

Out in the dark, the cold air felt good on my lungs and

skin. It helped wake me up but didn't help with the awful thoughts tumbling around my brain.

"What if there's more going on here?" I whispered to Nik. The smell of vanilla hit me hard and Heidi appeared, hanging behind Nik. She was the spirit who'd attached to Nik? Why? She didn't react as though she heard us. Maybe she was too new. What did she want with Nik?

Following my gaze, he checked back over his shoulder. "What? Do you see something?"

"Someone. Did you know Heidi Franklin?"

"Yes," he said. "She came to my meditation classes. Why?"

What the heck had Heidi been up to? She came to me for coaching, asked me about Nik, but already knew him and took his classes. Why come to me? Why was she with him now?

Nik raised his eyebrows and I waved him off. "Not important at the moment. What if someone from the cafe conjured the dybbuk and it got out of control?"

"Why would you think that?"

I pulled him farther away from the shop's front door. "Charles was really sick. What if he wasn't sick? What if the dybbuk's inside him and Ethan is to blame?"

"You've lost me," he said.

"Do you remember the floral chalk art in the cafe?" Nik nodded, so I went on. "Ethan did it. Darren got sad when he told me Ethan had drawn it. I think he drew it for his girlfriend, the one from Calgary who died. What if he tried to contact her? What if he succeeded?"

"Ethan? Charles' son?" His eyes narrowed slightly. "You think he contacted her and then got her to kill your clients?" Nik asked. "But why?"

Time for an uncomfortable truth. "I coached his mother, who then decided to leave his dad to move to the interior."

"Okay, unpleasant, but not bad enough to kill people over." Nik gave me an intense stare. "You know none of this is your fault, right?"

I poked him in the shoulder. "Are you coaching me now?"

He gave a small laugh and rubbed his shoulder as if I'd hurt him. "Do you know if Ethan has a history with this kind of thing? The dead, I mean? From Carme, it sounded like he didn't know much. Would he be able to do what you're talking about?"

I rubbed my hands together against the morning chill. He had a point. "I'm not sure. This all started when Ethan came back."

It hit me how much I felt Myst's absence. I'd not treated her well, and she had no reason to help me, but I missed her. Even if her insights came with copious amounts of snark and lesser amounts of usefulness.

I startled as Fidget appeared at my feet. "Geez. A little warning," I said, and Nik's eyebrows shot up. "Cat," I added, pointing down.

"Should I open a bag of chips?" Fidget asked. "That gets humans' attention, doesn't it?"

"Why are you out here?" I asked, ignoring the insults.

"Thought you might want to know it's back," the cat said.

"At the cafe? You can tell from here?"

"It's a strong being, so yes. I can."

He disappeared again and I worried I'd insulted him, then realized that was ridiculous. He was a cat who was always insulted by humans. Except for Carme. Through the shop window I could see her lift Fidget up and put him on the counter. I was pretty sure he could've materialized up there if he'd wanted to.

The cafe hadn't opened yet. The only people in there would be Charles, Ethan or Darren. Not only did I have to find and exorcise the dybbuk, I had to do it without hurting the person it was inhabiting. A person I cared about a lot.

# Chapter 22

Back in the Feathered Serpent, Carme handed me a bright purple, sparkly flask. When I tilted my head at her, she shrugged. "I like sparkles."

We had our flask and I had my conduit to an angel in Nik. It was time to find the dybbuk.

We'd agreed we didn't want the dybbuk to know we were on to it until we knew who it was in. If it guessed what we were doing, it would likely try harder to hide and deceive us.

Carme went pale as we stood outside the cafe.

"It'll be okay," I told her, not just for her benefit. I needed to believe it too. I stared at one of my favourite places on the planet. In the Artful Cup, I had always felt safe and at home. My business had flourished because of Charles and his generosity. These were our friends. Now I had to put one of their lives at risk.

Carme nodded at me and her strength encouraged me. She knocked on the door, a big smile on her face. Hopefully, the dybbuk wouldn't see how fake it was. Heidi hovered by Nik with a worried expression and continued to ignore me.

I peered down at Fidget but he shook his head. "Don't ask," he said. "I don't know which one. But it's in there."

"You'll be able to go in, even with the wards?" I asked the ghost cat. He didn't reply. The amount of disdain in his eyes did it for him.

From inside, Charles waved at us. He came to the door and unlocked it while my heart did acrobatics in my chest. He swung the door open with a warm smile. "How are you all doing?"

"Good morning," Carme said cheerfully. She held herself together so well, better than me, and I needed to take her example.

I cleared my throat and turned my nerves into focus. "I hope you don't mind us coming before opening."

Carme went inside, and Nik and I followed.

"Not at all. You're welcome anytime, of course." Charles closed and locked the door behind us. The click made my muscles tighten. For the first time ever, I didn't feel comfortable in the Artful Cup. This time, it felt like going to war. The smell of coffee combined with the mouthwatering scent of delicious baking. Darren gave us a wave as he wiped down the counter. We all waved back.

"Looking for something to go?" Charles asked as the three of us hovered in a clump.

Carme smiled at him. "We want to stay here. If it's okay."

Charles pointed at Nik. "Espresso, I believe?"

Nik nodded. "Yes, thank you. I was only here twice; that's amazing."

Charles chuckled. "Kind of my thing."

Was this a sign the dybbuk wasn't in him? Would he be able to think so clearly with a spirit in control?

The kitchen door swung open and Ethan's head popped

out. He gave a wave and a nod, like he was just checking what was going on, then disappeared into the back again.

It would have been easy to fall into old, comfortable patterns rather than seek out what might be different about them. Darren's smile was the same as always, most of it reserved for Carme. It plucked my heartstrings to see how much he adored her. Would that still show through so strongly if he was possessed by a dybbuk?

I'd only seen Ethan briefly, but he appeared perfectly normal. What did I expect? Glowing red eyes? A big sign around their neck, DYBBUK LIVES HERE? We had to hope our questions would be enough to bring it to light.

We moved to a table in the middle of the cafe. Carme and I exchanged nervous glances as we sat down.

Whoever the dybbuk was in, we were about to face off with it. Nik gave me a strong nod. We could do this.

Charles brought our coffees on a tray and set each in front of us. "You all look like you need these."

Fidget sat on the table directly in front of Carme, a ghostly sentinel, but didn't give me indication of where the dybbuk was. Even this close, it must have been powerful enough to hide who it was in.

Carme wiggled and sat taller, chair creaking. "Can we ask you a few questions?"

"Me?" Charles pointed a finger at himself.

"Ethan and Darren, too," I added.

"Is this for your blog thing?" Charles asked, appearing flattered.

"Yes," I answered, relieved he'd provided the perfect cover for us.

Charles flicked a hand at Ethan as he came out from the back again. "You guys keep working. I'll be here, getting famous." He pulled out a chair and sat down, smiling at Carme.

Ethan gave a small smile. "We could use the promotion," he said.

"What would you like to know?" Charles asked.

Carme swallowed hard. It was on me now to ask the right questions and bring out the dybbuk if it was inside Charles. Even this close to him, I didn't feel or smell anything, didn't see indication in his eyes.

"Are you feeling better now?" I asked him.

"Better than ever, thanks." He sounded relieved, typical of someone just over a horrible cold or flu and happy to be back to their old self. Was Charles himself, though?

"I'm glad. How are things at the cafe?"

He leaned forward and clasped his hands together on the table. "I think things are picking up." His words rang honest, thoughtful. "Ethan tells me we have to do more of this internet stuff. Keep business going."

"In this blog post," I said slowly, "we're going to tie in Aunt Jodene's shop with the cafe. Little double promotion."

Carme gave a nod. "Good for both."

"Fire away," he said without any hint of resistance.

"Have you ever wanted to talk to anyone who had passed away?" I asked.

He sat back hard in his chair. "Now, that's a big question for this early in the morning, isn't it?"

I watched him but tried not to stare as I studied his every move, every reaction. I felt Nik and Carme tense beside me. Carme smiled at Charles like we'd just asked him about today's specials.

"Who hasn't?" he replied. "I think we all want reassurance they're somewhere good. That they're somewhere waiting for us or here with us, able to look out for us."

He still looked and sounded like Charles, but something felt off. I wondered if Carme noticed anything. This was going to be harder than I'd thought.

Ethan worked his way over to us, wiping his hands with a cloth, expression curious. Or was the dybbuk inside him and it had realized what we were doing?

I focused on Charles. "I think if someone who died couldn't move on, they might need someone to talk to. Don't you?" I studied the man who'd been like a father to me, a real father, ever since I could remember. If that dybbuk was in there, I wanted it to answer me.

"Probably a question for Carme's mom." He laid a hand on her forearm. "When she gets better, which she will."

"But what do you think, personally?" I asked.

Ethan put a hand on his dad's shoulder. "We have opening duties."

Charles blinked as if he'd been far off in his head and Ethan had brought him back. "Right, yes." Charles got to his feet. "Are you done with me? I should get to it if we ever want to open." He smiled, but this time, it didn't reach his eyes.

My entire body felt cold. "Of course; we don't want to keep you."

It seemed the theory I'd told Nik had been right. Charles had the dybbuk inside of him and Ethan was in control. "Maybe Ethan could join us for a minute?" I asked.

Charles nodded absentmindedly. He got up and walked back behind the counter. Ethan continued to stand next to us.

I tried not to shake as I held my hand toward the chair. "We'd love to include you in what we're writing," I said.

He threw a glance over at his father and, let out a breath and sat down. "What do you want to know?"

What didn't I want to know? How had you done it? Was it the spirit of your girlfriend? Why was it in your father? Did you lose control? All things I couldn't ask or we wouldn't be able to get it out of Charles. Ethan wouldn't let us.

"We're interested in what you think," I said.

"For your blog," he replied slowly, as if he didn't believe our charade. He leaned forward. "I think you should drink your coffee and go back to that shop. I don't see how this in any way could be promotion for the Artful Cup. We sell coffee here, not silly human fantasies."

Carme's head swiveled toward me a little too fast. Ethan turned to her. "Do you think that's odd?"

Carme shook her head and stumbled over a few unclear words. My protective instincts kicked into overdrive, but Fidget was on it before me. He stalked over to stand directly in front of Ethan. Ethan sat back, but it could have been coincidence. If someone could die of cat glares, Ethan would already be in the spirit realm.

"Ethan," Darren called, half in, half out of the door to the back room. "Your cookies are burning."

As Darren's words reached us, so did the smell of burnt food, ushering images of smoke billowing out of a forgotten oven.

Ethan stood, slower than one would for burning cookies. He gave me one last glare and walked back to the kitchen. He threw a smile to his brother. "It's okay, Darren. I'm on it." He sounded more like himself. I worked hard to manage my breathing.

Darren came over and took Carme's empty cup, worry all over his face. "Ethan never forgets," he told us.

I grabbed Carme's wrist because she had started to shake. She'd probably had the same thought as me. The dybbuk wasn't being controlled by Ethan. It was in him.

# Chapter 23

It didn't matter how the dybbuk had ended up in Ethan. Maybe he had conjured it and then it had overpowered him.

Or maybe someone else sent it into him to get at me. What mattered was getting it out of him and never letting it harm him or anyone else.

It wasn't hiding well, which made me think it was confident and had a strong hold on Ethan. Maybe it didn't think we could do anything about it. Now I could even smell urine, the same smell from the attack at the shop when Mary had gone in to Aunt Jodene.

Darren carried Carme's mug away, my untouched coffee still in front of me. Carme clutched her necklace pendant. Nik gave us both worried glances but kept his mouth shut. Heidi hovered behind Nik, fixated on him. Why didn't the cafe's wards keep her out?

I leaned in to Nik and Carme, eyes firm on my cousin. "It's in Ethan." She shook her head at first, then squeezed her eyes tight and nodded. Fidget butted her hand until she petted him.

"I think there's another spirit here that's a part of this." It wasn't a solid theory, but I felt Heidi was here for more than just some crush on Nik.

Carme blinked back tears. She picked up Fidget, put him in her lap and hugged him close. It would've appeared strange to everyone else, but I understood. I'd hug my cats right then if I could.

I nodded at Nik. He shifted his chair to sit with his back to the counter. He rested his hands on his lap and closed his eyes. Carme let go of Fidget and pulled the flask out of her bag to rest it on her leg. She placed protection gemstones on the table in a small pattern in front of each of us. After the stones were set, she hid them under napkins.

My job couldn't begin until I got Ethan to come back out to talk to me. After a squeeze of Carme's shoulder, I walked to the counter.

Either my senses had gotten used to the burning smell from the kitchen or it had begun to disperse.

Charles wiped tables. Darren smiled at me and came over. I thought he was going to ask me if I wanted anything, but he didn't.

He leaned over the counter and kept his voice low. "You're gonna help him, right?"

I couldn't find my voice, so I nodded back at him. He smiled and disappeared through the door to the back. He talked to Ethan, but I couldn't hear the exact words. Several deep breaths later, Ethan reappeared.

"You know we have a business to run here, right?"

He said it with so much venom, it threw me a little. But this wasn't Ethan. It was the dybbuk who had killed my clients and scared Mary so badly, she now hid inside Aunt Jodene. It had to be stopped.

"Could I talk to you?" I asked calmly.

"Didn't we just talk?" The urine smell washed over me.

If I had needed more confirmation the dybbuk was inside Ethan, strands of orange now flashed across his brown irises.

"I meant, can I talk to whoever is inside Ethan?" I threw as much authority behind it as I could.

Ethan's eyes narrowed. Bursts of red merged with the orange streaks in his eyes, giving him a demonic look. It wasn't a demon. It was a spirit that needed to go back home.

A slow smile spread across Ethan's face and he looked nothing like himself. "Yes," he said, a strong edge in his voice. "This should be interesting."

Ethan turned to his dad and brother, who both watched us. "Let's delay opening, shall we? Just this once."

To my horror and disgust, they both bowed their heads, as if they were used to this treatment. For a moment, I worried they were somehow under control of this dybbuk or something else, but Charles met my eyes. His held sadness and fear but also strength. He gave me a slow nod. Darren smiled at me. The immensity of my task dropped onto my shoulders.

As I rejoined Nik and Carme, Ethan oozed confidence and superiority as he sat in the fourth chair at the table.

My thoughts jumbled but I told myself I could do this. I stared at Ethan.

"We agree, then. You're controlling Ethan," I said.

He laughed, then leaned assertively over the table toward me. "We do agree. What's next, exorcist?" Ethan's jaw clicked as the dybbuk talked through him.

Familiar anxiety cues crept to the surface. I had the advantage here, I reminded myself. These were my people. Good people, strong people. I had the upper hand and it was time for the dybbuk to leave.

"Why haven't you moved on to the spirit realm?" I doubted this dybbuk would be happy to tell me its woes and then go on its way, but I had to try.

"Well, now, how much time do you have?"

"There's more than one," Fidget said in my head. More than one? What did that mean?

"We're willing to listen," I said. "Tell us."

A grisly smile took over Ethan's face. "I don't think you really want to know."

Any hope this might go easily vanished. It was time to be more forceful. "What's your name? What's your unfinished business here?"

Red and orange glowed violently in Ethan's eyes. The dybbuk gave a horrible, spine-grating laugh as though it knew something we didn't. I feared we were about to find out what that was.

"What is your name?" I repeated, and watched for any signs it might be hurting Ethan. The dybbuk remained confident and full of attitude.

"You know my name," it said.

Panic rose from my stomach, into my chest and throat. "Ethan?" I tried. "Can you hear me?" The dybbuk grinned at me like the cat who'd swallowed the canary.

Pain gripped my chest. "Why don't you let me in on the secret, then?"

It wanted to tell me. I could feel it. We were getting closer.

Ethan crossed his arms. "You would like to know my name so you can get rid of me? I think you'll find it won't be that easy." There was a different tone in Ethan's voice now, somehow familiar.

"We want to help you move on. That's all."

"You can't force me to leave him, little Amy. Try as you might."

My mind and body froze. Only one person had ever called me *little Amy*. My vision blurred as panic took over me. I forced myself to take deep breaths. Moldy leather mixed with the urine scent.

"Carme," I said. "The flask."

Carme opened it and handed it to me. My hands shook. "You cannot stay here," I said. "You need to leave him. Now."

"I do applaud your efforts. You're going to need more than a few protection trinkets and an angel mediator to get rid of me, little Amy." Ethan's voice changed. It was no longer his. It was my stepfather's.

Heidi floated high, screeched, then flew into Nik. Nik's head fell back and he gasped for air. He fell forward, eyes closed, and his face smashed into the table. He was out cold.

Henry, inside of Ethan, stood. With one quick stroke, he swept all of Carme's stones and our coffees off the table. The mugs shattered on the floor; the stones scattered. He grabbed the flask from me and threw it, then laughed as it skittered across the ground.

I'd wanted to protect the cafe and everyone I loved, but I had failed. The weight of an anxiety attack fell on me, its claws deep in my chest. Flashbacks of Henry's torment paralyzed me.

Charles and Darren rushed over. My brain screamed at them to stay away, but I couldn't get any sound to come out.

Darren kept his distance, like he knew Ethan wasn't himself. Charles moved right up beside Ethan. "It wasn't supposed to be like this." His eyes brimmed with tears.

Henry used Ethan's hands to grab Charles' shoulders. He

lifted him off his feet and threw him across the cafe. Charles crashed into a table and knocked it on its side as he bounced to the ground, face down. He didn't move.

Darren ran over and knelt by his father's side. "Dad?" Darren shook him, but there was no response. Darren repeated his cry, louder and more anguished each time. Charles didn't open his eyes.

Henry pointed at Charles. "He didn't know what he was doing. That made it easy for me. He couldn't refuse my offer."

My brain tried to process his words. Henry moved toward Darren and Charles.

"Stop," I yelled at him. He slowly turned back to me.

"Don't hurt them." I hated the fear in my voice. Fear is what he wanted.

Henry pointed at Charles and Darren. "Not them? What about this one, then?" He turned the finger at himself. "What about that one?" He pointed at Nik. "You seem to care for that one a great deal, so I sent someone for him."

Heidi. She must have had feelings for Nik. Henry used that, killed her and then sent her to Nik. She resisted him near the end but it hadn't helped. She'd still gone into him so he couldn't call any angels.

This had to stop, but I could hurt Ethan and Nik if I tried. If I didn't do anything, Henry would keep killing people I loved until he took everything from me.

I dove for the flask, slamming my body to the ground. One hand touched it before my stepfather kicked me in the side. Pain exploded in my ribs.

"I do have unfinished business here, little Amy," Henry said. "It's you." He stood over me. "Once I gain more strength and you have weakened enough, killing you will be the final thing to set me free. I will so enjoy it."

A blur of brown flew toward Henry. Bloody scratches tore across Ethan's face. The orange and red left his eyes as Ethan's body went limp. He collapsed, fast and hard.

Carme cried out next to me, and she crumpled to the ground. I managed to reach out and catch her under the arms to slow her descent to the floor, but not by much. We landed together in a heap. Her eyes closed.

I shook her. "Carme? Can you hear me?"

Fidget put a paw on her shoulder, then backed away with a hiss. Carme's eyes opened, her irises a blend of orange and red.

"I hear you, little Amy," my stepfather's voice said from Carme's mouth.

Carme shoved me away, hard. I caught myself on my hands just before my face hit the floor. Henry walked Carme's body out of the cafe. Fidget disappeared.

The pain in my torso made it hard to get up, but I went to the door to follow Carme. When I opened it, several people who waited for the cafe to open peered inside with concern. Darren called my name. I spun. He stood between his fallen father and brother, holding clumps of his hair in both hands, like he would pull it all out. Tears flowed down his cheeks.

"Everything's fine," I said to the people trying to get in, and shoved them back out the door. I pulled the blinds down, then rushed along the front windows, drawing down all the blinds.

"It's okay, Darren," I said. "It's going to be okay."

He sat down on the floor beside Ethan and held his brother's limp hand. "Going to be okay," he echoed. He leaned over and rested his forehead on Ethan's.

# Chapter 24

Ethan and Charles were both still breathing. I got Darren a glass of water and made him have a few sips. I also gave him a cold cloth and asked him to gently put it on his brother's forehead. I didn't want us to touch Charles any further, not knowing what his injuries might have been. As I went to call 911, Nik stirred, but he didn't open his eyes.

"Heidi, get out of him," I yelled. "You can do it. My stepfather is gone. Fight whatever he did to you. Let Nik go."

It took a few breathless moments, but the ghost of Heidi lurched out of Nik's body. She met my eyes, hers full of fear. A second later, she vanished.

Nik pushed himself up off the table. He scanned the cafe with confusion and then worry.

"Are you okay?" I asked.

He shook his head no, then grabbed his head. "That was unpleasant. What happened?"

"Henry, my stepfather, used Heidi's spirit to try to control you. She's gone. He's gone too." I choked on my words. "He took Carme."

Nik started to reply but was upstaged by Ethan, who

rolled to his side and threw up.

I grabbed a handful of napkins and handed them down to him. Without moving his head, he reached up, took the napkins and wiped his mouth. Darren gave Ethan his glass of water.

"I have to call an ambulance for your dad," I said.

Ethan's eyes widened, and I watched him struggle to piece together what had happened.

"It's not your fault," I said.

Ethan ignored me and crawled to his father. Darren trailed behind him. Ethan's face remained haunted, vacant. He sat beside Charles and put a hand on his dad's chest, which rose slowly, up and down. Darren knelt and imitated his older brother exactly.

I called 911. Nik rested back on the table, this time his head cushioned on his arm. Ethan stared at his father, no readable expression on his face. What damage had Henry done by being inside of him? And who was the urine-smelling spirit? Another ghostly pawn of Henry's?

"Are you okay?" Darren asked his older brother. Ethan snapped out of it. One instant, he wasn't himself, then he was.

"Come here," he said to Darren. Still on the floor, the two embraced.

As I answered questions on the phone, I got Nik a water. He raised his head slowly when I set it down.

"Thanks," he said. "I'm fine. Or I will be. Just need my head to clear a bit. That was not fun."

"I'm sorry," I said. "I didn't know."

There was so much I hadn't known. The dybbuk was my stepfather and he had other spirits under his control. He'd killed Mary and sent the urine spirit to somehow use her, but she'd escaped into Aunt Jodene. He'd killed Heidi and used her instead.

I watched Ethan seated next to his dad, his arm around Darren. Was he really back to his old self? Maybe he never would be.

Numb from head to toe, I picked up the turned-over table, the chairs, and pieces of shattered mugs. I was aware of Nik's presence, giving me space while he cleaned up with me. Though I couldn't voice it, I was glad for his company. Carme's gemstones had scattered everywhere, and I began to pick them up.

I'm not sure at what point I started crying, but after Nik joined me, the floor and the gems became a blur. I sat back on my heels, salty tears on my lips, shaking with adrenaline crash, anger and worry for my cousin.

Even if I could find Carme and get Henry out of her, would she be changed forever? I needed Fidget, but he'd left with her. He wouldn't leave her side.

"We'll find her," Nik said.

I wiped my tears away with my sleeve. "We have to. We have to figure out how."

"To the shop?" Nik asked as we got to our feet with fistfuls of Carme's gems.

"Don't you have classes to run, a life?"

"Not right now. This is more important."

In that moment, I found myself wanting him to hold me in his arms and to keep saying exactly the kinds of things he was so good at saying. But that would've been selfish. I didn't have time for selfishness. I had to find Carme and figure out how to get Henry out of her before it was too late.

The first aid responders came and went straight to work on Charles. I pulled Ethan aside. Now there was help, I had to go. "I have to find Carme. What do you know?"

"My dad." His voice was so low, I could barely hear it. "I don't know details. Dad must have done something. Then I couldn't think much of anything for a while."

I believed him. I couldn't imagine what it had been like to have Henry inside of him. Was that how he was gaining power? Stealing it from the people he took over? "Do you know when it started?" I asked. "How long were you like that?" When was the last time I'd seen him? Had it been days? It felt like forever.

Ethan rubbed his forehead as if it hurt to think. "A couple of days, maybe?"

It must have been horrible, fighting to be himself while being taken over by something else. Having it control your actions, your words, your thoughts. Now it was happening to Carme.

"Do you know anything that could help me find Carme? Fight him?"

He shook his head, eyes exhausted and tormented. "I'm sorry."

I touched his arm gently. "If you think of anything, please call me." He nodded and went to be with Darren, to talk to the people getting his dad onto their gurney. I'm not sure what he told them, but there was no mention of police getting involved.

We left the cafe when Charles did. Ethan and Darren followed their dad to the hospital.

My ribs hurt but I could breathe without too much pain, so I was pretty sure there'd been no break. "Let's check Aunt Jodene's house, then my apartment, in case they went either of those places," I said to Nik. "If not, we go to the shop and find out how to get her." He nodded.

Both homes were empty, so we went to the shop and dug through Carme's notes. My heart pounded with panic for Carme, like an alarm constantly going off. I had to find her, had to get to her, now, now, now.

I focused on finding a way to call Fidget back, to get him to take us to Carme. He was a strong spirit and wouldn't leave her side willingly, even for a second. It would be on me to make him.

Nik found some older books in the back on summoning angels. "Maybe it was my fault," he said. "Maybe I could've done something differently."

"Please don't do that," I replied. "It definitely wasn't your fault."

He studied me for a moment, then smiled. "Understood." His smile faded. "I hope stuff like that isn't going to happen regularly. I mean, I said it was unpleasant, but that was an understatement." He paled a little and yet I admired his strength.

"I'd like to promise you it won't happen, but this is the world I'm dealing with. It's unpredictable. Dangerous, too. I'd understand if you want to just go home."

"It's not boring around you; that's for sure. I'm going to see what else I can find out about angels helping with exorcism." He smiled, but I could tell he was tired and still uneasy.

"Thank you."

Ethan called about two hours later. Charles had several bruises, a sprained ankle and a cracked rib. He was awake and wanted to talk to me. I wanted to talk to him, too.

Nik drove. On our way to the hospital, I reminded myself Charles was in no condition for an inquisition. Ethan met us in the main hallway of the wing where they'd put Charles.

Nik hung back but I felt his support.

"How's he doing?" I asked Ethan.

"He's tough. He's doing better physically than mentally, I think."

"Has he told you anything?"

Ethan shook his head. "He said he wanted to wait till you got here." His gaze dropped to the floor. "I should have done something; I should have seen what Dad was doing. Stopped him. I should've stopped it from leaving me and going after Carme. I should've been stronger."

"Don't do that," I said, echoing what I'd told Nik. "There's nothing you could've done. Blame me, if you want. It was my stepfather. It's because of me he's doing this."

Ethan put his arms around me in a hug. "I'll help any way I can." His body felt warm and comforting. I nodded in thanks as we separated.

"Focus on Darren, your dad, the cafe. If I need you, I'll let you know. A lot depends on this conversation with your dad."

Over my shoulder, I checked in with Nik. He gave me a nod and pointed to the floor. He'd stay there, wait for me, be there for me. Because that's who he was.

We walked into the semi-private hospital room, and I was grateful the other bed was empty. Charles rested in an inclined position, eyes closed. He had bandages across his chest, visible under his thin hospital gown. Tubes ran from the top of one hand and the opposite forearm.

Ethan touched the layers of blankets over his father's leg. Charles opened his eyes and saw me. For a moment, I thought he was going to try to get out of the bed. He pushed himself up and waved me forward.

"Come, Amy. Please. I need to tell you everything."

I approached carefully because I didn't want to bump any tubes, but I was also afraid of what he had to say. Regardless, I had to hear it.

"It's all my fault," Charles said. "When Beth left, I didn't know what to do. I know she's happier now, truly happy. It was the right thing for her, but part of me didn't want to believe it. Then he came to me."

"Henry," I whispered.

"We didn't have much of a relationship when he was alive, I barely met him, but it was his idea, to get me Beth back."

Charles told me he'd been all right when his wife had moved away. He'd said if she was happy that made him happy. I'd believed him, but my stepfather had still preyed on his grief.

How had Henry gotten out of the banishment Aunt Jodene had performed? However he did it, when he grew strong enough, he used Charles to get close to me. Of course, it hadn't gone the way Charles had thought it would. My stepfather didn't want to help anyone. Now I knew he wanted power, wanted it all along. He might have married my mother to get at my power but hadn't been able to when he was alive. It was possible he'd killed himself to get my power, but he'd been unable to and then we'd banished him.

Charles swallowed hard. "I wanted to convince my wife she was wrong to listen to you. If your clients weren't doing well with your help, then I could convince her. He wasn't supposed to kill those poor women." He paused and pointed. "My water, please."

Ethan grabbed the small plastic cup from a tray on the windowsill and gave it to his father.

Charles took a few sips through the straw. "He also

promised to help with the cafe. Keep it open. Ethan's been so worried. I wanted to leave it for my sons." He stared into the cup. "The only thing I have to leave them is that damn cafe."

Ethan didn't react to his father's gut-wrenching confession, and I worried for him. I hoped he and Charles could work through this. Right now, I had to get to Carme.

Charles drank in tiny, loud sips while my heart pounded in my ears, a tune mostly set to anger. I wasn't angry at Charles but at Henry. He'd used Charles, then he'd killed Mary and Heidi and had been about to kill Margaret. All to grow stronger, to weaken me at the same time so he could murder me, his unfinished business. It would set him free. Free to do what?

"Why did he go into Ethan?"

"To keep me silent." Charles's voice shook. "When those women died, I wanted it to stop. I wanted your stepfather gone. I wanted to tell you about it, so he took my son." He looked at Ethan, but Ethan didn't look back.

"It's you he wants, Amy. He thinks if he kills you, he'll have enough power to control the living and the dead." Charles' voice had another layer of sadness in his voice, either for me or for the rift now between him and his son. Maybe both.

"What else you can tell us?" I asked him.

"I don't know. He did say something about being trapped. Not sure what it meant."

I had some answers, more questions, and I wasn't any closer to defeating Henry. "What do I do?" It wasn't a question for Charles or Ethan. It was a cry to anyone, anything to help.

Charles thought it was directed at him. He teared up.

"I'm so sorry, Amy. I truly never meant for anyone to get hurt. Most of all Carme, my future daughter-in-law." He gave a weak smile.

Carme would've hated to hear him call her that. I would've given anything to have her there to tell him exactly what she thought of it.

"Is there something you can think of? Anything he did or said around you?"

Charles sank back into the bed, exhaustion set deep on his wrinkled face. "He said something once about guardian angels. I'm pretty sure that's what has kept him from getting to you, Amy. Keep those guardian angels close."

As far as I knew, I didn't have guardian angels since we'd vanquished Henry. It would be hard to keep them close if I didn't have any.

"Thank you for telling me," I said. "Get better."

"It's not any less than I deserve," he said.

I was tired and didn't have a response, so I gave his hand a squeeze and walked out of the room. Ethan followed me.

"Darren's with Mom," he said, tone flat. "I'll stay here with Dad."

"If he says anything else, thinks of anything else, please call me."

"I will."

"And don't be too hard on him. The problem here is Henry, not your father. He loves you."

Ethan remained stoic, and my heart bled a little for father and son.

To the contrary, I had to completely and utterly destroy my stepfather as soon as possible.

# Chapter 25

Nik insisted we hit a drive-through. We hadn't eaten all day and it was midafternoon already.

"I'm going to try to summon Fidget."

Nik gave me a sideways glance as he drove on to the shop. "He's a cat, right?"

I nodded. "Not just a cat. A cat who cares nothing for humans."

"Except for Carme," Nik said.

"Thank goodness." Fidget was with Carme; I had no doubt of that. He could keep an eye on her, but could he do anything else for her? Keep her safe? Keep her whole?

"You expect him to be difficult?" Nik asked as he squeezed us into a parallel parking spot on the Drive. "I don't know Fidget, but I know he's a cat. That's enough."

"I need to summon him and be able to hold him here long enough to talk to him. Neither will be easy. Maybe, since he is already in this realm, I might have less trouble contacting him. But like you said, it is Fidget."

We got out and he came around to the sidewalk to join me.

"I'd suggest you get some sleep, but I know you're not going to." He locked his car and put his hand on my lower back as we walked to the shop door. His hand felt warm and reassuring and I felt a pang of guilt for enjoying it while Carme was all alone. That wasn't quite true. She had Fidget, even if she might not know it at the moment.

Not surprisingly, she had tried to contact Fidget when he first died. It hadn't worked. It had taken the robed spirit's attack on her for them to be able to connect.

My aunt and cousin would want the shop to be open, but I couldn't deal with it today. I locked the door behind us and left the CLOSED sign where it was.

Carme had notes on every method of summoning spirits. She had tried everything. I felt lost without her help and decided to keep it simple. With Carme's notes from her attempts to summon Fidget, I grabbed a white candle in a secure, round base and settled down on the floor in the reading area. Nik came and sat across from me, knees touching mine. I lit the candle.

Nik reached across for my hands. "May I?" he asked.

"Please. I could use all the help I can get."

He held my hands securely, then let both our hands rest lightly on my knees. The warmth and strength of it gave me courage. I closed my eyes and focused on my breath.

Without me having to ask, Nik guided me through a meditation. His voice was calm and full of strength. After a while, I didn't feel tired anymore. I felt stronger and more determined than ever to save Carme.

I recited the summoning Carme had created for Fidget. As I repeated it, I kept a clear picture of Fidget in my mind. I poured all of my love and fear for Carme into the words.

I felt him, as though a string was drawn taut between us

and if I just pulled on it, he would come. I focused on the connection and pulled as hard as I could. As I'd expected, Fidget fought back. Stubborn as he ever was; I found myself in a tug-of-war with a cat. Maybe before, he would've won. But not now. I would win because I had to. I mentally yanked on the connection with everything I had.

Fidget appeared on the floor a few feet from us, pacing.

"He's here," I told Nik. He let go of my hands but I grabbed them back again. "I need to keep him here," I said. Nik nodded and held on tighter.

"What are you doing?" Fidget growled in my brain.

"Where's Carme?"

"She's in her house now. I can't bring her to you." He kept pacing and didn't look at me.

"Does he know you're there?"

"I don't think so."

"You don't have to bring her to me. Bring me to her."

He glared at me. "Then what? What do you plan to do?"

"I won't hurt her. You know that."

"I know you won't mean to. Doesn't mean you won't."

"I will find a way."

"We can't fight this alone," Fidget snapped.

"What do you suggest?" I echoed his tone, my patience thin.

"Get help. Strong help."

"Where—" I cut myself off because I knew. The vanquished ones. I had to collect an army to fight Henry.

Fidget raised his head in acknowledgment of what I had come to realize. "Good. Get help, then come get her. I need to go protect her however I can."

"My stepfather has been controlling Heidi. Does he have other spirits?"

"That Heidi one is tied to him. Made some deal with him when she was alive, about that one." He flicked his head toward Nik. "Ridiculous. Killed her to use her instead. He has another one with him."

The urine-smelling spirit. "Who is it and what's he doing with my stepfather?"

Fidget hissed at me, patience done. "I don't know. Now let me go."

"Take good care of her," I pleaded, and let go of my hold on him. He disappeared.

Nik didn't let go of my hands until I let go first. "He's gone," I told him. "Thank you."

"I feel like it didn't go well?"

"I have to go back to the spirit realm."

"Can you do it without Carme?"

"I don't have a choice. There are powerful spirits among the vanquished. There was one; it was the most powerful thing I've ever felt. All the spirits were afraid of it. I need it now."

"What if this powerful entity doesn't want to come? Or, worse, gets here and then decides it wants to do its own thing?"

He had a point. "I'll deal with it. Right now, nothing matters except getting my stepfather out of Carme and destroying him forever."

"I'm new to all this," Nik said slowly. "But what I have seen scares the shit out of me. Especially that you could get hurt."

It was an incredibly sweet thing to say, but it was a risk I had to take. "Thank you. I'll be fine. We need to figure out how we can send me to the spirit realm without Carme."

We both stood and ended up mere inches apart. He

gazed down at me and I wondered if he felt the same heat between us as I did. The tingling in my stomach told me I wanted to find out, but it would have to wait.

"We need a few things." I walked away, breaking the fiery connection.

Nik let out a sigh. "If we get through this, can we have a normal date sometime?"

If I was honest, at the moment I was more concerned with whether we could send me to the spirit realm with just the two of us. I trusted Nik, not as much as Carme, but I believed he would do his best not to let anything happen to me. I thought of Liam. Having a third person might help, but there was no way his grandfather would let him.

We got everything we needed and headed to my office. The sight of the red neon CLOSED sign in the cafe window tore at my gut. Would Ethan open it tomorrow? If I lived through this, I would do everything I could to help with the cafe's success.

I unlocked the office and flicked the lights on. Carme's desk remained set up from our last reverse seance. Panic rose for Carme's safety, but I pushed it aside. It wouldn't do me any good. If I could vanquish spirits, I could vanquish my anxiety. Carme needed me.

We followed Carme's procedures, sat down and held hands over the desk. Our plan was to try for multiple trips to bring back as much help as I could.

"You're shaking," Nik said.

"Little nervous."

"I know you can do this."

"I have to. Straight to that wall this time. I'll make it quick."

Nik gave me a nod. I closed my eyes and took deep

breaths as he recited the words of Carme's chant. His voice was calm and strong. I let the words wash over me and willed them to carry me away.

A stream of energy flew from Nik's hands into my arms, and he took in a sharp breath. He didn't waver in his chant, which made it possible for me to leave. I knew he had control of me and wouldn't let go.

When I opened my eyes, I stood before the frosted-glass wall between the vanquished and the rest of the spirit realm.

There was no sign of Aunt Jodene and also no opening in the wall this time. I reached out and touched it but nothing happened.

I summoned every bit of confidence and strength I had. "Let me in," I said into the thick air around me. "Now."

A small hole appeared and slowly expanded until I could walk through. Spirits rushed over. The anxious business woman was there, the mother and child, plus others I recognized. There was no sign of the robed man who'd attacked Carme. Maybe Fidget had done a great deal of damage to him.

My mom wove around and through other spirits toward me. Adam, Henry's ancestor, stepped aside and let her pass. She did not look happy.

"What are you doing back here?" Her voice was stern, just like a mom.

"It's Henry. He's back and he's taken over Carme. I need help."

She came as close as she could. "You can't fight him. Not if he's even stronger than he was. I couldn't beat him in life or death. I was sure he killed himself to become more powerful. I thought warding his ashes would help keep us both safe. I was wrong."

It hit me then. "Did he send you here somehow? Is that how he got out?"

"He must have switched places with me. I'm sorry. I guess I wasn't strong enough."

I grabbed her hands I couldn't feel. "Don't be ridiculous, Mom. You are strong enough. I'm here for help. As much as I can get."

"But how are you here? If Carme—" She didn't finish her question, but I knew what she meant.

My cheeks warmed a little, knowing what her reaction would be. "A friend is helping me."

Her eyes widened and she smiled. "A friend, huh? I know that look."

"Mom, stop. I can't stay long. I'm going to try to come back more than once. Come with me," I said.

She shook her head. "No. You need someone stronger."

"I need you. This is Henry. I know it turned out none of us actually knew him, but you were the closest. He might listen to you." Even in spiritual form, I could see the debate behind her eyes. "I don't have a lot of time, Mom. Nik is holding me here and I need to go back." This time, she nodded.

I pictured myself and my mom back in the living realm with Nik. When I opened my eyes, Nik was still sitting across from me, reciting my summoning spell. He stopped, rose to lean over and kissed me right on the lips.

"Hi." He sat back down. "I'm glad you're back."

There was no point trying to pretend I hadn't really enjoyed that kiss and the look in his eyes right now. "Hi."

My mom was there too. She hovered at Nik's shoulder, grinning at the kiss. "Just a friend, huh? I'll try to help him if I can."

"I'm going back," I said to Nik. "Are you okay?"

He looked tired, a little pale, but still had strength in his eyes as he nodded to me. He took a deep breath and began Carme's chant once again.

Dozens of spirits gathered as close as they could to me. Many called out to me to take them. Adam glared but remained silent. None of them were the one I wanted.

"Where are you?" I yelled. Most of the spirits quieted down. "Show yourself."

A breath later, I felt it. The spirit my mother had wanted me to run from.

"I want to talk to you," I said.

A ripple went through the spirits around me. None of them seemed happy with me. Many of them floated out of sight. I took note of the ones who stayed.

A being of dark, wispy smoke came forward. It felt like everything nightmares were made of. My hands shook and my chest tightened, but I told myself if things got bad, I would find my way back to my body.

My personal shield didn't hold it back. It swirled and wrapped me in the eye of a black, smoky tornado. I held my ground, focused on my breath and thought about Carme. There was nothing this spirit could do to scare me more than the thought of losing her.

"I need your help," I said. Its twirling movement made my hair and clothing flutter. Nik would only let me stay for our agreed time and I couldn't waste any of it.

"I won't control you; I don't want that," I told the spirit and meant it. "I will make you a deal."

"What can you offer me?" it growled.

I was sure I would hear that voice in my nightmares for years to come. "Your freedom. In exchange, you will help me stop a spirit from killing anyone else."

"How do I know you won't try to enslave me?" it asked.

I had its interest. "Because that's exactly the kind of thing I'm fighting against. I swear on my life, I will not try to bind you. But you won't hurt anyone or I will send you back here."

The smoky spirit rose up above my head and flew down a few feet in front of me, a thick pillar. It became human-shaped. A breath later, a woman stood there, an exact replica of me. It turned to black wisps again, swirled and turned into Nik.

"I get it. You're powerful. That's why I need you. We don't have time for this. Let's go."

The Nik shape dissolved. It turned back to its wispy form and wrapped itself around me. "Take me," it growled.

"You are agreeing to our terms? Your freedom in exchange for your help and you don't hurt anyone."

It growled again, but this time less like an angry beast and more like an annoyed businessman. "Agreed."

There were no hints of whether it was male, female, old, or young, but I felt it'd been dead a long time.

Nik's voice came to me and I closed my eyes. I opened them again to Nik's pained expression. The spirit I'd brought back flew up to the ceiling, hovering and rippling like the office was on fire. Nik let go of my hands and got to his feet.

"Are you okay?" I asked him.

He stumbled over to the window behind Carme's desk and waved me off. "Fine." He opened the window and put his face right out it. I was surprised to see the dark night sky. Travelling to the spirit realm was like crossing multiple time zones.

Mom came next to me and spoke in my head without

moving her mouth. "You brought that one? All the spirits were afraid of it, including me. I don't know why. We need to find out."

"We won't need it around long enough to worry," I told her, and glanced up. "Stop that. You're making my mother nervous."

The black cloud of smoke spun in a circle on the ceiling, flowed to the top of the filing cabinet and curled around itself like a snake.

"Thank you," I told it. "I'm going back in. Any input on who I should bring back?"

It emitted a small growl, not in anger but as if in thought. "The robed one is too damaged," it said.

Nik came back and sat down with an exhausted sigh.

"Maybe we should stop," I said, nervous about the glazed look to his eyes. "Maybe two will be enough."

He shook his head. "Three is stronger. We can do this. I'm fine." I wasn't sure he was.

"You need your guardian angel," the coiled spirit said.

"I don't have any."

"Yes, you do," it growled. "They can't be completely vanquished, so she'll be in the realm, wandering. She can help protect you from the one you want to fight. You need to go get her."

At first, my mind bounced aimlessly, but then I knew who it was talking about.

"Myst," I said.

# Chapter 26

Myst was my guardian angel.

That's why I couldn't find her in the vanquished domain. Maybe she didn't know who or what she was when she came to me because she'd been wandering the spirit realm since Aunt Jodene and I vanquished Henry.

How did she come back to me when I was trying to connect with Mary? If it was to come to my rescue, she would've remembered that, wouldn't she?

Now she was back there again and I needed to get her out. Not only because she could help us overpower Henry, but because it must have been a horrible existence. One that was my fault.

"How do I find her?" I asked the spirit.

"Have you tried?" it replied.

"No, I didn't know she was there."

"Go look for her, then. It's not like she'll be hiding."

"Mom?"

She kept her distance from the cabinet and the spirit. "Sorry, sweetheart. I didn't know any of this."

A wave of what my mom had also been through hit me then. She had been powerful, according to Aunt Jodene's notebook, until Henry had stolen it all from her and then killed her. She'd been trapped because of him.

Myst was now trapped again because of me. I filled Nik in on the plan. "What do you think?"

He sat back down. "I think you need to go in there and bring Myst out."

We clasped hands, he gave mine a firm squeeze and we began again.

When I opened my eyes, I was in the spirit realm. This time, I turned away from the opaque wall of the vanquished. I kept the wall at my back and walked forward.

"Myst?"

A spirit brushed my upper arm as it zipped by. More floated around; some ignored me, while others checked me out. Some were human-shaped, others mere wisps, all colours of the rainbow. Occasionally, one hovered and then disappeared. I was a novelty, a curiosity, but nothing worth their time. I continued to walk and call out for Myst.

I cupped my hands around my mouth and called her name as I slowly spun in a circle. But it wasn't her name. It was the one Carme had given her. Would that even work? Why hadn't I found out her real name? Who she'd been? I'd been too selfish, too afraid of helping her or any of the dead.

"Myst? Carme is in serious trouble. I'm sorry I didn't come sooner to get you. I didn't know where you were."

Nik's voice in my head called me back, but I couldn't go. Not until I found Myst.

A white vapor appeared in front of me. It hovered at eye level, long and thin, like a fine scarf waving in the wind.

Nik's voice became louder and I felt a tug at my chest.

"Myst?"

"I remember that name." Myst's voice came back into my head like a long-lost best friend. "Is that my name?" she asked. The confusion and uncertainty in her voice tore my heart.

"It's the name we gave you. You were a mystery, to yourself and to us. I think I know why now. You're my guardian angel."

"What? No, that doesn't sound right." Much of the old attitude returned, and I gave an inner sigh of relief.

"Carme really needs us. You have to come with me. Now." It was hard for me to hear anything but Nik's voice calling me back. It pained me to ignore the pull, but I did.

"Where?" Myst asked.

"To the human world. You can trust me." I shoved aside the guilt of having put her here in the first place. Twice.

"What if I'm supposed to be here? What if this is where I'm meant to stay?"

"It's not," I said.

"How can you know that?" Her voice held doubt, confusion and heart-wrenching desperation.

My time was up. "I know you're meant to help me save Carme."

"You keep saying that name. I know her, don't I?"

"Yes." I tried to say it encouragingly, but the pain of Nik's summoning overwhelmed me.

"She gave me my name," she said.

"Yes."

"You didn't want me around." She pulled away a bit.

"I was afraid."

There was a pause and she moved forward again. "You were afraid of me?"

"Of you. Of all of them." I waved a hand to indicate the other spirits.

"Why?" Myst asked.

Pain exploded through my chest and stomach. "Because my stepfather haunted me," I said through a clenched jaw as I doubled over. "He killed my mother, killed my friends, killed my clients and wants to kill me. Right now, he's hurting Carme. The longer we stay here, the more damage he could be doing to her."

"She wasn't afraid of me," Myst said.

"No, she wasn't."

"She liked me. I liked her. Your stepfather is hurting her?"

"Yes."

"I will go with you."

I gave in to Nik's call, then fell face-first out of my office chair and onto the floor.

My mom's spirit appeared at my side. "Amy?"

"Where are we?" Myst's voice said in my head. The scent of peppermint strengthened me to my core.

"We're in my office," I told Myst. "You've been here before."

"I don't remember it," Myst replied. "She's not here," she added with a forlorn tone.

"No, she's not, but we're going to get her. Nik?" Why hadn't Nik said anything yet?

As I sat up, my head spun and my stomach threatened to empty. I used the chair to pull myself to my knees. Nik had his head down on the table, arms stretched out where they'd held my hands.

"Nik!" I got myself into my chair and grabbed his hands. They felt like ice. I checked his wrist for a pulse.

"Relax, he's not dead." The smoky snake on the filing cabinet swirled.

The room spun as I tried to stand and had to sit back down. "What happened?"

"His spirit is worn out. He'll be like that for a while."

"How long is *a while*?" I snapped back.

The snake rose. "At least a day or maybe two."

"Does he need medical attention? A hospital?"

"No," it replied with impatience. "Your doctors wouldn't even know what was wrong with him."

"Is there anything we can do for him? Speed it up?"

"Just time." Its reply was so flippant, I wanted to send it back again.

Mom floated around Nik, examining him from head to toe. "I think they are right."

"Agreed." Myst gave me the triple confirmation I didn't want to hear.

I rested my forehead in my hand. "A couple of days? I can't leave Nik here in the office for a couple of days." I also couldn't carry him anywhere, not by myself. Doctors couldn't help him, and I was running out of living human allies.

With a steadying breath, I called Liam. He didn't answer. How sick was he? I left several messages, filled him in and said I needed his help.

The thought of having to leave Nik there, unsupervised, churned my stomach. I grabbed Carme's desk-chair cushion. The scruff of Nik's whiskers raked my fingers as I lifted his head, put the pillow under and lowered him back down.

"I can't find her," Myst said.

"Maybe she's being hidden from you," I told her. "We will find her."

My options were few. I pictured Fidget's furry, grouchy face and repeated his summoning spell. After several repetitions, the cat appeared at my side.

His back arched. His hair went on end and his tail puffed. I backed away, but it wasn't me Fidget had taken offence to. It was the smoky snake that now grew into a large cloud.

Fidget hissed and crouched, ready to attack.

"Stop," I said.

Fidget sidestepped, still facing the cloud. "This? This is what you brought back?" he yelled in my head, and I lost focus for a minute. Who was this spirit I'd brought back?

"You wanted me to get help, so I did," I snapped at the cat. "He was the most powerful."

"He's not a man," Myst said in my head.

"Not a man. Not anymore," the spirit growled.

The cloud streamed down and struck the floor with a force I didn't know it could have. A man, over six feet tall, muscles visible through tight black clothing, stood in my office. Fidget hissed again.

The man in black hissed back to show long, pointed fangs. "Stand down, little kitty."

Vampire? A vampire ghost? I fought to find my voice. But how? "Enough. We don't have time for this. I don't care what you two have against each other, I'm not playing referee. We need to work together." I turned all my attention on Fidget, still in his attack crouch. "Where's Carme now?"

"They've gone back to the store." Fidget's eyes remained solidly focused on the vampire ghost. "Henry is looking for something."

Aunt Jodene's shop. If we fought Henry there, Aunt Jodene's life's work, her beloved shop, would surely not survive. From what we'd experienced so far, this was bound to be a messy fight.

"We need to lure my stepfather out," I told my acquired army of spirits. "Somewhere we have the edge, not him. Somewhere no one else gets hurt in the process."

"Outdoors," growled the vampire. His ethereal fangs looked real enough to send shivers down my back.

"Fidget, does he know you're there?"

"No. I can hide from him. Just me, if that's what you're thinking. I wouldn't be able to hide them."

The vampire scoffed. "I can hide us from him."

Fidget hissed again. "They're moving." The cat disappeared and left me without a connection to Carme.

"Does anyone know where he's gone?" I asked Myst, my mom and the vampire.

"He's coming back," the vampire replied, a little edge to his voice. "You didn't tell me the cat would be here."

Fidget reappeared. "They're in the cafe. They're not alone and he is hurting people." He disappeared again.

The vampire turned back to black smoke and flew over my head as I ran out the door. My mother followed.

"Myst?" I said as I ran down the stairs.

"I'm here," came her reply, close to my ear.

It was time to face my stepfather again.

# Chapter 27

Carme sat on the counter beside the cash register, a queen surveying her subjects. Most of the cafe tables had been overturned. Those still upright held slumped bodies or people who were completely spaced out. Many of these early-morning patrons were familiar to me. Ethan stood behind the counter, as out of it as the others.

"Good of you to join us," Carme said. The posture wasn't hers. The condescending, angry look in her eyes wasn't either. It was all Henry.

Fidget paced the counter beside her. He stayed out of reach but close enough to leap into action if the opportunity presented itself. The vampire ghost and my mother remained behind me.

"Get out of her," I yelled as I weaved my way through overturned tables.

Carme threw her head back and my stepfather's laugh erupted from her. He continued to laugh as I checked on one of the semi-awake customers. We had to get everyone out of there.

I yanked a still-conscious young man to his feet and pushed him toward the door. "Go!" I yelled at him. He didn't move.

Ethan still hadn't moved. Had he become some sort of slave for Henry? Would he turn on us?

"Ethan, snap out of it," I called out. "We need you."

He blinked, like waking from a dream, and gazed around.

The young male patron resisted me, as if his feet didn't want to walk. I pushed him again. Eventually, I got him to the door and shoved him out, where he simply stood, staring down the street. I went for another customer. My stepfather laughed at me the entire time.

Ignoring him, I went to the older woman I'd seen every morning drawing. Taking her by the elbow, I walked her to the door. Once out the door, she met my gaze, eyes confused, but then they cleared.

"Can you help me?" I asked her.

She nodded. Before I could even blink, she turned to the young man I'd already escorted out and slapped his face. It sounded like it hurt. He blinked several times as his cheek turned bright slap-red. When she went to hit him again, he held up his hands.

"I'm okay," he said.

The older woman shooed him away. "Good, then go home." She came back inside to help get more people out.

Liam appeared at the door and my heart leapt with joy. He took in everything and, with a nod to me, jumped into action. He got his arms under one of the smaller unconscious customers and hoisted her up.

"How are you here?" I helped him adjust the woman so he could carry her.

Liam smiled. "I convinced my grandfather I had to help you, how important you and Carme are to me. Then I felt better." His grandfather appeared behind him and gave me a slow nod.

"Get them all out," I said to Liam.

"Smack them if you have to," the older woman said with a perky snap. Liam's eyes went wide.

"Whatever works," I told him, and he nodded.

Patrons taken care of, I rushed toward Carme. She flicked her hand at me. I fell back and hit the ground hard. Pain shot through my hip and the hand I'd tried to brace myself with.

"Those sheep don't matter," Henry said. Carme's eyes flared orange. "I have the power I need now."

My hip burned with pain as I got to all fours and then slowly stood.

Ethan went to lock the door behind the last customer, then stepped back. "Darren, what are you doing here?"

His younger brother pushed inside and stared at Carme. "I want to help."

A horrid grin spread across Carme's face. "Perfect," Henry said.

Carme jumped down off the counter, and Fidget followed after her. Carme's hand went back as if about to throw something at Darren.

I stepped in front of the two brothers and faced my stepfather. "You won't touch them and you'll let Carme go."

Carme stopped, head tilted, considering me.

I kept my eyes on her. "Ethan, you and Darren get out of here. I mean it. Liam, you too. Please, I need you to go check on Nik in the office."

"You got it," Liam said.

Ethan hesitated, debate behind his eyes. After a torturous moment, he nodded. He wrapped his arm around Darren's shoulder and guided the two of them out the door.

Carme's hand touched her necklace, her nervous habit. Maybe she still had some control.

"You made a deal with the dybbuk to switch places with Mom to what, be its slave?"

"We had similar interests. I wanted your powers, which I could only get if I got strong enough to kill you. It wanted one of your guardian angels. It let me get too powerful." He grinned again.

My heart squeezed. "The dybbuk wanted my guardian angel? Myst?"

"I have no idea what he is on about," Myst said. "As much as I would like to know who I am, we need to save her first."

"You must realize you're not stronger than me," Henry said, oblivious to my conversation with Myst. "Not any more, little Amy."

"Maybe not." I reminded myself to breathe. "But this time, I have help."

Fidget came to stand between me and Carme. Black smoke swirled to my left and transformed into the tall ghost vampire. He hissed at Carme, ghost fangs on full display. He scared me almost as much as my stepfather, but I fought not to show it.

Henry only laughed again. "An excellent attempt, little Amy. I do applaud your resourcefulness. It won't be enough."

"Maybe it will," my mother said as she appeared on my right.

Henry's reaction was not what I'd expected. I'd hoped for surprise or remorse, but he shook Carme's head and smiled.

"You weren't strong enough in life, my dear. Why do

you think you would be in death?" Carme's eyes rolled mockingly. "Disappointing, or I wouldn't have needed your daughter. You were something once. Now you're pathetic and weak." My mother's spirit wavered, retreating slightly from sight.

"Mom?" My throat tightened. The familiar weight of an anxiety attack settled onto my chest. It got hard to breathe and my head began to spin.

Fidget rubbed against my leg, only the second time he'd done that, dead or alive. It brought my focus back. We could do this. I had powerful spirits with me, including my guardian angel, who was proving more and more of a mystery.

"Mom," I said. "Don't let him do this. Not anymore. You are stronger than that." Coaching my dead mother wasn't something I'd ever imagined I would do. "You didn't deserve what he did to you, Mom. You didn't fail me. Not once. You're my hero. I love you and we're going to do this together."

My mom's spirit glowed and she gave me a smile full of strength. "We will do this," she whispered.

Henry laughed again. "You will lose." He pointed Carme's finger at me. "You shouldn't be giving her false hope like that. It didn't work for your clients, did it? Got them killed, didn't you? Just like those little friends of yours. All that blood on your hands."

It took everything I had not to give in to his manipulations, not to revert to that scared little girl. "People have died," I shot back, "but not because of me. Because of you and your sick, twisted ideas."

He shook Carme's head. "You managed to avoid death before because you were stronger than me and you had your guardian angel. Face it. It's over for you. Things are just beginning for me."

"I am here," Myst said, reassuring me. A tiny shower of light fell down around me in white droplets.

Carme's hand went to her necklace again. Message received.

"You're finished," I said, my voice strong. "I know your name. Henry Nilsen."

"You can't do this." There was hesitation in his tone. Carme's hand stayed tightly wrapped around her necklace. Her strength gave me strength.

"I know why you're here. To kill me, to gain the power you need to come back to life. You're going to be willing to leave that body because Carme and my spirits are going to make you." I brought Carme's sparkly flask out of my bag and began the exorcism chant.

"You will not stop me," Henry yelled. A tremor began from where Carme stood. It radiated outward and shook the ground. It vibrated the furniture and toppled the sales-item display. Mugs crashed from the counter to the floor.

The ghost vampire approached Carme but Fidget hissed at him. I couldn't stop my chant to let the cat know to leave the vampire alone to do what he must. The vampire wouldn't hurt Carme. Would he?

My mother scooped Fidget up and he didn't fight her. The ghost vampire, my mom with Fidget and I formed a triangle around Carme.

Black threads of smoke reached out from the vampire and entered Carme through her nose and mouth. I faltered for a moment, worried he might hurt her, even accidentally. Similar-coloured threads reached out from Fidget and my mother. The cat's were brown, my mother's red. All of them went into Carme, and I picked up my chant again.

Wind whipped around me, tearing at my hair and clothes. My eyes watered and my limbs became hard to control. I clasped Carme's flask with everything I had and continued the chant.

Carme's mouth contorted in agony and Henry screamed. In order to keep going, I told myself this was the only way. This would save Carme.

A twisted and blurry spirit streamed out of Carme's chest, then disappeared. The flask in my hand glowed red. Carme collapsed.

# Chapter 28

Stillness fell over the cafe but it felt far from peaceful.

"Carme?" I knelt beside her. Fidget leapt from my mother's arms and sniffed Carme's neck.

"She's alive." He bumped his head against her cheek.

I cradled Carme's head, looking for visible injuries, but didn't find any. She'd be bumped and bruised from that fall, but I was more worried about what would be left of her mentally and emotionally.

Frantic knocking at the cafe door made me flinch. It was Liam. Since I was the only one conscious with actual hands, I set Carme's head down gently and went to let him in.

"He wasn't there." He pointed at Carme. "Is she okay?"

"She will be. I hope." It took me a second to register what he had said. "You mean Nik? He wasn't in the office?"

Liam shook his head. "I even checked up and down the Drive a bit. I couldn't find him anywhere."

"Maybe he felt better and went home?" I didn't believe it even as I said it. I reached for my phone but Carme coughed and opened her eyes. Liam and I both went to her.

"Carme?" I asked. "Are you okay? Is that you in there?"

Her fingers found her necklace. "Not gone," she managed to say.

Fidget's hair stood on end. The vampire went into a slight crouch, searching the cafe.

"But we got him." I held the flask up to show her, sparkles scratching at my fingers. "It glowed red."

"No, I don't think so," Myst said, and my heart squeezed.

The cafe door opened. I hadn't locked it behind us when I'd let Liam in.

Nik walked in. Right away I knew it wasn't him. Not on the inside. It was Henry. Nik held his hands up high and clapped slowly.

"How?" I began. "Liam, get behind me."

The vampire moved closer to me. "He must have managed to overpower the spirit he let enter him when he was alive. When you tried to capture him, he sent it instead."

The urine-scented spirit. It had been the dybbuk, but it had no smell going in the flask.

"Clever dead vampire," Nik's voice said. "Now I can kill her and have more power than even you."

The vampire turned to black wisps and swirled around Nik.

"What do we do?" I whispered. Liam put a firm, supportive hand on my shoulder. His grandfather appeared beside him, but I didn't know if either of them could help now.

Fidget wouldn't leave Carme. His stance and glare told me his part was over. His human was safe. But for how long?

The vampire wisps floated quickly and smoothly toward me, then turned to human form again. "Let me devour him." His voice remained low and steady, but his eyes blazed with desire.

My skin prickled and every hair went on end. "You can do that?" What had I set free?

He gave a slow nod. Nik stared at us with a horrible smile. I'd worked with enough people who tried to fake confidence. I could see the doubt behind that grin. He watched us closely.

Fidget lifted his head from Carme's cupped hand. "Let the vampire do it," he snapped.

Mom closed her ghost eyes and nodded.

"What about Nik?" I asked. "What happens to him?"

The vampire ghost had the courtesy to turn his gaze down. "He may not survive."

"Nik has strong angels," Myst said, close to my right ear.

"Strong enough?"

I had to risk Nik's life to stop my stepfather? It wasn't only about destroying Henry. It was about saving Aunt Jodene and anyone else he intended to hurt or kill in the future.

"Open the flask," the vampire ghost said. His eager expression made me uncomfortable. Give him the dybbuk? We didn't even really know anything about it, except it used Henry and then he'd used it right back.

He pointed at the flask. "I will devour that one and be strong enough to get him"—he pointed at Nik—"out of that man and end it. Forever."

Fidget hissed at Nik as he walked past Carme toward us.

"Relax, pest." Nik's mouth moved, but it was Henry's voice. "You couldn't stop me if you tried. I want Amy. Then I'll take whoever else I choose." Fidget hissed again, back raised, hair on end.

Henry glared at me with Nik's eyes and patted his chest. "You like this one. That one, too." He pointed at Liam. Fury burned in my chest. "I will take them all," he said. "After you."

"Open it," the vampire hissed at me.

"I'm sorry," I whispered to the real Nik and the unknown dybbuk as I opened the flask.

It was all I could do to grip the flask as the vampire became something out of horror movies. It turned into a grey beast with emaciated limbs, long claws and fangs. The vampire ghost opened its jaws. The dybbuk streamed from the flask like a black and grey reverse waterfall. The vampire cried out in pleasure, and it turned my stomach.

My stepfather yelled profanities, but I didn't dare take my focus off the flask in my hand.

It finished and the vampire returned to his human form. He was different. More solid. Did consuming the dybbuk get him closer to regaining life? What would happen when he devoured Henry? Had this been his plan all along?

Nik stared at the vampire ghost as he backed up against the counter. I began to chant. "Henry Nilsen. You have come to kill me, but you will not. You will leave him willingly. His angels will make you." Or so I hoped.

"They are here," Myst said.

She didn't need to tell me. I could see them and they were everywhere, every shape and size, colour and gender. There must have been a dozen at least. They surrounded Nik. I chanted louder, drawing Henry out. Nik screamed in pain. I faltered and almost stopped. But it was working. Henry, as I remembered him, thin with a ragged grey beard and hateful eyes, began to be pulled from Nik.

The vampire moved so fast, he became a blur. In less than a human breath, he stood in front of Nik. The vampire changed again, and everything in me wanted to look away, but I didn't.

Nik fell to the floor, and I watched as the vampire ghost slowly devoured the spirit of my stepfather. Unlike the spirit in the flask, Henry put up a fight. Ghostly arms flailed, hands attempted to claw and scrape, but it was useless.

Henry's screams of pain and anger became anguished begging. I looked away then and met my mother's eyes. They held strength, and I blinked away tears Henry didn't deserve.

It ended. The spirit of my stepfather had been completely devoured. The vampire transformed back to his human shape, even more solid in appearance but still a ghost. I went to Nik's body collapsed on the floor.

He stirred, opened his eyes and pushed up onto one elbow. "I'm okay."

"Are you sure?" I asked.

A phone went off. Carme blinked and crawled to where her purse had dropped. She reached in and pulled out her cell.

"Mom!" she yelled into her phone. She smiled and nodded at me. Tears rolled down her cheeks as she spoke to her mom.

"Tell her we'll be there as soon as we can," I said, then leaned over and hugged Nik as hard as I could.

# Chapter 29

Charles stood at Aunt Jodene's bedside, holding her hand, when we arrived. We received a few stern looks from staff, as visiting hours were almost over. Aunt Jodene was thinner than I'd ever seen her and pale, but she smiled at us as we walked in.

We were a bit of a gang, Carme, Nik, Liam and me, plus the ones no one else could see. Myst, Fidget and my mom.

We stood back and let Carme rush to her mom, Fidget tight at her heels. They embraced, and I inwardly applauded Carme for hiding how much pain she was in from the fall she'd taken. The time Henry had been in control of her didn't seem to affect her. Or not that I'd noticed yet. He hadn't been in Carme as long as Ethan, but surely there would be some lingering effects. I planned to keep a closer eye on her from now on.

Mom had a small smile on her face and tears in her ghostly eyes as she lightly touched the top of her sister's head, then arm, then her hand. There was so much love in those ghostly touches, it made my heart weep. Aunt Jodene closed her eyes, took a deep breath and put a hand over her heart.

"Are you all right?" Charles asked, forehead scrunched.

Aunt Jodene opened her eyes and smiled. "I'm fine. Just feeling a lot of love in the room." She couldn't see my mom, but I was sure she felt her, which made me happy. "Glad to no longer have the company of your client," she said to me.

"I'm so sorry," I replied. "Fidget told us she did it to hide from the dybbuk so she couldn't be used."

Aunt Jodene's eyes went wide. "Fidget?"

Carme laughed. "He's here."

"Amazing," my aunt whispered. "I'm glad I could be a safe place for your client. She was strong to resist him."

I squeezed her arm. "You're the strong one."

"Not as strong as you." She adjusted herself in her bed. "Otherwise, Henry would've been after me for banishing him. I wasn't worth his time, apparently."

I was about to remind her how she'd raised an amazing daughter by herself and ran her own business, when there was a knock on the door frame. Ethan and Darren stood in the doorway.

"Hello there," Ethan said to Aunt Jodene with a small smile. "Nice to have you back." He pointed at Charles. "Dad, you're supposed to be in bed." Ethan acted normal and happy, but underneath I could sense he was far from either.

"Oh, shush. They're releasing me later today," his father said, back to his usual banter. I caught the guilt on his face when he looked at his sons. It would take us all a long time to heal physically and emotionally from this experience.

Darren came into the room and gave his dad a hug. He went to give Carme one but hesitated. She put her arms out and hugged him first.

"It's okay to just be friends," she told him. She couldn't

see his face, but I could. He wasn't thrilled with the idea, but wasn't too sad about it, either.

Liam elbowed Nik and pointed his thumb toward the door. "We'll leave you guys alone for a bit. I've got to text Andrea, who is doing well, by the way. We've got a date." He grinned down at my aunt. "She collects bones."

"Very interesting," Aunt Jodene replied. "I hope I get to meet her soon."

Nik, who acted as though he'd forgotten where he was, gave a nod. "Glad you're doing better," he said, his eyes still a bit dazed. They made their way out to the hallway.

Ethan stepped closer to me and smiled again at my aunt. "I know you'll be fine in no time," he said. My aunt nodded regally. I knew she was enjoying the attention and having us all together like this.

"You must be looking forward to getting back to the shop," Ethan added.

"I can't wait," Aunt Jodene said. "Not to mention the cafe. The coffee here is terrible."

"Tell me about it." Charles rolled his eyes and Darren laughed.

Darren held his arms out wide. "I'll make you a big coffee." Ethan wrapped an arm around his brother's shoulders.

They didn't know about the state of the café, and my breath caught in my throat. They'd tried so hard to get the cafe going again, and I'd all but destroyed their business.

Ethan met my eye and shook his head.

"He knows about the cafe," Myst said in my left ear. "He also knows you'll help him fix it before his father sees it."

I wanted to ask her how she knew that. Had she gotten stronger? Henry said the dybbuk made the original deal with him to get to Myst. Henry would get my powers; the dybbuk would get Myst.

When I was a teenager, they'd tried to terrorize me to weaken me, but thanks to my aunt, they hadn't succeeded. Yet even after Henry had gotten stronger, he still couldn't beat us. What was Myst's story? Questions for later, once I could get Aunt Jodene's help again.

"Come on, Dad," Ethan said. "Let's get you settled up with the nurses. I hear you owe them all cafe coupons, which apparently we give out now."

His dad chuckled. "Had to get them to keep coming in to see me somehow."

The three of them left, worn but safe. I hoped they could move on together. Ethan acted like himself, but I had to wonder how much damage had been done.

"Ready to go home soon?" I asked Aunt Jodene.

She eyed me, then gave an affirming hum. "How are you?"

A loaded question. I didn't know if I was prepared to answer it fully yet.

"I'm fine," I replied instead. "You don't need to hear all about it right now."

Aunt Jodene wriggled a bit, and Carme helped adjust the pillows behind her. "Carme told me a lot over the phone. I'm quite proud of you two." Carme beamed at her mother's praise. "I also hear you're going to be busy helping ghosts." Aunt Jodene's face lit up with one of those knowing smiles of hers.

I nodded. "It was the only way." We had a long road ahead of us, getting all those ghosts out, including Henry's ancestor Adam, who probably wouldn't be too happy with me. Plus, I'd promised to help them with whatever issues they had.

Aunt Jodene kept grinning. "Seems like you might have a new career path."

"What? No," I replied.

Carme, Aunt Jodene and my mother all smiled at me.

"I can't coach the dead for a living," I protested. "How could they pay? I won't have a business if I don't make any money."

"We'll figure it out," Carme said with her usual gusto.

"There could be ways, I'm sure," Aunt Jodene said.

I looked to my mother for help, but she shrugged. "There might be," she said.

"Vampires can pay." The vampire ghost stood in the doorway. Shivers ran through me at the thought of coaching vampires if they were anything like him.

I held up a finger to Aunt Jodene, Carme and my mom. "One second."

I went to the hall, waved awkwardly to Nik and Liam as I got out of their earshot. The vampire ghost followed me.

I crossed my arms and hugged them into myself. "Is that why you're still here? So I'll coach vampires?"

He smiled, strong and confident as though he already knew I would oblige him. "There are many in my community who don't deal well with being"—he flicked a hand—"undead. They could use help. It would make the entire community stronger and safer."

Could I make a difference to the dead? The undead? Maybe to the living people they'd left behind?

"I will think about it. If you tell me how you even exist. Is it from devouring spirits? You take their souls?"

He shrugged. "Something like that. I discovered it when I took the one who killed me as I died. Finding myself in the spirit realm was a surprise to me as well."

"How many have you consumed?" His eyes told me he wasn't going to answer me but the number was high. "Never mind. I'm going to look after my family. You're free to go." I shooed him with my hands, then realized how ridiculous that was for so many reasons. He was a ghost, a vampire ghost and an extremely powerful one. He would probably not be easily shooed by me. I cleared my throat. "Remember our deal."

"I will. But I have a feeling we will meet again. Take care of those ones. And get a leash for that cat." He turned into wispy smoke and vanished.

I should have felt relieved, but I felt a bit like I'd lost something valuable and important. I'd get over it. We were better off without him around.

"Vampires?" Carme whispered when I came back in the room. "Fidget told me," she added with a guilty smile for her eavesdropping cat. "First, we help the ones we promised," Carme said. "Then move on from there." She made it sound like a done deal.

I didn't think Carme could've looked any happier than she already did, but she beamed as she came over and gave me a giant hug.

"We'll do so much good," she whispered to me.

"You're hard to say no to," I whispered back.

"I know," she exclaimed as we let go of each other. "Nik is waiting." She pointed out to the hall, where Liam and Nik stood.

"Fine. But don't go changing my business cards just yet," I told Carme. I left her, Fidget and my mother with my aunt. Did someone who coached the dead even need business cards?

I walked over to Nik and my best friend. Nik watched me

approach, and I wondered if it all had been too much for us to ever be more than friends.

Liam threw a thumb over his shoulder. "I'll just go, uh, get us all some coffees. Even though I've heard it's horrible." He grinned at me as he backed up a few steps, then turned and walked away from us.

Nik stared down at me and I saw the conflict in his eyes. He'd been through a lot. I was a lot. But then his expression changed to one of heat and longing. It was as much as I could handle without throwing myself at him. He touched my cheek gently, and I closed my eyes for a moment at his touch. When I opened them again, he tipped my chin slightly, leaned down and kissed me. Not just any kiss, but an electric kiss to make my entire body tingle.

He finished the kiss, though I would've let him go on forever. "Now this is over, how about the subject of us?"

It was a bit difficult for me to think clearly, let alone speak. "Well, I think I could use some more of that private meditation coaching."

He tilted his head in thought. "I will also take you out for dinner. Somewhere bright and populated with living humans."

I laughed. "That would be fabulous. I need something to take my mind off all this talk of a new career."

"What new career?"

It was time to face up to it. "Coaching the dead," I replied.

"Sounds…" He paused and I could see the weight of the past few days flash over him. "Interesting," he concluded, and wrapped his arms around me in a tight, strong hug.

I lowered my head to rest against his chest. "*Interesting* is likely an understatement."

I had a feeling I would find out soon enough.

# The Ghostly Mysteries Continue

## Coming soon:

## Death Coach, Vampires

Thank you so much for reading Death Coach!

Please consider leaving a review on Goodreads or your favourite bookseller's website. It helps so much.

Want more? Great! Check out the following pages for a sneak peek excerpt from the next book!

# Death Coach, Vampires

Fidget jumped onto Carme's desk, staring at the door. His back arched, hair on end. Carme stood up quickly, looking at the door. Her face paled. As much as Carme loved the world of the dead, her experience of having my stepfather take control of her had left its scars.

We had strong wards on the office in order to keep the unwanted spirits out, but some ghosts could be strong enough to overcome them.

I didn't see or smell any spirits but something was going on. There were very few things Fidget was afraid of. The ghost cat let out a loud hiss.

Or, it could be the other thing Fidget didn't like. Vampires.

The vampire ghost walked into my office through the open door as though he had a living body. Or rather, an undead body.

My heart did two giant flip flops. One in relief because we knew him, the second because that wasn't necessarily a good thing.

Peppermint surrounded me. "What is he doing here?" Myst was back. Perfect timing. Or I guess she'd known I was in danger. I was still getting used to having a guardian angel.

The vampire ghost wore the same tight black shirt and pants as always but looked far less ghostly than the last time I'd seen him, which worried me. I still didn't know what his agenda really was.

"Amy." He gave me a nod, as though we saw each other all the time. The truth was, I hadn't seen him since he'd devoured the spirit of my stepfather. I'd hoped I'd never see him again.

I got to my feet and put myself between him and Carme. "What do you want?"

He hadn't ever done anything to threaten our lives, in fact, he'd saved them, but I still didn't trust him.

He gave a nod toward Carme and glared at Fidget. "If it makes you more comfortable, she and the cat can leave but I need to talk to you."

Fidget hissed. "Happy to, blood breath."

I grabbed Carme's coat and shoved it at her because I knew she'd try to protest. "Go get us some coffee, please." It was two against one and she gave in. Fidget disappeared and reappeared in the hallway, waiting for his human. Carme gave me one more concerned look before backing out the door and leaving with her ghost cat.

The vampire ghost sat on Carme's desk and crossed one leg over. He was tall, at least six feet four and made the desk look much smaller than it was.

"Why are you here?" I asked, hoping it was a simple answer but fearing it wasn't.

He clasped his hands and placed them over his knee. "I told you there were people in my community who could use your help. I helped you in exchange for your help in my community."

"He did," Myst put in. I didn't want to answer her with

him around. As far as I knew, he couldn't hear her.

I picked up my coffee mug and stared into it's emptiness, wishing he was wrong. He wasn't. I had promised to help any vampires he brought to me, but I hadn't really had a choice at the time. Without his help, we never would have stopped my stepfather from killing me and everyone close to me. Part of me never believed I would actually have to help any vampires.

"What do you want?" I asked.

"There is a young vampire who needs help."

"This could be very interesting or very dangerous," Myst said.

I flicked my hand past my ear as if swatting a fly, an action I'd developed when Myst interrupted. "Do you mean they're young in age, or they haven't been a vampire for very long?"

One side of his mouth turned up in a grin, an attractive look perhaps on someone who wasn't dead. I had seen what he'd become and what he'd done to my stepfather's spirit. Those were images I would never forget.

"In this case, both," he replied. "She's having issues with being a new vampire as well as fitting into her coven."

"You have covens? What does that mean, exactly?"

He clasped his ghost hands together on his crossed leg. "Consider it a chosen family."

"Oh, this is most interesting," Myst said.

I narrowed my eyes at him. "Chosen by who?"

This time his whole mouth turned up in a smile. "Clever," he said. "Which is why I'm sending this young woman to you. She can tell you her situation herself."

I wasn't done with the questions. "Why this vampire? What is she to you? And what will you consider me helping her? That can be a grey area in coaching. I won't fix her overnight. Also, how safe is it for her to be here? I need guarantees no harm will come to the people around me. How about some sort of guidebook on Vampires for me before I dive into this?"

He held his hands up, either in surrender or to get me to slow down with the questions. "I do not blame you for having these inquiries. If you didn't I would be less impressed with you than I already am."

My brain zipped. Did he just compliment me?

Myst gave a haughty laugh. "Don't get those knickers in a knot. He's not even flesh and blood. Or, well, not flesh at any rate." I flicked the imaginary fly again.

"I have an interest in her coven. It was mine before this." He waved a hand indicating his spirit body. "Whatever help you can give her to navigate things will be enough. I trust you."

"Why do you trust me?" I interrupted. "Why do you want me to try to help?"

He shook his head as though disappointed. "You got me out of the spirit realm I was locked in. And surely you haven't forgotten I have seen you in battle. I know what you are capable of."

More compliments. He had stood at my side while I'd confronted my stepfather but a vampire ghost trusting me to help other vampires was new territory. "Fine. How about some help with the world of vampires then? I know the living world, I am getting to know the spirit world better, but vampires are an unknown. How do you expect me to help?"

"Vampires are simply humans, with a few adjustments and rules to follow. Depending on their age, where they're from and whether they are in a coven or not, those rules will vary. Your cousin Carme already owns books to help you, in her mother's shop."

This did not surprise me, but it did bother me he knew that. My jaw tightened. "Stay away from Carme and Aunt Jodene."

He gave a single nod. "As you wish."

"I'm not sure if you're being genuine or mocking me. You might trust me, but I don't trust you."

"Fair enough. Trust can be earned."

I doubted that, but I didn't have much of a choice. I shuddered to think what he would do if I refused to keep my word to help his fellow vampires.

"As for your safety and those around you, I will guarantee that."

"Great," I said, perhaps a little too sarcastically. "How are you going to do that?"

It might have been a trick of the light, but his eyes darkened. "People do as I tell them, even now."

"I believe him," Myst said. "He is extremely powerful. What must he have been like when he was alive?"

"You will be safe," he said. "Vampires are not all monsters. For her safety, she will need to meet you after dark."

"You said not all are monsters," I repeated. "So some are." Again, he shrugged in a way I knew he wouldn't give more details. "When do you want me to see her?"

He stood. "Tonight."

"Tonight? That doesn't give me much time to get to know vampires."

He gave me a one shoulder shrug. "I'm confident you'll do your best."

He headed for the open door. He could have vanished,

gone through the wall or transformed into the smokey wisps he'd been when we'd first met. Clearly he liked being almost amongst the living undead again.

"Wait," I said to his back, "how will we know which books are accurate?"

"I've marked them," he said and walked away.

He marked them, in the shop? Whatever happened, I had to protect Aunt Jodene and Carme. I let out a long breath and sat back down. "I guess we're coaching vampires, now, too."

"Most, most interesting," came Myst's reply.

I sent a quick text to Carme to let her know I was okay and I'd fill her in later.

Vampires. I had to meet Ethan in the cafe, then it was time to go see Aunt Jodene.

Would you like to be the first to hear about more books in the series? Want sneak peeks behind the scenes, including an early look at the covers?

Join the mailing list here:
www.sandrawickham.com/list

You'll also get some great gifts for signing up! Free short stories, a free audio story, free printable colouring pages for book lovers and much more!

Thank you again for your support. Let's stay in touch on the internet, my links are all on my website:

www.sandrawickham.com

See you soon!

# Acknowledgments

This book has been a labour of love and thank goodness for the incredible people in my life who held my hand, let me scream and encouraged me to push throughout its birth.

Thank you to:

Clare Marshall for her expert publishing coaching.
Chadwick Ginther for his constant encouragement, gifs and Star Wars memes.
Kristene Perron for always being my bestie no matter what.
The Word Sisters for their unyielding support and input.
Kate Larking for listening to my freak outs.
Skyla Dawn Cameron for content editing and amazing cover design, all while putting up with me.
The Bruisers, Inkpunks, Rainforest Writers, Taos Toolbox 2013, WWC, Creative Ink Family, Paradise Lost, Fit 2 Write clients and followers plus everyone I have ever met in the publishing industry. You are my favourite people.
Last but not least, my parents for input, encouragement and babysitting so I could work on the novel.

# The Street Team

A big thank you to the Death Coach Street Team who helped me with development decisions and to spread the word about this novel. You're all amazing and I appreciate you so much!

Margaret Arsenault
Mary Brunk
Mary Cardle
Melanie Dixon
Judy Dufort
Lisa Gemino
Chadwick Ginther
Jeanette Montgomery
Sally D Simpson
Raeann
Krista Wallace
Andrea Westaway

Would you like to join the Street Team? They get involved behind the scenes, give input on creation and production, including the cover design!

Visit www.sandrawickham.com/team for more information or to join us.

# Meet the Author

**Sandra Wickham** is a fiction and nonfiction author, Founder of Fit 2 Write, Mom, Special Olympics Coach and Special Needs Advocate.

Her friends call her a Health Guru, Crafting Aficionado and Ninja-in-training.

Sandra has always loved all things paranormal. She still hopes her cat will speak to her one day, and ghosts will make themselves visible or that a unicorn and dragon will finally show up at her door with coffee and cookies.

She lives in Ontario, Canada with her son who has Down syndrome and their cat, Yoda.

In addition to writing fiction, Sandra works with writers who want to improve their levels of health and fitness to write more. She is the Author of *Feel Write Again, Crush Your Doubts and Write More, A Workbook for Writers*.

Connect with Sandra on her website:
www.sandrawickham.com

www.ingramcontent.com/pod-product-compliance
Lightning Source LLC
Chambersburg PA
CBHW031938210726
48290CB00006BA/1971